Here's what the critics are s̶a̶ about *The Color Red*...

"The complex investigation ir suspects... Potter makes Bourque, w̶ḥ̶o̶ ̶g̶ career in organic chemistry to hunt killers, a credible lead readers will root for. Fans of intelligent procedurals will hope for a long series run."
—*Publishers Weekly*

"An exhilarating murder mystery, The Color Red plunges the reader into rapid intrigue with clever insight and innovative twists. Creative and thoroughly entertaining."
—Bill Arnott, bestselling author of the *Gone Viking* travelogues

"A superb police murder mystery. The writing is crisp and the story compelling until the very end. I was hooked at Page One and couldn't put it down."
—David Hoath, Police Psychologist (Retired)

"A winning read with fascinating suspects. Detective Bourque is wry, intelligent, and sympatico. What a great main character for a series."
—P. W. Tilley, Former RCMP Detective

"Great story! Well delivered and really well written. Five shining ★★★★★."
—Vicky Coughlan, Instagram and Goodreads

"Potter keeps us guessing until the final chapter in this well-plotted clever mystery with a smart, savvy protagonist."
—Ken Haigh, Author of *On Foot to Canterbury*, shortlisted for the Hilary Weston Prize

THE
COLOR RED

Book One in the
Detective Bourque Series

by A.M. Potter

STARK
HOUSE

Stark House Press • Eureka California

THE COLOR RED

Published by Stark House Press
1315 H Street
Eureka, CA 95501, USA
griffinskye3@sbcglobal.net
www.starkhousepress.com

ISBN: 979-8-88601-021-3

Book design by Mark Shepard, shepgraphics.com
Cover photo by Sleep Music
Proofreading by Bill Kelly

First Stark House Press Edition: March 2023

*Before you embark on a journey
of revenge, dig two graves.*
~ Confucius

*It's not what you look at that
matters, it's what you see.*
~ Henry David Thoreau

DEDICATION
*To David and Penny:
Supporters and friends extraordinaire.*

Chapter 1

East Falmouth, Cape Cod, Massachusetts. May 14th

Swirls of mist rose off the infinity pool. The water was royal blue, the color of Adriatic tiles. Rollo Novak shed his robe, dove in and swam swiftly to the end of the pool. New Blue, he called it, the first outdoor swim of the year. Beyond the pool, the sun crested the horizon. He plunged underwater and returned to the deep end. Surfacing, he saw his wife Katrina on the deck. "Jump, *ljubezen*," he called. Jump, my love.

She grinned at him, dropped her robe and jumped in naked, cannonball style. The waves splashed over his head. Giggling, she grabbed his hand and led him to the shallow end. He heard a click at the back gate and another one.

Katrina pulled his swimsuit down. Forget about the gate.

Chapter 2

DAY ONE: *Cape & Islands Detective Unit, Massachusetts State Police. May 14th*

Detective Ivy Bourque roared up a long narrow driveway. Thick stands of umbrella pine shut out the sun. Her radio crackled, reporting another trooper on the way. A quarter of a mile later, the trees finally receded and the forest revealed a gargantuan house.

The white stone hulk featured a colossal central turret. The sun peered over it like a giant red eye. Rollo Novak, originally from Slovenia, had finished the faux Adriatic castle a year ago—another example of big money coming into Cape Cod. While big money was often entwined with big egos, by all accounts Novak was a true gentleman. He'd built the castle for his new wife. Bourque was more than happy with her man, but a gentleman and a castle, that could be a fairy tale come true. As she stepped out of her unmarked car, the front door swung open.

State Trooper Donnelly walked toward her, sidearm holstered. "Two hangers," he gruffly said. "Rich folks: the larger the fortune, the greater the misfortune." He shook his head. "It's the way of the world."

"You can't win," she commiserated.

"There's one man in there, unarmed." Donnelly winked. "Unless you count his stare."

"Lethal weapon?" she kidded.

"Oh yeah, loaded with attitude."

She followed Donnelly up the stairs, detecting no signs of a break-in. Inside, a vast foyer underscored the castle theme: gold-leaf paint, cognac-colored wood, Old-World tapestries. A few yards away, she saw a painting that looked like a medieval masterpiece. It could be an original. Novak was that rich.

Donnelly gestured toward a man sitting in a throne-like chair, guarded by a junior trooper. The man's face projected haughtiness. She pegged him at forty-plus: olive complexion, black hair, heavy crow's feet around the eyes.

"Detective Lieutenant Bourque, State Police. What's your name, sir?"

He stood. "Damijan Zupan. I am house manager. Butler, you can say."

The name sounded Slavic. Slovenian? she speculated. He wore an expensive blue-serge suit. With his wide shoulders and stony face, he looked to be cut from the mold of bodyguard *cum* butler. His slicked-back hair was shiny and duck-tailed. She pressed the recording button on her duty phone, preparing to listen forensically. "Did you call the police?"

"Yes, I call."

"Why?" An obvious question, but she wanted to hear his story.

"Mr. Novak, he is dead. Wife as well."

Bourque waited. A man of few words.

"He does not come for breakfast," Zupan eventually said, "nor wife. I go to look for him."

"Where did you find the bodies?"

"Outdoor pool. Shallow end. Half an hour ago. No, less." Zupan's dark eyes were empty. He'd called in the deaths, but levelheaded murderers sometimes did that. He pulled out a smartphone and aloofly showed her the call list. "I make nine-one-one at seven fifty-two."

Bourque glanced at her watch: 0821 hours. She'd been dispatched at 0758. Zupan's timeline seemed right. "Who else is in the house?"

"No one. It is quiet season. I look after whole house myself."

"Cooking, cleaning, everything?"

He nodded abruptly, his eyes suddenly indignant. They flashed like lightning, only black.

A reticent man with a temper. "Are there any groundskeepers?" she asked.

"No. They come next week. Wife, she is gardener. Mr. Rollo, he cuts lawn yesterday with rider mower."

Strange, Bourque thought. A billionaire on a rider mower.

"Mr. Rollo usually eats at seven-thirty," Zupan continued, apparently feeling more forthcoming. "I do not worry until fifteen minutes later. Then I start to look. I find him hanging beside wife, like from a tree." Zupan paused. "I am thinking. Who would do this? Šef, I mean, boss, he is good man."

She remained silent, hoping for more details.

Zupan obliged her. "Šef is happy man. Always content. Always, I tell you."

She waited again, but Zupan was done.

Leaving him with the troopers, she quickly surveyed the castle interior, taking in the area closest to the foyer: a great-room, a study, two sitting rooms. More heavy furniture. No evidence of fights or scuffles. The rooms felt abandoned, as if they hadn't been entered in years. In her experience, victims' houses were often useful clues. This one felt tired and stale, which was incongruous. The Novaks were said to be a gregarious couple.

Returning to the foyer, Bourque beckoned for Donnelly to join her. "We'll let Junior guard the butler," she quietly said. "Please control access to the driveway."

"Consider it done. By the way, I viewed the bodies from a distance. Didn't contaminate the scene. I was thinking of you."

She grinned. "Aw shucks. We'll make a detective of you yet."

"No thanks."

"You'd like it. No road patrols. No underage drinking parties."

Donnelly laughed. "No flying beer bottles?"

"Never say never."

□ □ □

Bourque motioned for Zupan to take her to the pool and remained silent, letting him hang on the hook. He didn't seem to mind. In fact, he seemed to welcome the silence. Outside the pool, she left him with the junior trooper and donned crime scene gear: shoe covers, gloves, and a hooded clean-suit. Instantly, she felt confined yet twice as big. She stepped through a sliding glass door.

The setting surprised her. Compared to the Old-World interior— cluttered and ornate—the pool was ultra-modern and utilitarian, about twenty yards long. The only common denominator with the house was the deck, blue-bordered white tiles that matched the hall floors. The area resembled a cloister—windowless, high stone walls—with one exception: the pool's infinity feature opened half the southern wall. She scanned the deck. No blood stains. No signs of bodies being dragged. Then she saw the bodies, two corpses hanging by the neck from a pool stair rail.

She approached methodically, mentally recording the details. The corpses were submerged from the mid-thigh down, suspended side by side, with no space between them. Their position seemed unnatural—too uniform, too perfect—as if the scene had been staged. Both were naked, except for the man's shorts, which were caught on one foot.

She recognized his face instantly: Rollo Novak, billionaire businessman, TV celebrity, a star on *Angels or Devils*, the hit show featuring financiers who funded startups, sometimes to the detriment of the startups. Angel investors often became devils, executing hostile takeovers. As for the woman, Bourque had seen her on TV as well, a beauty who'd hooked Novak two years ago and snagged him from his first wife. Bourque knew her name: Katrina Hayden. She'd been born in Falmouth. She was a former Miss USA, a dancer, about thirty years old. If Bourque remembered correctly, she was fifteen years younger than her new hubby.

The former Miss USA was closest to Bourque. Even in death, she looked exquisite, and with no makeup. Her skin was flawless. Although her blonde hair hung lankly, it was clearly expensively cut. Her large brown eyes looked like marble.

Bourque moved closer and examined the torso. To say Hayden's body was perfect was an understatement. Strong arms, muscular legs. No signs of trauma. Her bowels had loosened. Bourque ignored the smell. Hayden sported an almost hairless bikini wax. Although her head hair was blonde, her pubic hair was brown. Bourque looked again. A head dye job, she decided. Gentlemen preferred blondes, or was it that blondes preferred gentlemen?

Hayden had joined the ink club. She had a collection of "bedroom" tattoos, visible only when naked. The most noticeable tat was above her pubic bone: a signpost about an inch long, pointing south, with a "G" on it. Nice one, Bourque thought. *To the G-spot, Jeeves.* Two small G-signs adorned each breast, just below the nipples, pointing down. Bourque chuckled privately. Maybe Hayden had some directionally-challenged lovers. Nothing new there.

Bourque studied the victim's neck. It was lassoed by the broad end of a dark red necktie, about three inches wide. There was a silver-toned wire under the tie. She carefully moved Hayden's hair and inspected the back of her neck. The wire ligature was crossed just below the top spinal vertebra and twisted six times, very neatly.

Bourque's mind quickened. The victim couldn't have pulled the wire that deep herself and then twisted it—certainly not so neatly—which pointed to murder, not suicide.

Moving on to Novak, she found similar indications, but the MO, *modus operandi*, was different. There was only one ligature: the broad end of a dark red necktie, again about three inches wide. No wire. Perhaps Novak hadn't been murdered. She assessed the whole scene. Maybe he strangled Hayden and then hanged himself? Possible. More questions surfaced, buzzing her mind like bees. If suicide was in play, why didn't Novak just weigh himself down and jump in the pool? It'd be easier than hanging himself. Was he making a statement?

Slow down, she ordered herself. Let the crime scene reveal itself. She inhaled deeply, exhaled slowly, and repeated the cycle. It stilled her mind. Continuing her examination, she took in Novak's body. For a middle-aged man, he was very fit. Well-muscled yet slim. As with Hayden, rigor hadn't begun and his bowels had loosened.

Her eyes returned to the necktie. The end tied to the stair rail was about a yard long—long enough to enable suicide by hanging. Then again, someone could have used it to strangle him. The noose knot was at the back of his neck. She knew most male strangulation assaults occurred from behind. A frontal assault gave a fit man a chance to fight back. A rear assault suggested murder. However, there was no throttling wire. Given the Hayden MO, that seemed to rule out homicide. So, his death could be a suicide.

Bourque stepped back. As much as she wanted to, she couldn't offer the victims any dignity. They had to remain hanging until the forensic experts, the whitecoats, were finished with them. Either she was looking at two murders, or a murder-suicide. She didn't know which. She exhaled noisily. Her job wasn't to pronounce the cause of death. That was up to the state medical examiner. Her job was to find details that could reconstruct events and solve the crime.

She turned away from the crime scene but the hanging bodies were burned into her mind.

Whenever she encountered murder, she plunged into work mode—secure the scene and collect evidence—and later, when her duties stabilized, the corpses flooded her consciousness and became people: husbands and wives, fathers and mothers, sons and daughters.

Chapter 3

Pacing slowly, Bourque examined the deck area. Nothing except for two plush red robes, which she left to the experts. She stepped close to the infinity pool ledge, leaned out, and looked down. A sheer, smooth wall; a five-yard drop to the ground. The perps could have climbed it using grappling hooks or a ladder, but she didn't detect any scrapes or indentations.

Looking up, she noted it was clear all the way to the ocean, which formed the southern boundary of the estate. The perps might have used a boat, possibly motorless. Gentle waves were rolling ashore, breaking on a golden strand. Quite the location, she thought, close to New England royalty. The Kennedy Compound was barely fifteen miles away. Her mother Sarah, a descendant of the Puritans, had noted Novak's incursion into the area, mentioning his wealth, suspecting it to be "foreign and ill-begotten." Sarah didn't have anything against money—as long as it was old money. In her world, nothing trumped the past.

As a teenager, Bourque had rebelled against everything her parents represented. Nowadays, however, she had a soft spot for history. Incidentally, it happened to have a practical angle. Most New England murders had a link to the past. *Cherchez* the past.

Scanning southward, she saw no useful surveillance posts. However, the perps could have sent up a camera drone. Returning to the pool's shallow end, she strode to a backwall gate and turned the handle. It clicked open. Was it usually open?

She walked outside. A blue jay kamikazed her from the roof. She ducked. Another jay joined the fray, squawking proprietorially. It was slightly smaller. A nesting pair, she saw, a male and female.

Knowing her presence signified an intrusion, she stood completely still and closed her eyes. She felt the sun heating her face, yet just the surface of her skin. The midday air might say summer but the morning air said spring. It would have been chilly when the Novaks went swimming.

Opening her eyes, she took in the surroundings. If not for the murders, it'd be a hell of a morning. The dew-laden grass glittered with tiny diamonds. The beach sand magnified the sun, shining like a mini sun itself. A line of nearby red cedars was twisted helter-skelter, distorted by gales. With its two moods—one refined, one untamed—Cape Cod was as delicate as a lady and as drunk as a lord.

In due course, the jays resettled and she began surveying the gate area. No signs of forced entry. Manicured shrubbery, a path leading toward the ocean. She walked beside the path, leaving it untrampled.

As she paced, her senses logged the grounds. Ocean brine in the air. The smell of freshly-mown grass. A wide swathe of lawn. Not much cover for intruders. Thirty paces later, she turned back. No recent prints or obvious DNA carriers, like bottles or cans. However, considering the dearth of evidence in the pool area, the back gate and grounds were a prime zone for the whitecoats.

Preliminary inspection complete, she called her unit chief, Detective Captain Peabody. "Bourque here," she said. "Two fatalities confirmed."

"Identities?" Peabody asked. His voice was fast and high-pitched, like a whistling teakettle.

"Rollo Novak and his wife," she replied. "Could be two murders. Or a murder and a suicide."

"Suicide? Damn. Messy."

Bourque didn't respond. Peabody preferred murder over suicide. In the public eye, suicides were sad stories. In Peabody's, they were resource burners. Suicide was just another type of murder: premeditated and self-inflicted. His staff would have to probe for motive and opportunity.

"All right," he grudgingly said. "I'll call in two whitecoats."

She kept her counsel. It was a big property. They'd probably need more. Peabody wouldn't like that. Extra whitecoats would ratchet up his budget.

Bourque returned to the house and shed her crime scene gear, glad to be back in civvies—dark green slacks and a brown leather jacket—a bonus of being a non-uniformed officer, along with not wearing a trooper hat. She had her father's thick auburn hair. More than one man had said if she were a blonde, she'd pass for Uma Thurman. Bourque didn't know about that. Her hair certainly wasn't regulation. It was long, wavy, and free. Peabody called it unprofessional. She called it ideal. When he got bothered, she pulled it into a ponytail. In her eyes, a good strategy for a police detective was to avoid looking like one. With her competent manner and quick movements, people often pegged her as a thirty-something paramedic or doctor—which helped at crime scenes. The public tended to tell healthcare workers the truth. Even when she showed her State Police badge, people still seemed to see her as someone helping them, not grilling them.

Bourque motioned for Zupan to follow her. Back in the foyer, she began recording the butler's second interview. "Mr. Zupan, please tell me again. When did you find the bodies of Mr. and Mrs. Novak?"

Zupan appeared to be affronted. "I tell you," he said. "Okay. No problem." He stopped.

"Go ahead," she prodded.

"I am thinking. I want to tell exactly."

She waited, reflecting on Zupan's odd voice. It wasn't only his accent. It sounded like he was swallowing his words, holding them back, as if speaking English offended him. She took in his gelled hair. The comb lines were perfectly straight. He might be tough, but he was also vain. You didn't get hair like that without spending time in front of a mirror.

He referred to his phone. "All right. I know nine-one-one call was seven fifty-two. I found bodies three minutes before that, maybe four. Not more, this I can say. I am officer in Serbian army. Artillery captain. I know how to be exact. You police need precise and my time is precise to within minutes."

Perhaps too precise, Bourque thought. "When did you last see Mr. Novak or his wife?"

"Last night, maybe eleven p.m."

"Who was in the house last night?"

"Mr. Rollo and wife, and also Mr. Rollo's friend. I serve dinner to those three at eight p.m."

"What's the friend's name?"

Zupan's lips curled into a partial sneer. "Karlos Vega."

Bourque knew that name. Vega, another bigshot on *Angels or Devils*—for many viewers, the face of the devil. "The billionaire?"

Zupan nodded.

"Was Mr. Vega here this morning?"

"No. He goes last night, about quarter after eleven. I see his car leave from my suite over garage."

"How do you know he actually left?"

"I hear too. His car reached main road and turned left, to direction of Falmouth. I have window open. I can hear this."

"Why was your window open?"

"I sleep like that. The air here, it is clean, like in Slovenian mountains. I love to sleep here."

She switched to good cop mode. "Are you from Slovenia?"

"Yes. I am born there. Northwest of Ljubljana. Jesenice, very fine place, I tell you. Especially now, in spring. Trees come to life. Apple, pear, plum. Many blossoms."

"Sounds nice," she said. Despite his new volubility, she wondered about the open window. Although mid-May, it had been unusually cold at night. The heat in her house was still on. "You mentioned Mr. Novak was always content. Did he have any enemies?"

"Mr. Rollo is fair man, but not simple man. Some people think so. They *misjudge* him, I hear him say. He is not easy to fool. Sometimes he gives money, sometimes he takes. I am not business man," Zupan confided, "but I hear. Many dollars. Millions."

"How about personal enemies?"

"He does not have."

She took that with a grain. Everyone except angels had enemies. Probably even angels. "How about his family?"

"There is one son, Atlas. He does not like his father." Zupan's face hardened. "Of this I am sure. He want to run all of Šef's business. He want to takeover, you call it."

"What about the rest of Mr. Novak's family?"

"There is ex-wife but I never meet her."

"Do you know anything about her?"

He shrugged. "A little. Mr. Rollo, he still give her money. She has none of her own."

"How do you know?"

"I hear it from Mr. Rollo."

Bourque wondered about that. Either Zupan overheard a lot, or Novak told him a lot. "Do you have relatives in America?"

Zupan hesitated. "I have sister in Boston."

"Does she work there?"

"Yes. At pharma lab near MIT."

"What's her full name?"

"Snežana Marija Zupan."

"Did Mr. Novak know her?"

Zupan nodded. "They are friends. They share Old Country in common. Good food, good company."

How much in common, Bourque wondered. "Did your sister see Mr. Novak often?"

"When he is in Boston, almost everyday. She is also friends with his wife."

"Where was your sister this morning?"

"Airport. She is leaving for Slovenia."

Bourque's antennae went up. "When?"

"Ten-thirty."

She glanced at her watch. Snežana's flight was already gone—barely hours after the hangings. Coincidence? "Why did she leave?"

"Holiday."

Bourque would ask Boston PD, aka Metro, to question Snežana's employer. When had she booked her holiday? When was she due back? Given the territorial blue jays, Bourque suspected intruders had used the back gate, possibly intruders working with Zupan or his sister. The link seemed too obvious, but in homicide cases insiders raised red flags—whether they were relatives or people in the victims' orbit. She'd send Zupan's footwear and clothes to the lab. He could be the killer. On the other hand, he might simply be a person of interest, a POI.

Although Bourque had nothing concrete against Zupan, she decided to detain him, without arresting him. Always a tricky dance. "Thank you. You've been very helpful. You'll remain at the house for the time being, for your security. You can stay in your suite. I'm posting a trooper to secure your safety."

"I do not need," he boomed. "I look after myself!"

"Of course," she replied, "but we're going to err on the side of safety." The butler brought to mind a human stormfront: thunderous voice, lightning eyes.

□ □ □

While the junior trooper led Zupan away, Bourque's duty phone crooned Elvis Costello. She'd recently changed the default State Police ringtone, reminiscent of a submarine claxon, to *Watching the Detectives*.

"Watching the detectives," Costello sang. "Watching the detectives—"

She fished out her phone and answered. "Lieutenant Bourque, Cape & Islands."

"Eller here. They're parachuting me into the Novaks case. They want two lieutenants on it."

"Understood." She'd worked a few cases with Detective Lieutenant Victor Eller, one of eight roving lieutenants run by the State Attorney General's office, known as Central. Eller had an eighty percent solve rate, which made him the envy of Boston's homicide squad. They rarely cracked sixty percent these days, not from lack of trying. Her recently departed father, a Boston homicide superintendent, used to say that the main reason murders went unsolved was out of his control: *dead people didn't talk*. He had deeper roots in the New World than his wife, which annoyed her. Her ancestors had arrived in Salem in the 1630s, whereas his had settled Quebec City in 1608.

"I'll update Peabody," Eller went on. "I know how you hate filing reports."

"Always the gentleman." She smiled to herself. Reporting was a way for Eller to get ahead, yet she didn't care if he took the spotlight. She didn't want to climb the career ladder. The top brass were paper-pushers; they didn't do any actual detecting.

"What's your one-minute synopsis?" Eller asked.

"Two dead, either a double murder or a murder-suicide. Strangulations."

"What's your feeling, Double-M or M-S? Your intuition, that is."

Intuition? This was a new Eller. On other cases, it'd been weeks before he'd spoken of intuition. "Can't say yet. Too close to call."

Hearing a car in the drive, Bourque looked out a window and saw Dr. Andre Wozniak, the regional medical examiner, exiting his car.

She strode to the front door and let Wozniak in. His face was red. His nose was redder. The medical examiner had a love affair with Polish vodka. As usual, he wore a tight three-piece suit. His head looked like Humpty Dumpty's, shiny and comically wide.

The corners of his mouth turned up into a jovial smile. "Morning, Lieutenant Bourque. What a surprise," he teased.

She bowed good-humoredly. She worked most Cape Cod homicides.

Before entering the pool area, Bourque donned full crime scene, aka CS, gear and insisted Wozniak do the same. Although he always wore gloves and shoe covers, he was averse to wearing clean-suits. She had some idea why. After fifteen minutes, the suits made her sweat. She could imagine what they did to him.

Nearing the corpses, she took a series of CS photos before signaling him forward.

Wozniak began with Hayden's body, studying it intently. Being a long-serving medical examiner, he knew the drill. Don't move a body unless absolutely necessary. Finally, he spoke. "We have proximity to sufficient water for drowning, but there are no signs of drowning. Or blunt force assault or firearm injuries. However, there are two ligatures, a wire and a necktie. I haven't seen that before. The wire caused deep compression. Extensive bruising of the neck, extensive hemorrhaging of the infrahyoid muscles. I bet you know them?"

She nodded. "The straps. Eight muscles that help hold the head in place."

He smiled. "A in Anatomy. Look closely at the neck. The wire is the culprit, not the tie. The extensive blood flow indicates homicidal strangulation. Infrahyoids only bleed that much when a ligature is applied with sufficient force. If someone applies force to their own neck, they can certainly strangle themselves, but they don't usually cause that kind of blood flow. From what I see, the wire wasn't tightened by the victim. I see homicide, not suicide."

That's what she saw.

His eyes moved down the body. Eventually he glanced up at Bourque. "Regard the vulva. It shows evidence of recent intercourse, including the presence of semen. Sadly, strangulation is frequently associated with sexual interference. Make sure your technicians capture the semen."

Wozniak switched to Novak. As with Hayden, he studied Novak before speaking. "There are traces of semen on the penis. Advise your technicians. No signs of drowning, blunt force assault, or firearm injuries. I only detect one ligature, a necktie. There's not as much bleeding as with the female. Which could indicate either homicidal strangulation or self-strangulation. Unlike with the previous victim, this victim could have hanged himself."

Again, as she thought.

"We're lucky," the examiner stated, "the hat trick should work today."

"Good." Wozniak's *hat trick* was lividity, algor mortis, and rigor mortis. Lividity, or blood pooling, left bruise-like patterns on a corpse, usually reddish or purple. Algor referred to a body turning cold. When the heart stopped and blood flow ceased, body temperature dropped by about two degrees Fahrenheit each hour, until it reached air temperature. Rigor mortis, or body stiffening, took hours to become fully established. The triumvirate predicted PMI, post-mortem interval. If the team could place a suspect at a crime scene during the PMI window, they had opportunity; they could probe for motive.

Wozniak knelt next to Hayden. "Rigor hasn't hardened the largest muscles," he pronounced and pointed to the glutes. "Which indicates this victim died less than twelve hours ago. No sign of lividity, not to the naked eye. We'll use algor." He drew a liver thermometer from his medical bag and pierced the victim's right side. "Ninety-three-point-one Fahrenheit," he read. "Given ninety-eight-point-six is the norm, algor suggests the victim died roughly three hours ago."

Wozniak moved on to Novak. "I see the same indications," he soon said. "No large-muscle rigor. No lividity." He used his liver thermometer to read Novak's internal temperature. "Ninety-two-point-five." He stood. "I'd conjecture both victims died three to four hours ago. Approximately," he emphasized. "Cause of death is strangulation. Means are trickier. I'd rule homicide for the female. The male could be either homicide or suicide."

While Wozniak walked back to the house, Bourque lagged behind. The sun's rays ricocheted off the deck tiles, creating confusing reflections. Her thoughts were ricocheting around as well, flying in different directions.

Chapter 4

With the medical examiner gone, Bourque sat on the front steps. The castle was only four stories high yet it loomed above her, an alien presence in the pine forest. Dawn had become day. The cloudless sky was brighter and bluer. May warmth suffused the air. In a nearby red oak, grackles chattered vociferously, countering the presence of death. The blue jays were silent. Leaning against a stone balustrade, she went over what she knew with certainty. Not a lot. She had no firm leads on motive. There was no evidence of forced entry. From what she'd seen of the castle interior, it hadn't been ransacked. She could be looking at a botched B&E, a Break-and-Enter gone bad, but why would thieves string up the Novaks? They might kill them, but hang them with neckties? She didn't see it. The more time spent on killing, the less time left to pillage.

The population of Cape Cod was relatively small, about 200,000. In some places, like Nantucket, it increased more than tenfold in summer, which had yet to result in a similar increase in violent crime. In one sense, the Cape was like any region in America: most murders could be attributed to greed. In another sense, the region was very different: considering the amount of wealth, murders were unusual.

Bourque eyed the large reflecting pool facing the castle. It was as still as the air. Away from the ocean, there was no wind. She pulled up Google Earth on her phone. While the nearby properties were all under two acres, Novak's estate was 8.8 acres. The castle was isolated—a good locale for murder.

Before becoming a cop, she'd studied organic chemistry, a discipline based on the transmutability of carbon. The building blocks of life were the building blocks of death. All life was death. How could homicides unsettle her? Ashes to ashes, carbon to carbon. She found organic chemistry overly theoretical, which led her to seek more tangible work, like tracking down murderers.

She sat quietly, letting her mind cycle. There were suggestions from Zupan that financial gain was in play. The old chestnut. Money. Who'd benefit from Novak's death? His family would certainly be center stage. Ditto for his business partners. She wondered how often he'd become a devil investor. Depending on the money involved, an aggrieved partner could turn into a murderer. She'd subpoena all *Angels or Devils* footage, including the outtakes. Then there were Novak's many other business ventures. He'd been a billionaire well before rising to TV stardom.

Get your blinkers off, she chastised herself. What about Hayden? Just because she was a glamour girl, it didn't mean she had no money of her own. Someone could have killed her for financial gain, maybe Novak himself. However, that undermined the murder-suicide angle. Why would he murder her for money and kill himself?

Bourque shrugged. Perhaps he'd taken Hayden's money previously and left it with someone, who then murdered him to keep it. Enough, she told herself. You're getting convoluted.

It was time to marshal what she knew. Peabody's favorite saying was *a detective without facts is like a duck without wings. Lame.* As far as his bromides went, it wasn't bad.

While dictating preliminary observations into her duty phone, Donnelly puttered up in his squad car. He drove like a farmer piloting a hay baler: slowly and with deference. A grin was never far from his face but people didn't mess with him. At six-foot-five, two hundred-and-forty pounds, even in his mid-forties he still resembled a football player. He'd once played linebacker for the New England Patriots.

"I'll handle the butler now," he said. "By the way, that's a suspicious man. Fancy suit, but doesn't trim his ear hair."

She grinned. "That is suspicious."

"I know, only to a rookie. But I'm half-serious. He moves like a big cat. A killer cat."

"Agreed. You have a good eye."

"Listen, why don't we nudge things along a tad and set a few snoops in his suite?"

Bourque shook her head gently. Snoop cameras, she knew. In her undercover days with the Boston Police Department, she'd have done it. Back then, she'd temporarily *adjusted* rules to snag perps. She'd tried hard to be a successful criminal, and succeeded. That's when she knew she had to leave undercover and straighten out. It wasn't something she ever talked about. She'd been on the other side, and come back. As her mother's friends would have put it, where once she was lost, now she was found.

"We might catch him in the act," Donnelly continued, "flushing evidence or throwing it out."

"Appreciate the thought, but when your head tells you to play it by the rules, you do."

"I hear you. Don't get ahead of yourself, as in don't plow the driveway before it snows."

She chuckled. "Exactly. Besides, Zupan's story checks so far. And we don't have a surveillance warrant."

"Understood. If we found anything, it'd be considered 'fruit of the poisoned tree.'" He shook his head. "You detectives, you're all hog-tied."

She nodded heartily. Yet that was the system. As she now knew, the undercover way was easier, but it was also a good way to torpedo a court case. One glitch and a guilty perp could walk on a technicality.

Donnelly shrugged. "Wife says I'm too good for my badge."

"And too sexy for your uniform."

"*Me?*" Donnelly wiggled his butt, then sashayed away with an exaggerated strut.

She almost went inside to type her case notes. However, the sun was pleasant, warm enough to intensify the scent of pine. Pine sap was one of her favorite organic compounds. It smelled sweet yet sharp, it spoke of summer and winter at the same time. Seeing a patio table in the shade, she fetched her laptop from her car and began making case notes. When she'd applied to become a detective, she had no idea how much paperwork it entailed: case notes, warrants, subpoenas, reports. Stenographer City.

Having almost finished her notes, she looked up to see Eller's elongated black Ford Explorer roaring up the drive. His car reminded her of a hearse, which, given his job, was appropriate. While she was a generalist—handling major crimes as well as homicides—he was a specialist, a full-time homicide detective. In twenty-six years as a detective, he'd worked over 300 murders. In her eight years—three with Boston PD, five with the State Police— she'd worked ninety-plus. Jumping out of his hearse, he grabbed a crime scene kitbag and strode rapidly toward her. He wore a natty midnight blue suit and a blue-green tie.

Eller was a tall, fit man with a high-domed forehead and steel-grey hair. His visage was civil yet shrewd. He kept his home life to himself but Bourque knew he lived in a rambling bungalow near

Holyoke, far from Central. Although in his mid-fifties, he walked like a much younger man, one who got things done. He gestured at the patio table. "Nice HQ."

She winked, "Alfresco." She worked well with Eller. He was usually calm and even-tempered, although he could do a tough bad cop, which is what she wanted in a partner: a level-headed detective who breathed fire when it was called for. She waved him to the castle. "I'll take you to the bodies."

Leading him to the pool area, she kept her investigative opinions to herself. She didn't want to color his first impressions.

After donning CS gear, the two detectives walked the pool deck to the shallow end, Eller's eyes sweeping the tiles. Reaching the corpses, he knelt beside Hayden. He seemed lost in thought. Bourque almost asked what he was thinking. He was more unhurried than usual. Just as she parted her lips, he spoke.

"I see murder." He pointed to the wire ligature. "Can't cut it any other way. The necktie is a red herring. A very red herring." He gestured at Hayden's pubic area, then her head. "The front porch isn't the same color as the roof."

Bourque nodded. "Pretty common these days."

"A dime a dozen?"

"Depends on social circle and fashion trends."

"Sounds like a study unto itself." He turned to Novak's corpse.

She left him to his analysis and took in the complete crime scene. The dark red of the two neckties caught her eye. It reminded her of the bottom band of the Slovenian flag. She'd taken a few holidays in the Adriatic with her ex-husband Nico, who was born in neighboring Italy. Did the necktie color mean anything? Maybe it was a message to Novak's family. If so, from whom? Old-World connections? In the movies, she'd be jetting off to Slovenia to track down Novak's past. Not in real life. Too bad. She loved the Adriatic. People *respected* wine there; i.e., they knew how to drink it. In real life, two words got in the way of a jet plane: Central's budget.

Eller finally looked up. "Another murder," he stated. "I don't see suicide." His voice was measured and quiet. "Hangers sometimes change their minds, try to undo their neck ligatures, and leave evidence: broken fingernails, self-lacerations. There's no indication of that. Beyond that, there's the position of the necktie knot. In a hanging suicide, it usually jerks up when the body falls, ending above the spinal vertebra. But it's below that vertebra, which suggests murder, not suicide. What did the medical examiner rule?"

"Cause of death, strangulation. Means, homicide for Hayden. Either homicide or suicide for Novak."

"I don't like second-guessing a medical examiner," Eller mused, "but when you see something, you can't un-see it. Looks like two murders. I'll ask Peabody to release a press statement this afternoon. Let's hold off on what we actually know. We can announce a double suicide. Let the murderers think we don't have a clue." He chuckled. "We're useless idiots. Ruling possibilities out when we should be ruling them in. What do you think? Two suicides?"

She nodded.

"But we'll close with a little caveat: pending further investigation. Don't want to have egg on our faces when we announce the real McCoy."

She knew Eller was thinking aloud. She liked his MO. He didn't keep his ideas to himself. Other detectives she'd worked with kept their theories private, never airing missteps, believing the way to get ahead was to always look right, regardless.

Eller carried on. "Before I left Central, I looked up recent strangulation cases. There aren't many in the system. It's a rare form of murder in Massachusetts, less than ten in the last three decades."

"Good," she said. Rare was useful. It limited the known perp gene pool.

"All the cases were solved, not that that helps us. But we can use it to bolster the troops. Past victories point to future success and all that. *Now go and solve this!* You know the speech."

Bourque wasn't the rah-rah speech type. The "troops" didn't need someone on a high horse to lead them to victory. If finding murderers didn't motivate them, what would?

Eller turned back to the bodies. "I don't see Novak standing around while his wife was strangled, or vice versa. There were likely two perps. One to strangle her; the other to strangle him. And maybe someone riding shotgun. The corpses are hanging very close together. If more people were involved, it would crowd the scene, making close work difficult."

Bourque agreed. "I think we have a staging of sorts. Perhaps there's messaging in play."

He nodded thoughtfully.

"Let's talk to the butler," she said.

"There's a butler?" Eller grinned. "The butler did it. Case closed."

She chuckled. "If only."

"What's your read on him?"

She shrugged. Again, she'd didn't want to color Eller's first impressions. She didn't believe everything Zupan said. Although people preferred to believe each other—belief built cooperation; it was a societal glue—on a case, she walked the fine line between treating POIs with respect and treating them like liars.

Bourque led Eller to Zupan's studio, delivering a synopsis of her two previous interviews with the butler. Damijan Zupan was Slovenian, like Novak. He'd been an artillery captain in the Serbian army. He had a sister in Boston who knew the Novaks. He'd served dinner to the Novaks the previous evening, and to a guest, Karlos Vega.

Eller stopped her. "*The* Karlos Vega?"

"Yes. From what I know, Vega is one of Novak's best friends."

"Hard to believe. Oil and water, those two, with Vega the oily one."

"Very greasy. I'll email you the audio of my interviews with Zupan."

While Eller listened to the audio files, she retrieved her laptop, sat outside and resumed her notes. Her never-ending notes. Despite the ideal spring weather, she felt trapped. Fortunately, the trap was soon sprung. Eller approached her half an hour later.

"So," he said, "it appears Vega was the last POI to see the Novaks alive. I'm thinking he should be at the front of the POI line. You?"

"Good place to start."

"I talked to Vega. He's at his Boston condo. Back Bay area. He'll *entertain us*—his words—at eighteen-hundred."

"Kind of him."

"He's granting us thirty minutes, no more. Apparently, he has to fly to Miami this evening. Private jet from Logan but, still, there's the limo to the airport and the pilot needs runway time."

"Poor Vega." She shook her head in mock sympathy. "So little time to add to his billions."

"And the likes of you and me, we'll have to hoof it to Boston."

"How about my car this time?"

"Sure. Let's stay in Boston tonight. Atlas is there, as well as his mother. They live downtown, but in different neighborhoods. By the way, I hooked Atlas for ten-hundred tomorrow. I hope you don't mind. I also hooked the ex-wife for thirteen-hundred. Let's leave as soon as we're done with Zupan."

"It won't be right after. The local forensic crew is on the way. I have to debrief them." One side of her wanted to stay behind to work the crime scene and consolidate the evidence. On the other hand, they had to gather new evidence. The first forty-eight hours were critical. A murder case was like an avalanche. If it lost its momentum, it ground to a halt.

□ □ □

Unlike the rest of the castle, Zupan's studio apartment had no medieval art. The furniture was white ash; the window coverings, peach-colored—didn't match anything in the castle. In Bourque's view, the mismatch was potentially suspicious. Maybe the suite was an afterthought, like the butler himself. Would Novak, a man who mowed his own lawn, hire a butler? Had Zupan wormed his way into the job to eventually kill the Novaks? If so, was Snežana part of the con? It'd be a long con but, as Bourque knew from her undercover years, a long con was the best con. She filed her thoughts away.

Eller preceded her into the studio. She usually let him lead interviews. It allowed her to focus on a POI's body language.

Eller invited Zupan to take a kitchen chair and remained standing. "Detective Lieutenant Eller, Central Homicide. I'm curious, Mr. Zupan. Did you know Mr. Novak was swimming in the outdoor pool today?"

Zupan said nothing for a few long heartbeats. "Yes. He advises me yesterday."

"I wonder if you can help us. Why do you think Mr. Novak hanged himself?"

"He did not." Zupan's eyes flashed. His voice had descended a few octaves, almost to a growl.

"Why do you say that?" Eller placidly asked.

"Is complete truth. This I know."

"How can you know he didn't kill himself? Not to get philosophical, but no one knows what goes on in someone else's head."

"This I agree. I know only what I know. And, in this case, I know.

Is good enough for me."

"But not for a court of law."

"This too I know. We are caught between inner truths and outer truths. But I am responsible for knowing. And for making correct choices."

Okay, Bourque thought, enough of the existentialism.

Eller seemed to agree. He switched topics. "Tell me about Karlos Vega."

"He is loud, but he is rich. Much richer than Mr. Rollo. I hear Mr. Rollo say this. Also he says Vega is sometimes, what is word, tactless. But Mr. Rollo, he likes Vega."

"Do you like Vega?"

"Not so much. But I do not dislike either. He is like older brother to Mr. Rollo. He is watchful. No, is not correct word. I am now remembering my English lessons. Better word is *protective*. I hear Mr. Rollo say to wife, 'Karlos and I are good together.' Vega is making sure boss makes more money. Much more. Mrs. Katrina likes that. She showed much interest in making money."

Bourque read his tone. Disapproval. Wives shouldn't sully themselves making money.

"Did you like her?" Eller asked.

Zupan shrugged. "Snežana likes her. They cook together, they laugh."

"Are you responsible for the security of this house?"

"I am very responsible," Zupan haughtily replied. "I set and monitor security system. Mr. Rollo shows me how. He trains me. System is powerful. Has twelve cameras, all outward-facing. They see everything."

"And inside the house?" Eller asked.

"There are no cameras. Mr. Rollo want privacy inside."

"What about the artwork, such as the three-piece painting in the foyer?"

Zupan snorted. "You mean triptych? Is *altare portatile*. Reproduction of *Dresden Triptych* by Jan van Eyck. Mr. Rollo try to buy original, but they would not sell."

Dresden Triptych, Bourque thought, *altare portatile*. Zupan was no goon. In the same vein, Novak wasn't a typical nouveau riche New Englander. He bought devotional art, not big-screen TVs.

"Is the *altare*," Eller mildly asked, "secure?"

"Yes, same as all art in house. Is protected one-hundred percent with force fields. You try to remove art, fields zap you. If power goes out, there is backup, run by generator."

"Is it fail-proof?"

"No. No system is fail-proof," Zupan stated matter-of-factly. "But I am here. I am trained in other things. Hand-to-hand, guns, knives. I know them all."

"What about the grounds? Do you monitor the grounds?"

"Yes. Grounds are secure."

"Then why was the pool gate unlocked?"

"Is not unlocked."

"It was this morning."

Zupan's face reddened. "Is not possible. Not possible, I say." He jutted out his hefty chin.

Bourque contradicted him. "The gate was unlocked. I went through it about half an hour after I met you."

Zupan studied her, seemingly judging her words. Eventually he shrugged. "Is strange. Is, as you say, suspicious."

"So," Eller said, "the grounds weren't secure."

"I am surprise."

"I'll take your word for it." Eller's smile said the polar opposite.

□ □ □

Outside the studio, Eller gestured at the closed door. "Good idea to pen him. Let's keep him as long as possible."

Bourque called Donnelly over and gestured inside. "He doesn't leave."

"Roger. A butler in hand is worth two in the woods. Running like hell."

Eller smiled at Donnelly. "Can't say you're wrong."

While Bourque and Eller headed to her car, he informed her Peabody had booked the autopsies for the next afternoon. "The fan's starting to spin," Eller said with a wry grin. "Shit will fly."

"Oh yeah." Autopsy openings usually took several days. As they both knew, when Peabody got directly involved, although the budget didn't go up, their pace did, not that she minded a fast pace. A good murder investigation had the pulse of a Blondie song: hard-driving, made for moving down the highway.

Chapter 5

Boston. May 14th

Early that evening, Bourque and Eller pulled up to the Regency Private Residences in Back Bay. The sun sat low in the west, tingeing the condo tower burgundy red. The sky was robin's-egg-blue. A valet sluggishly walked their way, in no mood to service them. Bourque assumed it was due to her car: an eight-year-old Mazda 3, unwashed to boot. These days, she didn't get to Boston often. To some, it was open-minded, even radical; to others, past its best-before date. To her, it was the city she'd grown up in, a melding of the old and the new, riding a wave of tech and healthcare—unrecognizably glitzy in places, stately New England in others.

Eller powered the passenger window down. "We're here to see Mr. Karlos Vega," he snapped.

The valet's back instantly straightened. "He expecting you, sir?"

"Yes. We have a six o-clock appointment." They were five minutes early.

The valet bowed and pointed to the lobby. "Go right in. I'll take care of your car."

Inside the lobby, a liveried attendant escorted them to a quiet alcove with a pair of luxurious coffee-brown leather chairs. "Please, have a seat."

Thirty minutes later the two detectives were still sitting. Bourque had begun researching Zupan on her phone. The butler was born in 1973, which made him Novak's age. Maybe Novak talked to him because of their shared past. They came from a fractured region. Yugoslavia had disintegrated in the 1990s, giving way to seven nations, Serbia and Slovenia among them, adding further complexity to the historical divisiveness of the Balkans. Though Slovenia was the same size as Massachusetts, its population was two million, as opposed to the state's seven million. She scanned a Balkans topographical map. It was no wonder the Balkans were divided. There was little geographic continuity. The region resembled a maze. The valleys ran in all directions—north, south, east, and west.

Moving on, she determined Zupan had arrived in the U.S. three years ago and worked a year as a security guard in Boston before joining Novak. Snežana, who was eight years younger than Zupan, had arrived just after her brother joined Novak and had begun working as a lab assistant. On the drive to Boston, Metro had called to report on her employer. Snežana had requested her holiday two weeks ago, relatively short notice. She was due to return in five days. She was an excellent employee: a hard worker, on time, always pleasant.

Bourque looked up the siblings' addresses. Zupan lived with Novak at his main residence on Avon Hill Street, Cambridge. Snežana lived three blocks away, where she rented a coach house. Excellent employee or not, that made Bourque suspicious. Coach houses in Novak's neighborhood were beyond the means of most lab assistants.

Switching to Wikipedia, she checked out the Serbian Army, which, she soon learned, had supported the Bosnian Serbs during the Siege of Sarajevo, at three-plus years, one of the longest sieges in modern history. She remembered it and the bitter Bosnian War. She wondered if Zupan had taken part in the Siege. He was an artillery man. He was old enough: nineteen at the start. The team would question the siblings separately and simultaneously to see if their stories held together.

For now, she zipped off a secure email to her old friend Tom Gronski, a captain in Organized Crime with Metro, asking for a global search on Zupan and his sister. Research done, she sank into the lobby chair. Very nice. She'd like to buy two for her living room. Then again, the likely price—a fortnight's salary—wasn't on. She sensed someone close by and looked up to see a beefy man approaching them. Given his severely broken nose, she took him for a brawler. He wore his expensive dark suit and polished shoes proudly, but they didn't make him a gentleman. His wide neck said *muscle, pure muscle*. Unlike with Zupan, she wasn't expecting any existential musing from this man.

"Show me your IDs," Wideneck bluntly ordered.

The detectives obliged. "And who are you?" Eller asked.

"Mr. Vega's Security Manager. Follow me."

No name offered, Bourque noted, no pretense of welcome. The three rode up an elevator in silence. It opened onto a huge private foyer. Vega owned the Residence's only penthouse, the entire top floor. Wideneck ushered them forward, leaving them in another placid alcove. A huge rococo vase held dozens of fresh tiger lilies. The stamens were glossy and engorged. The petals glowed like they were lit from within. Bourque eyed the vase. She'd bet it was solid gold. She was familiar with ostentation. Nico had expensive tastes, yet Vega's condo orbited another planet altogether.

A waiter appeared bearing a gold drink tray. He wore a gold-braided uniform. "Champagne or Cognac?" he asked.

Eller waved him off.

Bourque asked if he had water. A minute later, he reappeared with sparkling water served in a gold-rimmed glass. More gold. A Midas theme.

Within seconds, Karlos Vega joined them. She didn't hear him coming. Taking in his last step, she saw he walked like a puma, on the balls of his feet. She and Eller stood. The famous man was about her height, five-foot-seven, above average for a woman, but subpar for a man. He wore a sleek ebony-black suit, white shirt, charcoal tie, gold cufflinks, and crocodile-skin shoes. His long dark hair was tied back in a ponytail. It shone like buffed onyx. His face radiated health—wrong, Bourque decided—it radiated money. She felt distinctly underdressed.

Vega shook hands and sat in the chair opposite them. His eyes said he could buy anything, including them. According to the celebrity rumor mills, what you saw of him in public was what you got in private: a take-no-prisoners smart-ass. "I could have met you on time," he divulged, "but I decided to keep you waiting." His voice was loud yet silky. "Don't be offended, Lieutenant Eller, I wanted to find out about you. With some people, it takes less than a minute. With you, longer. In my world, the longer you wait, the more important you are." He smirked. "Sometimes."

Eller said nothing.

Vega turned to Bourque. "You, Lieutenant, are a bit difficult to plumb. Keep out of the limelight, don't you?" He scrutinized her frankly. "Not likely from any lack of confidence. Yet you prefer to lay back."

He'd nailed her on that one, Bourque admitted. Was it that obvious? In any case, it seemed to be his nature. From what she'd seen on TV, he was a man of quick judgments that were often correct. He liked to probe people for weaknesses and show right away he'd uncovered them.

He glanced at his watch. "What do you want to ask me?" His tone was somehow both arrogant and agreeable.

Eller leaned in. "Was Mr. Novak on edge lately, worried about anything?"

"The old standard." Vega waved dismissively. "The *old wives* standard, I should say. Haven't you detectives gotten past Agatha Christie?" He huffed. "To answer your question, Rollo wasn't a worrier."

"Did he mention any business deals that were troublesome?"

"All deals are troublesome," Vega replied with condescension. "Contrary to what most people think, a deal is not sealed with a handshake. That's just the start."

Bourque shook her head inwardly. Most POIs acted deferential or nervous, even fearful. Not Vega.

"I mean," Eller said, "was he involved in any deals that might have made enemies?"

"All deals have that potential. However, he had no enemies that I knew of, business or personal."

Eller tried a new tack. "Do you know why Mr. Novak committed suicide?"

"Suicide? That's ridiculous. Where do you detectives get your theories? If one can call them theories."

"Forensic science," Eller said.

"You call that science? Imprisoning people based on a fingerprint pattern? Excuse my bluntness. That's bullshit."

Bourque couldn't argue with that. The man was right. Fingerprints were unreliable.

"That was the past," Eller stated. "We've learned."

"I hope so," Vega shot back. "Move it along." He shook his head as if they'd kept him waiting, not the opposite.

Bourque stepped in. "Apparently, Mr. Novak had no enemies. Given the detection you do on TV—the *theories* you form—why don't you tell us why."

"Touché, Lieutenant. And I will tell you. Because Rollo was fair in everything, often too fair. Not a patsy, but too much of a gentleman for his own good."

"For his own profit, you mean."

"Let's not waste time. You two have a lot of hard work ahead of you."

She nodded accord but not acquiescence. Like many arrogant

people, Vega shut down topics he disliked. "When did you last visit Mr. Novak's house in East Falmouth?"

"Yesterday. Only for the day. I arrived around eight a.m. and departed about eleven-thirty p.m."

"Where did you arrive from?"

"Here. I left just after seven. Some people think Rollo and I spent all our time drinking champagne. Incorrect. We worked. We got up early."

"What can you tell us about Melanya, Mr. Novak's first wife?"

"Very little. She's beautiful, but everybody knows that. I rarely socialized with her." Vega stopped and regarded his hands, then looked up. "We didn't talk, other than to say hello, and Rollo didn't talk about her with me. I didn't visit him much at home until he married Kat."

Kat, Bourque noted. No one else had called her Kat. A small thing, but Bourque looked for small things. She committed the tidbit to memory. "When did you meet Mr. Novak?"

"About five years ago, on the set of *Angels or Devils*. We became fast friends, which surprised some." He grinned mischievously. "To extend a theme, to many people, Rollo's an angel and I'm a devil. I'm not all ego, Detective. I have some self-knowledge."

She nodded. "What about Katrina Novak?"

"Let me put it this way: she is—was—" he corrected himself and sighed heavily. "She was both an angel and a devil. Both heavenly and earthly. Tall, blonde, and beautiful, like Melanya, but a lot more worldly. Despite the bombshell appearance, one might say bimbo appearance, she was as smart as they come. And as tough." Vega glanced at his watch.

"Did Mr. Novak have many female friends?"

"Of course. A handsome man like him."

"Did he have any special ones?"

"I can't think of any."

Or you're not saying. Bourque wouldn't be surprised if Novak had a lover or two tucked away. He was handsome *and* rich, an irresistible combo for many women. "Very good, Mr. Vega. We'll need to speak with you again."

"That won't be easy to arrange. After Miami, I'm due in São Paulo. Two days later, I'm back here for a night, but I fly to Hong Kong the next morning."

"We'll book a time."

Vega shrugged.

"I thought Mr. Novak was one of your best friends. With all due respect, I think you should make time."

Vega studied Bourque silently. Eventually he nodded. "You're right. Here's my card. Call me."

"In the meantime, we need to take a DNA swab and fingerprint you."

Vega's eyes narrowed.

"Standard procedure," she explained. "We have a kit."

"I'm going to call my lawyer."

"By all means," she said. "We simply want to eliminate you as a suspect. We don't want to confuse your bio matter with anyone else's."

Vega considered her words. "All right."

□ □ □

As Bourque approached the Sheraton on Dalton Street, Eller perked up. He'd won their hotel debate. He'd insisted on the Sheraton. She'd voted for the Holiday Inn Express on Boston Street, but he said it was too down-market. She hated splurging, even when it was taxpayer's money. In that respect, she took after her mother and a long line of no-nonsense Yankees. Nico used to joke that being part-Yankee, her cheapness was inevitable. *I'm frugal*, she would counter. In her view, you were frugal if you pinched pennies on your own behalf. If you pinched them when buying for others, you were cheap.

She didn't miss Nico Rizzi in the least. His family, on the other hand, was a great loss, especially his mother, who was a magnificent cook. The Rizzis were from Brindisi, the heel of Italy's boot. In *mamma's cucina*, the tomato reigned supreme, whether sun-dried or roasted, stewed or grilled; whether flavored with basil, rosemary, or oregano. Then there were her fish stews, cioppino-type marvels chock full of tomatoes, garlic, scorpion fish, squid, mussels, and clams. Bourque counted herself lucky to be living in Massachusetts, where first-rate tomatoes, garlic, and seafood were plentiful. While she could cook a decent cioppino, it didn't hold a candle to Mamma Rizzi's.

Having reached the Sheraton, the detectives checked into their rooms and went to the hotel steakhouse for dinner. When they were away from home overnight, they could expense their meals. Nonetheless, Bourque kept things simple. They rushed through their mains—filet mignon for Eller, fettucine with chicken & wild mushrooms for her (disappointing)—and passed on dessert in order to reach his room for a teleconference with forensic officers Dan Munro and John Wolf from Central, known as the ninjas, as well as Barnstable forensic officers Paul Magnotta and Tamara Miller.

All communication lines encrypted, the ninjas began the proceedings. They worked seamlessly together, as if they were a single unit. They reported the Novak security system was state-of-the-art, but it wasn't wireless. The wire arming the back-gate alarm had been cut at 0622. They swept the path from the pool which ended at the beach, 260 yards away. They only found three workable shoeprints.

Miller went next, relating that she videotaped the crime scene and took over 200 photos. She searched the house for personal electronic devices and discovered a laptop and two smartphones. Having powdered the complete pool deck, she found shoeprints leading from the sliding pool door to near the hanging rail, and back. She also uncovered eleven partial shoeprints, eight clustered around the rail, three leading to the back gate. Magnotta then summarized his work. He recovered blood, skin, and hair from the wire around Hayden's neck as well as both neckties. He conducted an intensive DNA sweep of the pool area, hoping to at least find perp hairs, skin flakes, or nail slivers, but found nothing.

Bad luck, Bourque thought. Killers often left DNA signatures near bodies, especially when struggles occurred. She took over, described Zupan's interviews and concluded with his Serbian Army background.

Eller thanked everyone and signed off. She left him at the main hotel bar and walked to a nearby pub, a favorite haunt from her undercover days.

Although she'd grown up in Boston, the city center felt alien. The stars that illuminated her home in Falmouth were absent, devoured by a massive urban corona. She loved Falmouth, an eclectic mix of low-rise brick buildings and wooden houses, of steep gabled roofs and deep porches. She walked on, wishing she were there, hearing plovers chattering and waves crashing, rhythms older than human cunning.

At the pub, Bourque ordered a half-pint of Samuel Adams stout. Murder didn't swell her thirst; it suppressed it. Nursing the stout, she checked her bank account on her personal phone. Hell! Two hundred and eighty-two dollars left for the month of May.

Her money troubles were a recent development. She was beholden to two banks. She'd let Nico talk them into buying a huge house in Falmouth. She'd also paid off his crushing grad school debt, which put her deep in the hole before the house came along. Prior to university, he'd raved about American art. He'd finished university claiming the only thing that mattered was the Italian Renaissance. Matisse, Gaugin, and Picasso were pretenders. In his view, there wasn't an American artist worth mentioning.

These days, after shelling out for an enormous mortgage, what was left of Bourque's decent pay packet barely covered utility bills, work lunches, and groceries. Being half-Yankee, she knew how to weather financial trouble. "Avoid" spending money. Eat dinner at home. Eying her account balance, she shook her head. What could she do? She wasn't going to quit her women's hockey team. She loved ice hockey. She had no choice. She had to cut back on wine and groceries. She knew what she'd cut first: groceries. If she'd learned one thing in her misspent youth, it was 'wine has calories.'

Thinking of wine, her mind turned to Marty Dalton. She'd share a bottle or two with him anytime. They'd been "seeing each other" for eight months. More to the point, as she teased, they'd been smelling each other. And Marty Dalton smelled very good.

She'd moved a few outfits to his place, and a few more. Now she spent most nights there, happy to inhabit his world. He had the laugh of a younger man, genuine and hopeful. His house was a ten-minute drive from hers. It was shipshape and modern. In comparison, hers felt dark and haunted. She'd commandeered his small backyard and planted high-bush blueberries, which would take years to yield fruit. Presumptuous of her, but sometimes you looked ahead.

Marty, a journalist, generally worked from home but with a murder investigation on the boil she'd rarely see him. So far, he had no strikes against him. Being a former Navy Seal, he was calm and capable. Her mother Sarah didn't like him. Another point in Marty's favor. In Sarah's eyes, he was a nothing. He didn't wear suits. His car was older than Bourque's. Bourque's best friend, Gigi Lambert, loved him. Two more points. Bourque and Gigi had done their detective training together. Gigi, a brainy dynamo, soon went to the big leagues—the FBI—which everyone knew was going to happen.

These days, the two only saw each other once or twice a year, when Gigi got home to Boston for a few days off. They didn't call each other often. When they did, they gabbed long into the morning, yet their bosses had nothing to fear. They never talked specifics, just feelings and thoughts, ruing the way the Old Guard tended to go full speed ahead, often in the wrong direction.

Chapter 6

DAY TWO: *Boston. May 15th*

Over a working breakfast at the Sheraton, Bourque dug up details on the Novak family, starting with Atlas: twenty-four; single; MBA with Distinction from Harvard. You can't buy one of those, she reasoned, but you can buy help to get the marks. Two DUIs, both unsuccessful prosecutions, no doubt due to daddy's lawyers.

She switched to Google. In Marty's eyes, it was a decent 'first-look tool,' if you critiqued what you'd gathered. In her eyes, it was a detective's wet dream. Where else did people reveal the minutiae of their lives, usually with no regard for filters? Atlas had over 20,000 social media followers; he posted on everything from Zumba to foodporn to international trade. As for his digs, he lived two blocks from Karlos Vega's condo. She wasn't surprised. The rich consorted with the rich. Atlas's address translated to a full-floor penthouse suite, like Vega's. It was registered to Rollo Novak, but the utility bills were in Atlas's name. Tough, she wryly thought, papa didn't pay all the bills.

Unlike the Regency Residences, the Novak tower had no valet. When Bourque and Eller entered the foyer, no attendant rushed up to them; no security manager met them. The concierge waved them to a private elevator.

The all-glass conveyance afforded an uninterrupted view of the Charles River and beyond, to MIT and Harvard. The doors opened to reveal Atlas Novak: lustrous dark hair, clean-cut, commanding. He graciously beckoned them in.

Patrician already, she reflected, even in his fledgling years. He wore a perfectly tailored navy suit framing a crisp silver shirt and dark blue tie. Understated yet impressive. If clothes made the man, they made this one manlier.

Eller pulled out his badge. "Detective Lieutenant Eller, State Police. Homicide."

"Detective Lieutenant Bourque," she added.

If Atlas Novak was disconcerted by the presence of two detective lieutenants, he didn't show it.

"Sorry for your loss," Eller politely said.

Atlas's eyes went vacant.

Bourque saw a rudderless ship. However, Atlas could be playing them.

He seemed to recover his bearings. "A terrible loss, but we'll move on. Father would want that." His tone was grieving yet pragmatic, as if he truly accepted what had happened. Bourque couldn't get a read on him. On the one hand, his words sounded trite. *We'll move on.* On the other, they sounded heartfelt.

They followed him down a long, wide corridor flooded with natural light from floor-to-ceiling windows surveying the north shore of the river. Boston's twin jewels, MIT and Harvard, dominated the view, standard-bearers of both her past and future. No doubt the vista was meant to impress, and it did.

Atlas ushered the detectives into an oak-paneled study, gestured to two guest chairs, and sat behind a massive desk. "Coffee?" he asked.

The detectives nodded.

Silver shirt switched on an intercom and called for coffee service for three. Bourque scrutinized him as he spoke. His voice was breezy and confident. He looked self-possessed, yet not completely at ease.

"Mr. Novak," Eller began, "where were you Sunday, May thirteenth?"

"Here. I was working until about nine p.m."

"What about after nine p.m.?"

"I had dinner. I went to Strega."

"How was the food?" Eller genially asked.

"Excellent."

"What did you have?"

"*Capelli d'angelo con aragosta.*"

"Angel hair with lobster," Eller said. "Nice. Cream sauce?"

Atlas nodded.

"Dessert?"

"Tiramisu. It's outstanding at Strega."

Eller smiled. "Always *perfetto.*"

Good smokescreen, Bourque thought. She knew Eller wasn't simply playing good cop. They'd check Strega's menu to see if angel hair was on it. If required, they'd subpoena the restaurant for a copy of Atlas's bill.

An elderly uniformed maid entered with a silver coffee service. She had the eyes of a Mother Superior, kindly and inquisitorial at the same time. Her skin tone was strangely off-pink, like a white rose dipped in blood.

"*Hvala*, Branka," Atlas said. "Thanks. We'll look after ourselves."

Coffees poured, Eller restarted the interview. "Mr. Novak, what did you do after dinner on Sunday?"

"I came back here, watched a little TV, and went to bed about eleven-thirty."

"Can someone verify that?"

"Yes. Amber. My girlfriend," he explained. "I called her just before bed."

"She wasn't here, Mr. Novak. How can she verify you were?"

"We were on video chat. My room and bed were in the background."

"As you may know, we can subpoena your call data stream and your location."

"Be my guest. I have nothing to hide." Atlas grinned. "I was under the covers."

Eller ignored him. "What did you do yesterday morning?"

"Amber came here for breakfast. Afterward we took a walk, then I started my workday."

"When?" Eller asked, his normally mild voice getting harder.

"About ten-thirty. I work from home."

"Can someone verify that?"

"Yes, Amber. And Branka too. She served us breakfast at seven-thirty, then brought me coffee at ten-fifteen."

"Where was Branka born?"

"Slovenia. She's my father's aunt."

"Does she reside here?" Eller asked.

"No."

"What's her full name?"

"Branka Taja Novak."

Eller changed tack, addressing Atlas bluntly. "Why did your father commit suicide?"

"He didn't," Atlas flatly stated.

"How do you know?"

"I know Dad. That's absolutely impossible. Absolutely. Absolutely and unconditionally."

Bourque noted the repetition. Atlas was laying it on thick. On the other hand, he sounded forthright. Maybe he was trying to spare his family the stigma of suicide. She studied his mouth. A good liar, or a good son. She couldn't tell which.

Eller remained quiet, trying to bait the POI with silence.

Atlas stepped into the trap. "Why would he hang himself?"

"How do you know he hanged himself?"

Atlas shook his head. "I know that gambit. I listen to the news, Lieutenant. I can also read. The media says he hanged himself. But that's ludicrous. Why would he?"

"You tell me," Eller said.

"I should think you'd know. If my father had any ruinous debts or debased business liaisons, you'd know. Financial forensics."

Bourque nodded to herself. Although they had nothing yet on Novak's money trail, they would. There'd likely be a rabbit warren of numbered corporations. Men like Novak didn't use corner banks. They moved money around with the click of a mouse, depositing it to offshore shell firms, transferring it to other shell firms, then dissolving the original firms.

Eller left Atlas's assertion unanswered. "Mr. Novak, I'm interested in what *you* know. Do you have any insights into your father's recent past?"

"No. He was a private man."

"You said he wouldn't commit suicide. Why not?"

"He, well, he had everything to live for." Atlas fidgeted with his coffee cup. "A platitude, I realize, but he did."

Eller held his fire. The silence deepened.

Good move, Bourque thought. Keep the POI waiting, wondering what's next. You had all the time in the world. You weren't hiding anything. POIs often were, even the cooperative ones. If they knew the victims, they usually wanted to shine a good light on them, which wasn't the same as the truth.

Atlas eventually broke the silence. "Dad loved his work," he hesitantly began, "and his new wife. His properties too. Especially the Falmouth one." He shook his head. "What a terrible irony. Dad died in Falmouth."

Eller switched to good cop. "How do you get along with Mr. Zupan, your father's butler?"

"Butler? Axe-man is more like it."

Eller smiled. "I take it you two don't get along."

"What can I say? He's a Neanderthal man. Look at his jawline."

"Do you know his sister Snežana?"

"No."

Eller switched gears again. "Who stands to benefit from your father's death?"

"How would I know?"

"Because," Eller replied, "you worked with him."

"So?"

"Because," Eller said, "you're his son."

"So?" Atlas repeated.

A common reaction, Bourque noted. People should know by now it didn't work with the police. If you got your back up when questioned, cops got their antennae up.

Eller scrutinized Atlas. "I said, 'Who stands to benefit?'"

"I heard you. How do you expect me to know? Talk to his lawyers." Atlas pushed his chair back. "You can talk to mine too. We're done."

Eller stood, his stance saying *now it's my move*. "Mr. Atlas Novak, you are not permitted to leave the state of Massachusetts."

"What?" Atlas sputtered. "Are you kidding? Am I a suspect?"

"No," Eller replied, "and yes. As in *no* kidding and *yes*, at the moment, you're a suspect."

"Fuck!"

Eller grinned. "That you can do. Only in Massachusetts, of course. I have a suggestion. It would help your cause if we take a DNA swab and fingerprint you."

"You don't have a court order."

Eller turned to Bourque. "These amateur law buffoons, pardon me, law buffs, they should do more reading." He turned back to Atlas. "You don't have to cooperate, but it's to your benefit."

"What if my lawyer tells me not to?"

"He wouldn't."

"She," Atlas corrected him. "Amber Luu's her name. My girlfriend."

"*She*," Eller stated, "would likely advise you to do so. One, if we don't find your bio matter in any compromising locations, it could eliminate you as a suspect. Two, do the job here and you won't have to see us again."

A good lie, Bourque thought. They'd certainly be seeing Atlas again. She wasn't thrilled to hear his girlfriend was a lawyer. Luu could coach him. If she knew his movements or his past, even part of it—she might keep him from divulging valuable details.

Atlas leaned back and regarded the library wall behind the detectives. His eyes travelled the book spines, seemingly searching for counsel. Finally, he nodded. "Let's do it here."

Eller dug into his crime scene bag. As he deployed his fingerprint kit and took a DNA cheek swab, Bourque watched silently, leaning nonchalantly against the doorjamb. Seconds after Eller finished with Atlas, Branka entered the study. It appeared the maid had been following the proceedings on a security camera. She approached Atlas's chair and addressed him quietly in what Bourque took to be Slovenian. Her mouth barely moved as she spoke; her teeth didn't show. Leaning closer, she scolded him, her tone saying *you know better*. Atlas's face reddened. Message delivered, the maid marched out.

"Mother's here," Atlas said.

Eller looked at him quizzically.

"When we heard from you yesterday, I asked her to come here. To make things easier for you."

Really, Bourque thought. Atlas appeared to have a decent side. Then again, maybe he'd ordered his mother here to keep the police away from her residence. Circling the wagons.

□ □ □

Melanya Novak sailed into the study like a runway model: hips forward, shoulders back. At forty-four, although five years older than Bourque, she looked ten years younger. She was undeniably beautiful. Beyond beautiful. Unlike many women over forty, the closer she came, the more stunning she looked. Her blonde hair was Southern-belle-big. She wore a sleeveless linen dress, definitely haute couture. It showed exactly what was under it.

As with the son, Bourque had done a preliminary search on the ex-wife. Melanya Carola Novak, née Kemet, was a year younger than Rollo Novak. She had no sheet.

"Please, have a seat." Eller stood and gallantly pointed to his own chair.

As Melanya sat, Atlas asked if she'd like him to remain. She waved her son off. Eller gave his usual introduction. Bourque followed, maintaining her post by the door.

"My condolences," Eller began. "Sorry for your loss."

"For this I thank you." Melanya's voice was low and wistful. It barely extended beyond her body. On an audiotape, it'd be easy to think she was across the room, not two yards away.

"I understand you still call yourself Mrs. Novak. Why?"

"Why not?" Her chin rose, wafting her perfume their way. It reminded Bourque of Budapest, Mitteleuropa in a bottle, a flowery, cloying scent not typically worn in Boston.

"Do you know why your ex-husband committed suicide?" Eller asked.

Her eyes glazed over. She shook her head.

Bourque read Melanya's face. She looked doubly detached, as if her ex's death was both unreal and none of her business.

"Any idea?" Eller prodded.

Melanya's detachment morphed to haughtiness. "Why you are asking me?" Despite the haughtiness, her reply was still quiet.

"Because," Eller said, "you were married to him for over twenty years."

"Do you think I know everything about him?"

"Perhaps you can tell us where you were yesterday?"

"I was home," she softly stated. "I have apartment on inner harbor." She recited the address.

Bourque wondered, parenthetically, about Melanya's accent. It was as thick as Zupan's. She and Rollo Novak had escaped from the former Yugoslavia just before the Berlin Wall came down, when she was seventeen. Although she'd lived in America twenty-seven years, she sounded like a recent immigrant.

"Were you there all day?" Eller asked.

"Yes."

"What about Sunday, May thirteenth?"

"Same."

"Can someone verify that?"

"Many people. I swim in pool every morning and afternoon. I meet neighbors there."

"Names?" Eller asked.

"Some I know only their first name."

After writing Melanya's response down, he eyed her. "You swam twice both days?"

"Yes." She crossed her shapely legs and looked away, as if she'd said all that was necessary.

Was she wary, Bourque wondered, or just self-contained? With her wide Slavic eyes and tentative manner, she wasn't the usual society beauty. She didn't seek the limelight. But maybe that was because she spoke heavily-accented English.

"What times?" Eller asked.

"I go at nine in morning. I take sauna too. I also swim at four p.m."

Some people, Bourque thought. She hadn't had time for a sauna in years. The ex probably had a personal trainer and a masseuse too. From the look of her, she jetted to Swiss spas for blood transfusions and vitamin boosters. What was wrong with a home juice extractor and an oatmeal mask?

"Where were you Sunday night?" Eller asked.

"At dance class in social room."

"Do you have a boyfriend?"

Melanya bristled. "None of your business."

"I'm afraid it is. You see, Mrs. Novak, *everything* is our business—until we find out what happened to Rollo Novak and his wife. Do you have a boyfriend?" Eller repeated. "Let me rephrase that, a man friend?"

She shook her head. "And this woman is *not* his wife. I am his wife."

"The law says differently."

"It can say what it wants."

"It does." Eller gave his canned speech about fingerprints and DNA. "You can come to a precinct or we can process you here."

"Please do here."

Chapter 7

Maynard, Massachusetts State Police Crime Lab. May 15th

Bourque had always loved forensics. As a teen, while girlfriends giggled over heartthrobs, she watched shows about ballistics and insects that augured when a person died. Now, when she walked into Maynard's crime lab, she felt expectant. However, being a cop, she knew forensics wasn't enough to convict a felon. You needed a complete case: motive, opportunity, and evidence. What did the prosecuting attorney say to the whitecoat? *DNA might be damning, Doc, but it doesn't put a perp in jail. A trial does.*

Bourque pulled her hair into a ponytail and led Eller into the autopsy lab. She liked the venue's transparency. Ashes to ashes, carbon to carbon. The chemistry of death was the same as the chemistry of life. Nothing was hidden on an autopsy table, a reminder not only of humanity's physicality, but of the physicality of crime. When a crime occurred, it always left a trail—no matter how faint. It was just a matter of finding it. She nodded hello to the forensic pathologist, Dr. Donte Aloysius King. Under his lab coat, he wore jeans.

"Let's get to it," he amiably said. "As usual, we're taping this, but please stop me if you have any questions. I concur with most of Dr. Wozniak's findings. Most of them. We'll follow the spirit of *autopsy.*" King smiled. "I believe you know the word's meaning: to see for oneself."

He led the detectives to the table. "We'll begin with the female." The red necktie and wire had been removed from Hayden's neck. What remained was badly bruised skin and a deep ligature imprint.

King hit the recording button. "The victim was strangled by a wire ligature. To be more technical, she was garroted. The lab determined the wire was an uninsulated aluminum-nickel composite, a type favored by jewelers, to make necklaces, for example. Malleable yet durable. You can twist it and it won't snap." King paused. "Carried out long enough, garroting blocks the carotid arteries, which eventually results in brain death. In this case, it also blocked the larynx and caused oxygen deprivation below the neck. Let's consider what likely happened."

Bourque leaned in. Reconstruction was King's forte. He was usually able to tell what had happened to a victim and in what sequence. Just as with a medical autopsy, a homicide autopsy was conducted for the future. While the medical version was often done to make sure a similar death didn't reoccur, the homicide version was conducted to help track down a killer.

Being a big man, King handled the corpse by himself. He gently turned Hayden's body over. "According to the CS photos, the wire was twisted six times." He used his pointer to indicate the uppermost spinal vertebra. "The imprint you see there is consistent with the photos. The wire was pulled so tight it sank deeply into the neck. The necktie did not cause bruising, which indicates the victim was dead before it was used. Dead people do not bruise. I surmise the victim was garroted and then suspended with a necktie after she was dead. Regarding defensive wounds, there are no signs she put up a fight. However, I found a hypodermic syringe wound. See there—" King pointed to a small puncture on Hayden's neck above the left collarbone, "—that wound was formed by a needle with a very narrow width, a thirty-gauge. Due to the wound's reddish-brown color, it melds with the victim's tan. Furthermore, it was under the necktie. Hence, Dr. Wozniak did not see it."

Bourque looked closer. She hadn't seen it either.

"I suspect the needle was used to inject a tranquillizer," King stated. "Likely a date-rape type drug. We're screening for ketamine, among others. Typically, thirty-gaugers are short. Unless an air gun or blowgun-type apparatus was used to deliver the needle, the assailant got very close to the victim. A woozy victim would make it easy to apply a garrote."

"Why sedate her?" Eller serenely asked. "Why not kill her with the needle?"

"Good point. An assailant could have injected a deadly cocktail like succinylcholine, SUX for short. Why garrote someone when you can SUX them? Unless you want to make a statement."

Exactly, Bourque said to herself. Someone had made a statement, though she couldn't fathom the message.

"By the way," King continued, "I didn't find any assailant DNA or defensive wounds on the male corpse. I didn't see any evidence he put up a fight or was sedated with a needle. However, he may have ingested a tranquillizer with food or drink. We're screening him as well."

"He was bigger and stronger than Hayden," Eller noted. "He could put up more of a fight. He's the kind of target you'd want to sedate."

Bourque immediately thought of Zupan. The butler fed Novak.

"Valid point," King granted, "but not necessarily true. Let me hypothesize why. Dr. Wozniak reported the presence of sperm on the female corpse, both in her vagina and near it. He also reported sperm on the male's penis. We ran rush DNA tests on both sperm samples. It's the same sperm, from the male. It appears the victims were engaged in sexual intercourse. Lucky buggers. They went out with a bang."

Bourque suppressed a grin. It was mildly disrespectful to the dead, but pathologists were known for their gallows humor. King was no exception. He'd once told her the only way to keep sane in his job was to jest whenever he could. She knew his partner Dmitri, one of her first forensic friends, a ballistics specialist who joked about warm guns and "ejaculation" trajectories. Most of the Old Guard shunned the couple, which only made Dmitri more flamboyant.

King reassumed a serious demeanor. "Although they may have been attacked during intercourse, I conjecture they were attacked afterwards, during the so-called post-coital state, when the male was, let's say, not ready to fight off predators. The female was likely less relaxed. Females are more vigilant than males after intercourse. The maternal instinct. Thousands of years of biology. Regardless, I suspect the garrotters approached the victims from behind and tranquillized the female. By the time they were cognizant enough to fight back, it was too late."

Eller wasn't convinced. "How would the perps know Novak was post-coital? Did they have an inside view of the pool? Did someone setup a spy camera for them?"

Or, Bourque reflected, use a drone camera.

King shrugged. "They didn't have to be spying. They saw semen on his penis."

"I don't buy it," Eller evenly said. "It doesn't add up."

"I read bodies," King replied, "not minds. You know how it is. A pathologist's answers aren't supposed to add up. They're supposed to make you think." He smiled. "I'm not going to break with tradition. All right, final step." He selected a scalpel and made an adroit Y-incision in Hayden's chest. The body released a rancid odor: roadkill mixed with rotten eggs. Even after years in chemistry labs, Bourque's stomach churned. Being organic molecules, body odors were particulate. She was inhaling microscopic particles from Hayden's innards. King handed out safety glasses to protect against airborne bone slivers and sawed through the ribcage, excised the chest plate and extracted the inner organs. After dissecting the heart and lungs, he looked up at the detectives.

"No signs of water ingress. Consistent with Dr. Wozniak's findings," he concluded, "I do not detect any evidence of drowning." King stepped back. "Excuse me, I'll call my assistant now. We'll take this body away and bring Mr. Novak's."

When Novak's corpse was positioned on the autopsy table, King beckoned the detectives forward. As with Hayden's corpse, Novak's neck was free of encumbrances. Bourque did a double-take. There was a deep inset wound in the neck, the kind imprinted by a wire, not a necktie.

She glanced at Eller. He'd seen it too. His eyes were wide open.

King wasn't watching the detectives. "Contrary to what Dr. Wozniak reported," he said, "this victim wasn't killed by a necktie. He was garroted by a wire, which was later removed. The wire makes sense. It'd be harder for him to fight off a thin wire than a wide necktie. We analyzed the wire inset characteristics. Both victims were killed with the same type of jewelry wire." King carefully rolled the corpse over. "Again, we have an imprint on the anterior neck below the uppermost spinal vertebra. Unlike with the female, this victim's hyoid bone is intact. It usually takes an expert to choke out a victim without cracking the hyoid. On the other hand," King cautioned, "the strangler could have used constant, measured pressure. They were strong but gentle, as strange as that sounds."

Strong but gentle. Like a woman? Bourque wondered.

King pointed to the base of Novak's neck. "The victim has a protruding upper spinal vertebra. The tie was placed below the vertebra and pulled so tightly it stayed in place. Hence, it didn't ride up the neck, as occurred with the female victim."

After completing the rest of Novak's autopsy, King ruled murder by garroting in both cases, pending toxicology reports. He stood back from the table. "There's something to bear in mind. The medical examiner reported Hayden's body temperature was zero-point-six degrees higher than Novak's. Algor causes a two-degree Fahrenheit drop roughly every hour, which suggests Hayden lived eighteen minutes longer. It's possible the murderers let her live longer on purpose, to make her watch her husband being strangled. Then again, Hayden had a very athletic build. She likely had a slower heartbeat, so it would take longer for her core body temperature to fall. That could cause a cooling difference of perhaps ten minutes. The remaining minutes could be attributed to perpetrator actions." King raised his hands regretfully. "I'm sorry, I can't be definitive."

□ □ □

Can you give me fifteen?" Bourque asked Eller as they walked out of the crime lab.

"Sure. I'll grab some coffees."

While less than an hour west of Boston, Maynard felt like it was in another state. It was noticeably warmer than the Cape. Dozens of beech trees lined the parking lot. Reaching her car, she sat inside. Although she'd been working the Cape & Islands region for five years, relatively speaking, she was still a new kid in town. She had gaps in local knowledge. After breakfast that morning, she'd asked Peabody to identify locals who worked at the Novak castle. Checking her duty phone, she read his email reply and cc'ed it to Eller: no locals worked at the Novak castle. She wanted to crosscheck that. She could do it on her own but it might take hours. She'd likely spend ten minutes with her neighbor Cal, a retired newspaper reporter.

At eighty-two, Cal Knowlton had lived his whole life on Cape Cod. He was a typical Caper, nonchalant about most things. Capers knew death could get them any day of the year—when they were on the Atlantic, when driving icy roads, when swimming or surfing and a great white came along. He'd grown up on the Outer Cape and now lived in Falmouth, where he claimed to know almost everyone. In truth, he joked, he knew everything and everybody but was too humble to say so, things like who just bought a dozen bottles of whisky and rum and when the shindig was. The shipping news for landlubbers.

She called him. "It's your neighbor, Lieutenant Bourque."

"Lootenant? Where have you been?"

"Boston."

"Baastan," Cal drawled, elongating the vowels with the city's signature accent, "that bastion of false modesty. You see any Brahmins or Blue Bloods up there?"

"Oh yeah. Daughters of the American Revolution too. Listen, can I ask you a few questions about the Novak castle?"

"Always."

"Do you happen to know if any locals work there?"

"Let me think." He didn't think for long. "No locals. Novak used Boston help for most things."

"Who did the housework?"

"You want the short answer?" Cal asked.

"Yes."

"His wife."

"How do you know?"

"I guess you want the long answer."

"Okay, tell me."

"My granddaughter lives in East Falmouth. She pitched her maid service, but Novak didn't bite. Not that he was ungracious. He was friendly to everyone around here. You know what I liked better? He paid no special attention to any of the local Blue Bloods. I admired that. But back to the housework. I heard three others pitched their maid service and Novak always declined. Said his wife did the cleaning. The whole shebang, even when there were guests."

Hell, Bourque surmised, that was a huge job. She wouldn't want it. So much for the fairy tale castle. And so much for Hayden being a spoiled glamour girl. She'd worked hard.

"Thanks Cal. One more thing. What do you know about Katrina Hayden?"

"Not much. She was born in Falmouth. Apparently, she insisted Novak build the castle here instead of Nantucket or Martha's Vineyard, the usual summer playgrounds of the rich. When she became a celebrity, people started calling her a Cape heroine. At least, some did."

"Not you."

"Fast, Lootenant, aren't you."

"Oh yeah. What's the scoop?"

"She was an only child. Her father was a local; her mother, Romanian. They left about twenty-five years ago. It ended in a tragedy. The parents were found dead in Spain fifteen years ago. Both were reportedly suicides. Rumormongers say Katrina was trafficked for sex by her parents."

"What do you think?"

"I knew her father a little. Nestor was his name. I see him as a joiner. If the rumors are true, his wife was the leader. By the way, I know Nestor's father better. Nathaniel Hayden once ran an illegal still up the National Seashore near Truro. And that's not hearsay. I sampled his wares a few times."

"I might have to arrest you." Bourque grinned to herself. "Ah heck, what's done is done."

"Whew," Cal whistled in fake relief.

"Thanks, Cal. No more questions."

"Don't you like my answers?"

"I like them."

"Then I must be boring you. The worst crime of the old is to bore the young."

She smiled. Nice to be thought of as young.

"No more?" he pressed. "What's a man to do?"

"Start a rumor. Thanks again." She didn't mind if Cal talked about their chat. In fact, she hoped he'd spread the word that the State Police were interested in Hayden's background—it might send someone to their tip line.

Leaning back, she did a thoughtful drumroll on the steering wheel. The team had let Katrina Hayden fall between the cracks. That was going to change.

□ □ □

Driving toward Barnstable Detective Unit, Eller broached the subject of Zupan. "There're a few things stacked against the butler," he began. "Consider the castle. No local workers, which implies the back gate wasn't disarmed by an insider. Unless it was Zupan."

"Go on."

"He was a soldier," Eller noted, "a trained killer."

"All soldiers are."

"Remember what Zupan said about security? No computer system is fail-proof, but he's trained in hand-to-hand. The chokehold is one of its main maneuvers. If you want stealth, it's a good way to render opponents unconscious or kill them."

"True. Zupan has the pedigree of a killer."

"A strangler, in theory. I'm talking theory, thinking out loud, if you will."

"Good idea. Keep going."

"He's a meticulous type and Hayden's garrotter twisted the ends of the wire around her neck precisely and six times. Zupan appears to genuinely respect Novak, but not Hayden. Perhaps he killed Hayden and a comrade killed Novak."

"If Zupan respected Novak," she said, "why would he let someone kill him?"

"I don't know the answer to that."

"I'll admit, it's possible Zupan disarmed the gate and let the killers in. I made a little call that corroborates no locals worked at the castle. However, even after three interviews Zupan looks clean."

"He could have fed Novak a sedative," Eller said.

"Novak didn't eat breakfast."

"He could have dosed Novak's liquids. Water, juice. Whatever."

"Possible, but how could he be sure Novak would drink them? Beyond that, if sedated, could Novak walk to the pool? I've been thinking about the sedation scenario. There's no evidence Novak slipped or fell on the deck due to a tranquillizer. If killers wanted to sedate two victims, they'd likely use the same mechanism on both. Simpler. Anyway, pending toxicology results, there's no proof anyone tranquillized Novak. I suspect the patho is right. Novak wasn't sedated."

"Doesn't mean Zupan is clean," Eller pointed out. "I think we should bring him into the unit. Get him on videotape as well as audio. Look for some body language we didn't hear in his words."

She glanced at her car clock. "How about we book him for twenty-one-hundred?"

"Okay. I'll call him in."

She concentrated on the road, giving her mind a break from the case. A wall of clouds began massing on the western horizon, blocking out the setting sun, which flared livid red. She winced. The clouds seemed to be burning. They looked like a wall of fire. The sun sank and the wall bled into the Earth.

Chapter 8

Barnstable, Cape & Islands Detective Unit. May 15th

Bourque entered Barnstable Unit to find Zupan sitting in the foyer, looking far too comfortable. She immediately hustled him to an interview room and directed him to the suspect's chair, the Slider, which had a heavily waxed seat. The front legs were half an inch shorter than the back ones, making suspects slide inexorably forward, into the face of their interviewer.

Despite the venue, Zupan appeared unflustered. Bourque left and cranked the room thermostat to the max. That'd make him sweat. Tom Gronski, her friend from Metro, dealt with Serbian gangs. He'd told her that Yugoslavs were aloof and severe, and they loved to drink. She was no fan of generalizations—they were useless as end points—yet they could be useful as on-ramps, giving inroads into what made people tick.

Fifteen minutes later, after reviewing the audio of Eller's exchange with Zupan, she dropped the thermostat down to forty-five Fahrenheit. Heat 'em, then chill 'em. Annoy 'em, then interrogate 'em.

Eller had decided to begin the interview. While he usually chose the friendly approach—get a POI to open up by being pleasant—he wanted to irritate the butler, figuring an emotional Zupan would be a more honest Zupan. Bourque agreed. It wouldn't hurt to push his buttons. Afterward, she'd flip the script and deploy a little pleasantness to open the door.

Sitting in the shadow room, she watched the console screen as Eller entered the interview room. He eyeballed Zupan disdainfully. The butler gave back as good as he got. Showdown simmering, she settled in.

Eller nonchalantly sat across from Zupan. "I'm sorry to bring you in so late," he lamely said, clearly indicating he wasn't sorry at all.

Zupan snorted. His face was wet with perspiration.

Eller pretended he hadn't heard the snort. "Mr. Zupan, do you know Karlos Vega?"

"I tell you already," Zupan said with exasperation. "Yes."

"Do you like him?"

"I tell you already."

Eller feigned forgetfulness.

Zupan shook his head, obviously not impressed. "I do not like," he snapped, "but I do not dislike."

"I understand you were in the Serbian Army. When did you join?"

The old switcheroo, Bourque saw. Irritate the suspect, then change topics.

"September 1991," Zupan grunted.

"Why did you join?"

"I am young. I find no work in my town."

"No work? Really? Seeing you today, I assume you were a strong young man."

Zupan pushed himself back in the Slider. "After 1990 Yugoslavia fall apart. Little work."

"You're Slovenian. Why the Serbian Army?"

"My mother was Serbian."

"Where did you serve?"

"Belgrade."

"That's the capital," Eller stated. "There was no fighting there. After Belgrade?"

"Sarajevo."

"How long were you there?" Eller asked.

"Until end of siege."

"You served at the Siege of Sarajevo?"

Zupan nodded.

Possible red flag, Bourque thought. The infamous siege. Gronski, himself of Slav descent, had given her a better idea of the Balkan's twisted past. Yugoslavs, meaning the "Yug" or "South" Slavs, had fought, among others, Ottomans, Turks, and Austrians. They'd been subjugated for centuries, and held grudges for centuries. *Scratch a Slav,* Gronski had said, *and he'll bleed brooding stoicism. He won't show his hand. He'll wait to strike back—as long as need be.*

"I believe," Eller said, "that over one hundred thousand people died in Sarajevo."

"You are wrong. Over one hundred thousand die in Bosnian War."

"How many in Sarajevo?"

"They say fourteen thousand."

"And you say?"

"I do not say." Zupan's eyes flashed black lightning. "One is too many."

"And yet you remained in the army."

"Yes, I remain. I am only boy."

"You saw a lot of death and destruction."

"I saw. But not, how you say, oversaw."

"Weren't you a captain?"

"Much later. I am plain soldier during siege. I obey or they kill me."

Eller harrumphed.

"You know nothing. You are American. Always happy with yourself, yes? I tell you, the river at Sarajevo runs the color red—blood red—from all time past. The siege is inevitable. Foretold from history." Zupan eyed Eller, his look saying *you are fool. You will never understand.*

Eller stared back. *Forget about me, you're in deep shit.*

Shit, Zupan's eyes said, *you eat.*

Bourque watched the show, wondering who'd blink first.

It was Zupan. He forced himself back in the Slider, clearly annoyed.

"How long have you known Mrs. Melanya Novak?" Eller asked.

"I do not know her. Mr. Rollo was with second wife when I start to work for him."

"Apparently, you monitor the security system at the Novak house in East Falmouth. If you maintain systems, I assume you know the difference between electric wire and normal wire."

"Electric is insulated."

"Coated with plastic material?"

Zupan nodded.

"It would be relatively slippery then. It wouldn't sink into the neck. Not the best wire to strangle someone with—such as Mr. Novak and his wife."

Zupan snorted again. "You are like bull. Wait, I know better word. You are 'obstinate.' More to point, you are barking up wrong tree. Why you suspect me?"

"I ask the questions, Mr. Zupan. Not you. You're an organized man, a trained soldier. The wire around Mrs. Katrina Novak's neck was crossed and twisted very neatly. Who would do that?" Eller answered his own question. "Someone precise. Someone who wanted to ensure the wire wouldn't loosen."

"You are barking again."

Eller looked down his nose. "Did Katrina Novak give you any reasons to dislike her?"

Zupan shrugged.

"Any reasons?" Eller pressed.

Zupan shrugged again, then nodded half-heartedly.

Eller waited, but Zupan appeared disinclined to speak. "What reasons?" Eller asked.

Zupan regarded Eller for a long time. To Bourque, it felt like minutes, but was probably less than ten seconds. "All right," the butler said, "I tell you. She was always bossing me. Clean this, pick up that. Too much bossing. I know job."

"Anything else?"

"She love to spend the money. Spend, spend. Mr. Rollo is not like this."

Eller said nothing and shuffled and reshuffled some papers, maintaining silence. Eventually, he stood and circled the room, hands behind his back, and abruptly left.

Bourque kept her eyes on Zupan. He looked relieved. She decided to keep him waiting. Time was on her side, not his. Donnelly called it "curing the carcass." Thirty seconds later, Zupan drew out a large comb from his suit jacket and carefully aligned his hair, then realigned it. Having pocketed his comb, he sighed. She let him cure a few more minutes.

Upon entering the interview room, she sat across from Zupan and smiled pleasantly. "I have a few questions about Katrina Novak. Did you talk to each other?"

"Not much. She talk to my sister."

Šef talked to him, Bourque reflected, but not the wife. That might get to Zupan. He was too proud to be treated like a mute slave. "Did she dislike you?"

He waved a hand dismissively.

"I think she disliked you," Bourque said. "Did you dislike her?"

"No."

"Didn't you want to get even with her, pay her back for bossing you around?"

"Now you are barking." He eyed Bourque as if he'd expected better from her.

"When did you know Snežana was leaving for Slovenia?"

"She tell me two weeks ago."

"How long is she staying?"

"Five days."

"Why didn't you go with her?"

"I cannot take time away from Mr. Rollo."

"When was the last time Snežana saw him?"

"Friday. She come to Avon Hill house for dinner. She is teaching Šef's wife to make Štruklji, rolled dumplings, most famous Slovenian food."

"Was Mrs. Novak a good cook?"

"Not bad. Snežana help her."

Bourque moved on. "You said Mr. Vega left the Falmouth property around eleven-fifteen p.m. on Sunday. How can you be sure?"

"I cannot."

"You sounded sure yesterday."

"Yes. But I think again. For police, I must be precise. I hear his car reach main road and turn to direction of Falmouth. But I do not see."

"I'd like you to cast your mind back to the crime scene. Red neckties were used to hang Mr. and Mrs. Novak. Does the color mean anything to you?"

"Red is very common color of necktie in my country, not just Slovenia, in all Yugoslavia. Pardon me, was common. Was most important color during time of Tito. Communist Party color. Most important," he repeated.

Bourque sat back. She had no more questions. As for Zupan, they had nothing on him. They had to release him.

With Zupan gone, Bourque contemplated the red neckties and Tito's Yugoslavia. Perhaps the neckties had a connection to communism. Maybe Novak had "Red" enemies before he defected. Or maybe he made enemies when he defected.

She glanced at her watch. She figured Eller would want to deconstruct the Zupan interview and/or the Novak family interviews. Peabody had assigned Eller to the spare desk in her office, a spacious room with double windows facing a small park. Approaching her office, she heard him pecking forcefully on his laptop, his four-finger typing juddering the desk.

When she stepped inside, he looked up. "We better complete our case notes now. Peabody wants them ready for a team meeting tomorrow at oh-eight-hundred. Damn Peabody."

She nodded. Case notes, again.

Eller held her gaze. "I have a question for you. Do you like my plan about keeping the public misinformed?"

"Yes."

"Keeps the perps misinformed too. No news can worry perps, but misdirection is better. It screws with their heads. That's my theory. Does it fit the facts?"

"Like a pair of Speedos."

"Okay." He laughed. "Not that I'd be caught dead in Speedos."

□ □ □

Exiting the unit, Bourque found Cape Cod under a natural light dome. She freed her ponytail, shook her hair out and let it cascade around her shoulders. The moon ruled the western sky. The cloud wall had dissolved. The stars twinkled like votive candles. Unlike in Boston, the sky was so full of light it was almost white. The only dark patches were beyond the Milky Way.

She thought about heading home to Falmouth. Instead, she reached for her personal phone to call Marty. No, she decided, surprise him. Naked. Well, almost naked. She smiled to herself. She'd slip into his bed with a blue sapphire pendant winking between her breasts. *La dolce vita.*

Chapter 9

DAY THREE: *Falmouth. May 16th*

Bourque's favorite time was pre-dawn, the precursor of a new day. Leaving Marty to sleep, she got up and tiptoed naked out of the bedroom. The kitchen clock read 0502. She had two hours before work. Marty's place on Menauhant Road faced the ocean. Looking out the window, she debated if she should swim off Bristol Beach. It'd be cold but, hell, she had a wetsuit. And she was half-Canadian. Her paternal grandfather had left Quebec in the 1920s to work in Lowell's textile mills. Although he'd adapted well to life in New England and his eldest son had become a high-ranking police officer, he'd had one consistent complaint: they called school off for a few inches of snow. In his youth in Quebec, if you woke up and the snow was up to your waist, you shoveled for an hour or two and went to school.

Outside, the night lingered. The last stars were still visible. The Atlantic was unusually calm, a wide mirror reflecting the even wider sky. She'd seen the ocean off Cape Cod in all its moods. It wasn't just blue. It held every color: grey, green, white, silver, violet, even wine-colored, as Homer wrote of the Mediterranean. Today the Atlantic looked turquoise. She pulled on a thick neoprene hat and gloves and waded gingerly in. Cold water seeped through her full-length wetsuit.

Donning her swim-goggles, she took a deep breath and plunged in.

Time slowed down. In the water, she was often gripped by a sense of Cape Cod's past. The Cape had been formed 23,000 years ago, after the last Ice Age, well before 1620 and the Mayflower. A retreating glacier had deposited millions of tons of rock and sand, which were sculpted by the sea into a massive sandbar, one of the largest glacial peninsulas on Earth. That morning, the moon was in perigee, the closest it came to Earth, not only raising tides, but also tugging at human emotions. Swimming freely off Bristol Beach, she could almost believe death had no place on Earth, let alone murder. If more Americans saw murder and violence in person—actually *saw* it, not on TV or online—she felt there'd be more live-and-let-live in their souls. More mercy, even from hardened perps. The feeling didn't last long. When she was on a case, it rarely did.

Returning to land, the Novak murders began to seize her mind. Even after years as a detective, she still found it jarring to move from "normal" life to detective life, from convivial person to driven homicide cop. Luckily, she had her father's example to turn to. He'd been the same person at work that he was at home.

She entered Marty's house to find him making breakfast: porridge with dried cranberries, her favorite. He smiled but didn't talk, letting her eat in silence, allowing her to think. She liked that when she was on a case. He looked utterly carefree. His mop of brown hair hung over his forehead. He was naked under his robe.

"Hey," she eventually said, licking her spoon, "better than ever."

Marty winked. "Extra cranberries."

"What's up today?"

"Working from home."

"Lucky you."

"You find the murderer yet?"

She shook her head.

"There has to be one in Boston."

She chuckled despite herself. "Oh yeah, one or two." She avoided talking "business" with Marty. While some detectives chatted privately with their partners about cases, she didn't. To her, it was a sign of love. Having served in Afghanistan and Iraq, Marty could certainly handle death but she didn't want to burden him with homicide details.

□ □ □

Bourque pulled into Barnstable Unit well-fueled and wide awake. The air smelled of lilacs. The sun had breached the horizon, its rays magnified by the pure ocean air. It was the kind of day she loved— one of the things that had made her take a post on the Cape. She'd twisted her long auburn hair into a bun. For a change, she wore lipstick: Dusty Rose, duty-approved. As an undercover operative in Boston, she'd usually worn black, often black leather, essentially her uniform. She'd been the only straight female on the undercover squad. Some of the guys had been "overly frisky." The black leather didn't help. Now, on the Cape, she rarely wore black.

That morning she was dressed in dark-blue slim fit slacks and a matching blazer. Peabody wouldn't approve of the slim fit but he'd like the color: traffic-cop blue. Most of the male detectives she knew wore expensive suits. She didn't want to appear elitist, but accessible. Her father had climbed the career ladder quickly. He believed a cop's best tool was an unpretentious manner. Marty concurred. In his eyes, a humble cop was a good cop. He'd kissed her on the way out the door. "You're not only a good detective," he'd said, "you're beautiful." The man and his words. She didn't believe them, but they worked.

On the way to her office, she checked the Overnight Incident Report. One entry for assault, passed on to the detective unit. Carla Rutler, a local streetwalker, had been found by neighbors with a black eye and a bloody face. Supposedly, she'd "waltzed" off her porch again, her dancing partner this time being Señor Bacardi. According to Donnelly, it was usually Captain Morgan.

Bourque sat at her desk, booted up her laptop, and navigated to the video of Zupan's fourth interview. She'd been thinking about the red neckties. She replayed his last sentences. His voice had been neutral at first, and then become more insistent than she'd thought at the time. He'd said "most important" twice. Was he trying to tip them to a communist connection? Or was he trying to set them up, send them running after red chimeras?

As she pondered Zupan's words, Eller stepped into her office with two takeout coffees. He wore a chic light blue suit. "Morning, Bourque. Brought you a Dunkin'." He smiled. "Two milk, no sugar. I remember."

"Thanks very much."

"Do you have time to review POIs before the meeting?"

"Sure."

The two detectives rolled their desk chairs to the windows and sat side-by-side overlooking the park. One window was open. Bourque could smell the sweetness of honeysuckle.

"I'm wary of Vega," Eller began. "Could be his money or his fame. Or it could be I don't like him."

"He's a hard man to like."

"I wonder if Novak actually liked him. Were they true friends, or was Vega using Novak? As in one rich man using another to get even richer." Eller held up a forefinger. "Sorry. One superrich man using another. I checked out their money trail early this morning. Nothing yet. And no one can rush M and M, not even Peabody."

Bourque agreed. M&M, the Money-n-Murder unit, was part of Central's financial forensic bureau. It was under-staffed and over-burdened. A lot of murders in the state had a money trail. The Novak-Hayden trail would be longer and more circuitous than most.

"By the way," Eller continued, "I ordered cellphone records for Novak, Hayden, and every POI we interviewed. Three-month metadata traces."

She nodded. The usual. Phone numbers, datetime stamps, call/text durations, but not the actual conversations or messages. They'd need a warrant—probable cause—to search those.

"I also made a direct request to Vega's condo for video to verify his movements on the thirteenth."

A common ploy, she knew, side-stepping a warrant, digging into a POI before they had judicial approval.

"For the moment," Eller went on, "Vega allegedly left his condo just after seven that day, the day before the murders. He arrived at Novak's Falmouth house at oh-eight-hundred. Even allowing for quiet roads, a fifty-five-minute drive to Falmouth is very fast. Over the speed limit fast. I checked his driving record. Five speeding tickets in the last two years. If he keeps that up, he'll soon be license-free. He can hire a chauffeur, but he seems to like driving. He owns two Bentley SUVs." Eller's tone was reverent. "Bentaygas."

She raised her shoulders. Greek to her.

"Next time we interview our heavy-footed friend," Eller advised, "let's keep those tickets in mind."

Might be useful, she supposed. Then again, it was likely a blizzard in a beer mug. If they hoped to intimidate Vega with innuendos about speeding, or anything else, it would probably fail. It made sense to approach him with subtlety rather than browbeat him. Let him think he was an alpha male. If they fed his ego and guided him correctly, he might trap himself.

Eller kept going. "I slotted Atlas Novak at the bottom of the family list, after Melanya. He can be mouthy, but all youngsters that age are mouthy."

Bit overstated, Bourque deemed, but she understood Eller. In many ways, such as dressing the part and driving a big car, he was a "traditional" detective, which wasn't surprising. He'd trained almost twenty years before her.

"What do you think of Melanya?" he asked.

"She's led a sheltered life. I don't think she's dumb, not by any means, but she's not street smart. Seemingly," Bourque added. "She said she doesn't have a *man friend*. I don't believe her. We should look into her male friends, past and present."

Eller nodded. "Since we're on that topic, Central is going to look into Novak's lady friends. Then there's Atlas. I'd say he's bent on making money. Let's see what M and M finds. We need to know more before we can ask him the right questions."

"Agreed. What about Katrina Hayden? So far, she's slipped through the sieve. She might have some secrets."

"Such as?" Eller asked.

"Suspicious connections. Her own money, as in a lot of it. Blackmailers who didn't get what they wanted."

"Hmm. I watched her on TV. She looked like she was on the make. I know, that was Reality TV."

"Exactly."

"I'm not saying she was a slut, but that doesn't make her a saint."

"That's what makes you a good cop. You observe the world through a wide lens."

"Only on Wednesdays."

Chapter 10

Bourque and Eller followed Peabody into the murder room, a room frozen in the 1970s: grey broadloom, tan walls, two rows of fluorescent lights. Nothing could rescue the room, not even the former courthouse's high windows and fine wooden trim. It smelled like a new murder beat. Everyone was freshly showered and deodorized. In three days, it would ooze fast-food grease and reeking feet.

The room's noise level instantly dropped. All attendees were present. Magnotta, Miller, Munro, and Wolf sat on the far side of the boardroom table. Central had allocated four junior detectives to the case, no doubt due to the high-profile victims. The four detectives would arrive at noon. They'd been assigned computer hutches lined up along the back wall. In addition to Donnelly, two local troopers had been seconded to the case full-time. Bourque sat next to Eller.

Arthur Peabody, a thin man with a pinched nose, resembled a bureaucrat rather than a cop. He routinely wore wide suspenders. When he took his suit jacket off, as he did today, the suspenders made him look even thinner. Conversely, his eyes were large and deep blue. After calling the meeting to order, he took attendance and motioned for Munro to proceed.

"I'll open with Prints," Munro said. "We made good progress, *we* meaning Miller." He nodded toward her and smiled.

Bourque watched her smile back. She was a good-looking redhead, the kind you saw on CSI shows: slim, busty, legs to the ceiling. If Bourque wasn't mistaken, Munro, who always looked chipper, looked even more chipper. Maybe it had something to do with Miller. Nothing like a new romance to spice up an investigation. *CSI: Detectives in Love*. Should be a TV series.

"Miller," Munro said, "established Zupan's shoeprints weren't in the kill zone. Turning to the eleven shoeprints near the CS, there were three different sets. Hence, there could be three perps. *Could be*, I stress. Jumping to conclusions is counterproductive."

Donnelly chimed in. "That's what my wife says."

"She's right." Munro grinned. "We might have a place for her."

"Oh no, we don't." Donnelly shook his head vehemently yet comically.

There were a few chuckles.

"Got it," Munro said. "Recruitment offer rescinded."

"Thank the Lord," Donnelly rejoined.

Peabody coughed loudly. "Stick to the agenda," he commanded.

Bourque glanced at Donnelly. He'd puffed up like an irate animal—in his case, a bear, one ready to confront Peabody. She knew Donnelly's opinion of Peabody. He'd labeled the captain a *FOP*, code for *Fucking Old Prick*.

"Re the eleven shoeprints," Munro quickly went on, "one set has been identified as a male size ten Adidas Athletics shoe. Another set, as the same shoe make, male size eight. The third set is a male size ten Reebok CrossFit. As a reconstruction, we have a start."

Munro nodded toward the local troopers. "For the benefit of the non-forensic folks, I have a little spiel about DNA. The first rule of a CS is that anyone who's been there leaves something behind and takes something away. They might leave behind DNA in a carrier like hair. And they might take away blood or skin, transferred from a victim. Leave. Take. That's a useful rule to remember. Back to the Novaks Case. At this point, we don't have any takeaways. Zupan didn't carry anything away from the scene. There was no blood on his clothing. The skin and hair on it matched his own DNA."

Fast lab work, Bourque thought. On her cases it often took a week for DNA results to come back. Technology wasn't the issue. It was the DNA queue. She knew Peabody had something to do with that.

"Considering leave-behinds," Munro continued, "we bagged hair and skin from two robes but it belonged to the victims. Ditto for the blood, hair, and skin found on the wire around Mrs. Novak's neck as well as on both neckties. In short, we have no potential perp DNA." Munro sat. "Over to you, sir."

"No perp DNA," Peabody repeated for the room. "Don't take that as a minus. No data is still data. It tells us the perps were smart. They wore the right gear or cleaned up after themselves. Or both."

Peabody moved on, reminding attendees the case was under a press blackout. No posting to social media, no talking to reporters.

The usual media spiel, Bourque saw. The team sat through it like obedient schoolchildren.

"As you read in the autopsy report," Peabody stated, "we have two murders on our hands, not two suicides. The two-murder update is internal information, for your eyes only. Let me stress that. *For you alone*. Not your wives, husbands, girlfriends, boyfriends. Not even your sex toys."

A few sniggers.

Peabody smiled slightly. "The suicide angle is for public consumption. For now, we want the killers to think they got off scot-free." He pursed his lips. At first, Bourque saw a kissing codfish. Seconds later, his face morphed into a pondering sage. "This is a high-profile case. One of the richest men in New England is dead, and his wife. No expense will be spared. Some might assume that's because Novak was wealthy. Wrong. It's because he and his wife were brutally killed. We'll conduct a soil analysis of the Novak property. Its bio-signature will be compared to dirt on POI cars and clothes." He raised a professorial finger. "But that doesn't excuse us from old-style policing, ground work, as they used to call it. Lieutenant Colonel Hyslop enlisted our Metro brethren to help us process Boston contacts. For our own purposes, henceforth we'll refer to Rollo Novak as *Novak* and his second wife as *Hayden*, not Novak. We don't want anyone confusing Katrina with Melanya, who still calls herself Mrs. Novak."

Peabody took a short sip of coffee. "No neighbors saw or heard anything on the day of the murders. So far, Central's E-Forensics Unit has no leads either. They couldn't crack the laptop or smartphones we found. Par for the course. Novak was an e-security titan. All right, on to the murder scene. The perps used jewelry wire. No similar wire was found on site. It appears the wire was brought to the scene. Which speaks to perp organization. What's the toughest type of perp to crack? The organized type." He nodded sagely. "We have one more thing to consider. The pathologist reported a needle was used to sedate Hayden, but not Novak. In most cases, with sedation in play, killers would inject both targets or the bigger of two targets, the one likely to cause trouble. Not in this case. It's a puzzle, an important puzzle, one we have to solve."

Peabody surveyed each attendee individually, fixing them with his deep blue eyes, underscoring his request. "The public believes it's easier to murder someone in the country than the city. No CCTV cameras, no big detective units. But you know what they don't know? Per capita, we have more boots on the ground. Use that to our advantage. I've posted a list of actions. Please attend to your actions."

□ □ □

Peabody signaled to Bourque and Eller that he wanted to chat. He led them to his office, where he sat and sighed heavily.

"You know that needle," he began, "it kept me awake all night. Only used on Hayden, not on Novak. Why didn't the killers use a needle on him? Makes me think Novak could be the person who used the needle. He sedated Hayden, and then he strangled her."

"Novak?" Bourque asked. "Why?"

"Let's forget the why for now. Consider the how. Using sedation makes sense. Hayden was fit and strong. If Novak sedated her, there'd be no struggle, no need to fight her off. No wound marks on him. No assault marks on her."

Bourque shrugged. "They were lovers. She wouldn't be alarmed if he stepped behind her. From there, he could garrote her without sedation."

"Set that aside for now. I suspect Novak wanted to keep his money from her. We'll see what kind of prenup they had. We'll dig into their bank interactions."

"What if she had her own money?"

"Good point. Then we have another story."

"And why was Novak murdered?"

"That's the question I kept asking myself last night. If his plan was to dispose of Hayden, you'd think that would be the end of it. But he gets killed too. Why? Who did it?" Peabody's brow was furrowed. "Anyway, whether Novak is Hayden's killer or not, it smells like an inside job. The pool gate was disarmed. That says inside job. In addition, outsiders would be conspicuous. Quiet town, early hour."

"Consider the murder date," Bourque countered. "May weekends are always busy on the Cape. People don't take notice of new faces."

"Valid point," Peabody conceded. "But here's the odd thing. The current DNA picture fits the Novak-killed-Hayden scenario. The only DNA we have from the scene is from two victims. And Novak is one of them. Convenient, isn't it? Nobody doubts his DNA should be there." Peabody held up a hand. "I know, he's dead. I'm suggesting it's convenient for his killer. What if Novak didn't expect to be killed? What if he murdered Hayden, expecting to be free, but instead got killed?"

Bourque had considered a similar scenario two days ago, wondering if Novak had taken Hayden's money and left it with someone, who killed Novak to keep it. Novak's guilt was a stretch, but it wasn't impossible. It had a strange symmetry.

"All I'm saying," Peabody continued, "is that the peripheral can become pertinent. The apparently incidental can crack a case open. That needle looks innocuous, but I'd bet it isn't. Intuition."

"You're beginning to sound like me."

Peabody smiled. "I'll never get that far, Bourque." Almost immediately, he regarded her and Eller seriously. "Not so long ago, the incidental was king. If a perp looked or sounded guilty, they booked him. Guilty until proven innocent. Some of the brass still think that way. Terrible business." He shook his head. "A detective's job isn't to prosecute, but to substantiate. Remember that. Gather facts and details, then let the courts decide."

Eller nodded.

Bourque echoed him. She'd seen what a prosecution first focus did. It resulted in closed minds—and, even worse, miscarriages of justice. She admired Peabody's fairness. Although a bureaucrat, he was an impartial one.

Chapter 11

Cape Cod National Seashore, Outer Cape, Massachusetts.
May 16th

Reaching the end of its run, U.S. Route 6 followed the Cape Cod National Seashore along the Atlantic coast, passing a string of sand dunes resembling a series of knuckles on a long finger pointing north. Bourque opened her car window. The warm air suggested a distant sea. Her sailing nose told her it was Caribbean air, propelled northward by the Gulfstream.

The surrounding land seemed to be asleep. A mile or so to the west, the shore was relatively protected, forming the outer side of Cape Cod Bay. To the east, the Atlantic shore bore the brunt of ocean storms. Gales and hurricanes could be dormant for months but when they roared in, they had no mercy. Compared to the lushness of the Berkshires—or even Falmouth—the Outer Cape was sparse and hardy, a narrow sliver of land caught between two seas. Bourque had a special affinity for it. She liked the elemental simplicity. The wind ruled. Everything was huddled close to the ground. The sun climbed lazily, nearing its noonday zenith as she approached Truro, roughly an hour from Barnstable.

She'd researched Katrina Hayden's local relatives before leaving the unit. Katrina's paternal grandfather, Nathaniel Hayden, was seventy-three. The Haydens, who'd arrived in the 1650s, were among the Outer Cape's first English settlers. The men had been coastal sailors and whalers and finally cod fishermen until the 1980s, when, in effect, they'd washed up on shore. Nathaniel owned a campground called Bluefin Bay. His wife, Calypso Hayden, née Payne, was dead.

Bourque turned off Route 6 and drove up a lane bordered by thick red cedars—your usual Cape cedars—not tall and elegant but squat and square, each distinctly different and yet somehow the same. The lane felt ageless, as much a state of mind as a road. Then the campground office emerged, and the spell dissolved. The building, a low beige box, was firmly set in the 1980s.

She parked and walked toward it, taking in the property: stands of wind-blown pitch pine, low-lying scrub oak, dunes fronting a wide beach. Though she couldn't see the ocean, she could hear breakers roaring ashore. Overhead, three hawks rode the mid-day thermals, with a larger one circling in their wake, as if batting cleanup. A map outside the building showed 120 sites. Entering the office, she saw it resembled an army barrack: poorly-lit, faded blinds, worn floorboards. Three stag heads hung on the back wall. She modified her assessment. Army barrack *cum* hunting lodge.

The young man behind the counter eyed her churlishly. Early in the season, she figured, for the help to be surly.

"Got a reservation?" Surly asked.

"No." She glanced outside at dozens of empty sites.

"You need one," Surly said.

An older man stepped into the office from the attached bungalow. "I'll get this, Hank. Good day, Miss. I'm Nate, the owner."

She pressed the recording button on her duty phone. "Nathaniel Hayden?"

He nodded. He looked to be in his sixties, not his seventies. He was imposing: tall, ruddy-faced, and barrel-chested. Incongruously, his lips were thin and as straight as a ruler. He wore his weight like a sumo wrestler—in his chest and stomach. His lumberjack shirt had two missing buttons and patched elbows. I'm a local, it said, not a weekend warrior. He'd only had one child, Nestor, Katrina's father. The rest of the family was on his wife's side. She had a brother who had two local sons, Tobias Payne and Jebediah Payne, who had seven children between them. Bourque pulled out her badge. "Detective Lieutenant Bourque, State Police."

Hank grunted. "I knew it," he said, "I smelled bacon the second she came in. A big side of bacon. Enough for breakfast for a month."

Hayden waved abruptly. "There's firewood to pile."

Hank gone, Nate sat in a creaky office chair. "Can I help you?" he growled.

"Are you Katrina Hayden's grandfather?"

"Yep. Took you a while to get here."

"Did it?" she gruffly said. Charm wasn't going to work on this man. "What's Hank's last name?"

"Payne."

She recalled the name. Hank Payne had been busted a year ago for dealing ecstasy in Provincetown. He was arraigned with his uncle Tobias. "When did you last see your granddaughter?" she asked.

"Four-and-a-half years ago," Hayden replied.

"Where?"

"Here. She was visiting her gran. My wife. Dead now."

"My condolences."

"A bit late."

Bourque let the barb fly over her head. "Tell me about Katrina."

"Not much to tell. She was a good kid. Messed-up parents, but that wasn't her fault."

"Whose fault was it?"

He sniffed with disdain. "You cops. As shuttered as social workers." He shook his head as if to clear his mind. "If it was anyone's fault, it was mine. However, I can't take full blame for it. Pardon my mouth, but your shit comes out of your own arse. You hear what I'm saying? You can't hang it on your ancestors."

"What about her father, your son Nestor? Can he take any blame?"

"Yes. Less than me, though. Same for her mother. They were lost souls."

Bourque eyed Hayden dubiously. He didn't speak. She waited.

"You should have seen this place in the fifties," he declared. "In some ways, it was the end of the Earth, a lost peninsula."

Bourque could see that. The campground still looked lost. As for Hayden himself, he could pass for a tar from centuries ago, from the Cape's time as a whaling hub.

"When I was a kid," he continued, "we did what we needed to get along. It was no picnic up here." He grinned unreliably. "All right, let's move on. We bought this place sixteen years ago. Everything has come up roses. I'm a model citizen."

"And Hank?"

The grin faded. "Don't worry about him. He won't get around me. You can't shit a shitter. Pardon my—"

She waved him off. "When was the last time you heard from Katrina?"

"When we saw her. Four-and-a-half years ago. She didn't invite me to her wedding. She didn't invite any of us."

"Rumor has it her hubby built the Falmouth place because she had roots there."

Hayden huffed. "That's an old wives' tale. You people relying on rumormongers now?" Said like, *You relying on assholes?*

"What do you know about it?" she asked.

"Nothing." He shrugged. "Sorry."

"No, you're not." She'd intended to interview Nate with no animosity. It wasn't working.

"That's the problem with female cops. That attitude. Next time, leave it in your cruiser."

"I don't drive a cruiser. And, in case you're wondering, I don't have a purse. All I have is a Smith & Wesson and handcuffs."

Hayden's ruddy face reddened even more.

"Where were you on Sunday, May thirteenth?"

"Here. I didn't leave the *premises*, as you cops say."

"Can someone verify that?"

"We have seven or eight seasonal RVs near the office. All the occupants saw me that day, some more than once."

"What about Hank? Did he see you?"

"He was off."

Sure he was. "Where was he?"

"None of my business. He's over eighteen. That makes him an adult, as I'm sure you know."

Bourque moved on. "Where were you on Monday, May fourteenth?"

"Here. Before you ask, Hank can verify that."

Right, she thought. "What about Hank and Katrina? Was he in touch with her?"

"Nope. They had nothing in common."

"Aren't they first cousins?"

"Yep. But she was twelve years older. And Hank's not a bootlicker. He wouldn't go begging."

"Call him back in."

"That's my flesh and blood," Nate warned. "Don't mistreat him."

"Not my intention."

"He doesn't need any more *help* from Social Services. You hear me?"

She didn't respond.

☐ ☐ ☐

Sitting across from Hank Payne, Bourque held her fire. Let the carcass cure. Nate Hayden exited the office with a huff, but left the sliding door to the bungalow open. Bourque studied Hank: heavily-muscled, buzzcut hair, a scar on the right temple, the beady eyes of a wolverine.

"What's your full name?" she asked.

He ignored her for a few seconds. "Hank Jackson Payne," he grunted.

"What's your date of birth?"

"You could ask for my license, you know."

"I could, but I want to see if you can remember it." She smiled evenly. "Drugs, Hank, they mess with your memory."

He sniffed. "You think I'm a hillbilly?"

"Not at all. No hills around here."

"That supposed to be funny?"

"Your date of birth, Hank."

"What the hell. June second, two thousand."

Although she'd already reviewed his record, she brought out her phone and viewed it again. Her MO was to treat everyone with respect—until they showed her some reason not to. Hank had already shown her a few. She wanted to keep him hanging on the hook, to generate a little angst. Young bucks hated waiting for the *man*. In this case, the *woman*. That often rattled them more. Eventually she spoke. "I see you've been out seven months, Hank."

"Yeah?" He sneered. "Don't you cops always travel in pairs?"

"No."

"Be safer."

"I don't need to be safer."

"You might need help."

"Help? I'm not Miss Marple."

His face went blank.

"Let's start again, Hank. Where were you on Sunday, May thirteenth?"

"Don't you need a warrant to ask that?"

"No, I don't, and you don't need to be served a warrant to answer it. You just have to make an important decision. You can either help or hinder a murder investigation. I repeat, where were you on May thirteenth?"

"In Truro," he hurriedly replied, "hanging with Jim McVey and Randy Connors."

She didn't trust him. Maybe he figured quickness conveyed innocence. Not in his case. "Where were you on Monday, May fourteenth?"

"Here."

"Doing what?"

"Not much."

"I have an idea," she sincerely said, trying to give him another chance. "Rather than tell me 'Not much,' give me the details and maybe I'll say, 'That's not much.' Okay?"

He sneered again.

"What were you doing?"

"Piling wood. What else?" he scoffed.

"Was anyone with you?"

"Nope. But my grandfather was supervising me," he added, realizing the meaning behind the question.

"Was he?" Her respect quotient had hit bottom. "When was the last time you saw Katrina Hayden?"

"Let me see." He pretended to ponder the question. "Memory issues. Oh, right, two days ago."

"Pardon?"

"Two days ago. The late news on TV."

Bourque suppressed a grin. She'd walked into that one. "The last time you saw her in person."

Hank pretended to think again, then answered. "About four years ago, when Gran was sick."

"Well, young man, you've got me thinking. You see, I'm a detective. We ponder, we cogitate."

He regarded her warily.

"We listen too. And I don't like what I'm hearing. I think you're bullshitting me."

He shook his head.

"If you're lying about anything, it'll come back to bite you. Like a pack of wolves. Now, what's Katrina Hayden's phone number?"

"How would I know? I never called her."

"Did she call you?"

"Nope."

"Well, we know her number and we're tracing her calls. If any of them end up here, I'll be back to see you." She stood. "Not that I want to be near you. You should take a shower. You smell like rancid bacon."

Chapter 12

Bourque left Bluefin Bay behind and drove south into Chatham. There were only a few tourists—aka *cidiots*—in sight. She loved Cape Cod towns in May: the unhurried pace; the feeling that nothing needed to change. The sea still had equal billing with the land.

Reaching downtown Chatham, she ordered takeout fish and chips and sat on a bench overlooking the harbor. Gulls patrolled nearby wastebins like prize fighters, jawing and posing. The charter and tour boats were freshly painted, shipshape, and ready for business. The town possessed an aura of confidence and prosperity, as befitted an area with some of the best beaches in Massachusetts.

Eating her lunch, Bourque put her phone earbuds in and listened to Hank Payne's interview. Another youngster without boundaries. Wanting things 'everyone else' had, plotting ways to get them—*easy* ways, *fast* ways. She concluded he could be a suspect. Then again, he might simply be a garden-variety bad boy. Donnelly would call him a weasel: slippery and opportunistic. She phoned Peabody to request McVey and Connors be questioned by a junior detective. The seasonal RVers had all corroborated Nate Hayden's whereabouts.

Back in her car, she googled "Massachusetts campgrounds for sale" and made some comparisons. Bluefin Bay was worth over two million. She researched Hank's siblings. None of them had sheets. The father, Jeb, was a widower. His sheet was clean too. Nonetheless, she ordered a financial trace on Nate Hayden, as well as Jeb and Tobias Payne. In particular, she wanted to know who owned Bluefin Bay and how it was financed. Bootlegging? Drugs?

Bourque drove toward Falmouth with a heavy foot. The highway was both straight and freshly sealed. No wonder people sped. Her mother Sarah used to say, "You make good highways, you make speeders." She'd been stopped for speeding by a Texas trooper on a recent trip across the country. When he wrote her a ticket, she told him it was the road's fault. He laughed at her. A minute down the road, she tossed the ticket out the window, then reported him for being rude and overbearing.

Bourque shook her head. *Overbearing.* Her mother was the epitome of overbearing. She'd have made a good detective captain. She was always pushing Bourque to wear nicer clothes and find a rich husband, not an "over-educated" one. If she encountered a book shelf, she raised two fingers in a cross, yelled "Devil," and ran the other way. It was no wonder the two saw so little of each other, even though Sarah lived relatively close by, in Salem.

Continuing west on Route 28, Bourque tried to give herself a mental break. She forced the case to the bottom of her mind. It didn't stay there. Approaching East Falmouth, the Novak castle began tugging at her. She passed the driveway. A few seconds later, she screamed to a stop, pulled a one-eighty and sped up the driveway.

□   □   □

Although the sky was cloudless, the passage was as dark as two mornings ago. The strong sun barely filtered through the umbrella pines. Outside the house, she stopped at the State Police checkpoint and signed in.

Walking the blue-tiled hall to the pool, she felt a pall of gloom weighing the house down. She didn't believe in tales of murdered lovers becoming immortal ghosts, but for once the Gothic got the better of her. She sensed the Novak castle would become haunted. Wrong. It already was.

At the sliding pool door, she quickly donned her CS gear and approached the crime scene. When she returned to a scene, small details often surfaced, details she'd miss the first time. The pool area was empty. No deck chairs. The sun's glare bounced off the deck tiles and burned her retinas. No wonder there were no chairs. Who could relax in that light?

The blue water was motionless. The tiles near the scene were still dusted with black print powder, as was the stair rail. There were two rings around it, the color of stainless steel, where the neckties had been cut away after Miller's dusting.

Bourque stopped a yard from the rail and dropped to her haunches. Her clean-suit crinkled as she moved. She shut out the sound. She heard no grackles or jays. There was no such thing as silence—breezes usually stirred; tiny motors whirred—yet the pool area was as silent as any crime scene she'd known.

Her nose picked up something she hadn't noticed before: no chlorine smell. She dipped a finger in the pool and tasted it. Salty, and cold. Novak used salt to treat his pool water, not chlorine. Perhaps the absence of chlorine meant something. She let her mind cycle.

There was one small thing. Chlorine could be used to sedate someone. Maybe its absence had something to do with the hypodermic needle? If Novak was involved in Hayden's death, perhaps he used a sedative because he had no chlorine on hand.

Bourque shook her head. Is that the best you can do? A weak supposition. Most rich people used salt to treat their pools. Her ex used to say she saw guilt everywhere. According to him, she manufactured it. Of course, he'd say that. Being an inveterate womanizer, he was often guilty himself.

Staring at the rail, she envisioned the hanging corpses, recreating the crime scene. The outlines of the two bodies materialized in her mind, and then the bodies came into focus. She slowed her heartbeat, trying hard to see something new.

Nothing. No fresh details. Some days, the sky rained clues. Not today. She was in a dry zone.

She reached out and touched the surface of the tiles, expecting them to be warmed by the sun, but finding them still cold. Despite the afternoon hour, Novak's pool area hadn't warmed up. She dipped a finger in the water again. Very cold. Novak didn't heat his pool. Not so strange, she decided, for a billionaire who mowed his own lawn. She wondered about Hayden's nakedness. Hayden was frisky, no doubt about that, but making love on those tiles? Why not go inside? Why freeze your butt?

Bourque exhaled noisily. Why? She shook her head. Forget it. The woman was in love. Cold didn't matter. Bourque knew that feeling. She'd dragged Marty out to the back deck a few times in November. Cold butt, warm heart.

Shifting gears, she leaned forward and stared at the crime scene. The cold seeped up through her shoes. Her body wanted to leave, but she kept staring, to no avail. She was still sightless, like a ship sailing through thick fog.

Abruptly, she stood and eyed the scene again, hoping to jog at least one tiny detail loose. The sun danced across the pool. A cloud passed over the sun and stayed there. She felt her mental fog thickening. With each passing moment, it seemed more difficult to envisage anything. This was the time she dreaded: the blindness at the beginning of a case, when nothing made sense.

She trudged back to the house. If there were no clues outside, she'd search inside again. There had to be something there, maybe slight signs of a scuffle: a barely misaligned piece of furniture, a smudge on the wall. Stop, she told herself, don't look for specific things, just *look*. When you looked for specifics, other things eluded you. Victims' houses often provided the best way of knowing them. While family and friends might not intentionally mislead you, they tended to speak out of the corners of their mouths. Houses spoke directly, revealing things victims never wanted anyone to see—caches of old photos, clothes hoards, secret hobbies—not to mention slipups the perps didn't want anyone to see, especially any detectives.

She began re-examining the first three floors, fixing the map of the house in her mind, hunting for missing links. What had she or the whitecoats overlooked? Had they mistakenly downgraded any details?

Two hours later, she hadn't detected any missing links or mistakes. The three main floors were dead-ends. The same dark walls and ponderous furniture, the same feeling of another century and another continent. The castle was stultifying. How could a woman like Hayden—young and fashionable—find excitement or happiness here?

Bourque climbed the narrow stairs to the library spanning the top floor. Given the castle's sharply peaked main roof, the library was a third the size of the first floor. Though the ninjas had processed the room and found nothing, she hadn't inspected it. Entering the room, she whistled. Quite the book collection. If her mother saw it, she'd howl and run for days. The bookcases were fashioned from thick maple, the kind milled in the eighteenth century. The leatherbound books lining them looked older. Unlike her mother, her father had been a big reader. Although not university educated, his home office was lined with books, including Greek and Roman classics. Bourque had read many of them in her youth.

She walked to the nearest set of shelves and scanned the authors. Teilhard de Chardin, Confucius, Ralph Waldo Emerson, Krishnamurti, Hans Küng, Plato. No Homer, no *Iliad* or *Odyssey*, her favorite, the epic tale of the wise wily human who was tossed hither and yon but found his way home. She perused the next set of shelves. Bertrand Russell, Saint Augustine, Saint Paul, Henry David Thoreau, Zoroaster. Nothing about commerce or money. Not what she'd expected. Novak was a business titan, yet she was standing in a philosopher's den.

She moved on. In the far-right corner of the room, she noticed a framed quote on the wall:

> "The gentleman is conversant with righteousness; the small man is conversant with profit."
>
> ~ Confucius

The back shelves held adventure tales. Edgar Rice Burroughs, Ian Fleming, Marco Polo, Tolkien. Continuing her perusal, she found the collection rounded out by two additional shelves. Aristotle's *Nicomachean Ethics,* Buddhist sutras, more Confucius, Catholic theology, Greek tragedies.

Bourque left the castle in a thoughtful mood. Novak was another conundrum: an apparently ethical rich man. Thanks to his book collection, she had a better handle on him, not that she'd ever mention that to Peabody. Her book insights wouldn't interest him. In his view, if an investigative angle couldn't deliver some facts, it was a dead-end. What facts could Novak's books yield? In her eyes, what a detective needed most was a wide-open mind. Curiosity was queen. Uncertainty was a prod. When you were unsure, you kept searching. As her father used to say, a detective was an explorer, always on the lookout for unknown lands, always searching for strange clues.

Chapter 13

Barnstable. May 16th

Driving toward Barnstable, Bourque thought of Marty. She fleetingly considered detouring to his place for an early dinner. And a roll in the hay. She glanced at the car clock. 1610. Why not? Wine, Get Naked, Dinner. Or Get Naked, Wine, Dinner. Both good. But she knew it was out of the question. Her day was only half-done.

The sun, once high in the sky, had transitioned to the western horizon. It was a good time for a sail. If you were a busy person, it might feel like it took forever to sail from Falmouth to the Elizabeth Islands. If you had all the time in the world—if you weren't working a case—it would be an enjoyable few hours. With the afternoon light softening, the eye could linger and focus. Out on the Atlantic, big birds would be visible for miles, flying high across the sky, following the curve of the earth.

Passing by Barnstable's post office, she noted its flag snapping in the wind. A northeasterly was kicking up. She and Marty had bought an old sailboat, a Tartan 30, and berthed it in Falmouth Inner Harbor. They could reach Woods Hole in a flash. It'd be a fun ride, but not for her, not today.

Back at the detective unit, Captain Peabody was waiting for her near the main entrance.

"Come into my office," he said.

Come into my parlor, she thought. The spider and the fly reprised, with Peabody the spider. There was no humor in his blue eyes today. His hair was severely parted; his pants perfectly pressed. The creases looked like knife blades. He led her to his office and pointed to a chair.

"Coffee, Detective?"

"No thanks." She wanted Spider Peabody to pick her legs off as soon as possible. One today, she wondered, maybe two. What had she forgotten to do? Many things.

"I heard Eller is staying in Barnstable tonight," Peabody began in his fast-paced voice. "He booked two nights at Days Inn. Do you know why?"

"No." While Eller's booking was news to her, she wasn't surprised. He liked to work late and stay put, not drive home. At least he'd gone down- market; Days Inn wasn't the Sheraton. "You know him. He burns the candle at both ends."

"Huh," Peabody said, "he can do that at home. I wish I could cancel his expense account."

She didn't reply. At times, she felt for Peabody. While she didn't know exactly what he believed, she knew his idea of the good-featured *sacrifice and selflessness*, which weren't bad maxims for a public servant.

Peabody pursed his lips. His face appeared to be split vertically down the middle, a chiaroscuro of philosopher and codfish. "How's the investigation going?"

"It's moving along."

"Moving? That's it? Get cracking. As they say, *information is king*. What's the best source of information, Bourque? Not the internet. It's people. Get out there and talk to them. All of you! You're not paid to sit on your butts. Next time I drop by the murder room, I don't want to see anyone there."

She didn't reply.

"You do good work, Lieutenant. I'm not saying that to flatter you. You'll go the distance—and not many women do. But remember this: don't lose sight of the job. You're more idealistic than you let on."

"And that's a bad thing?"

Peabody huffed. "For a police officer, it is. Don't overthink things." He stomped out of the unit.

As Bourque walked down the hall to the staffroom, Eller emerged from the men's toilet.

"How did you know he was gone?" she asked.

"I saw him leave. Gotta love this building. Windows everywhere."

"Oh yeah. Let's get a sandwich."

"Sure. Dunkin'?"

She nodded. It was their go-to place, a five-minute walk away.

"What'd he want?" Eller asked.

"All of us out there, talking to the locals."

"Boots on the ground. All that jazz?"

"More or less."

□ □ □

After eating at Dunkin', the two detectives returned to the station and headed to Bourque's office. She could tell by Eller's look that he was back in work mode. He'd tightened his tie. She smiled to herself. Eller was like most coworkers. It was just a matter of time before they revealed their tells. Too bad suspects weren't like that.

"Any leads on Katrina Hayden?" he asked from his chair.

"Not yet. I'm still looking into her family."

"What's the angle?"

"I wonder how Nate Hayden got the money to buy Bluefin Bay. He was a bootlegger with a captive market, but it wasn't a big one. It's possible Katrina had part ownership in the campground. If so, she might have borrowed money to buy in—which might have left her open to danger. As in murder."

"By Novak?"

"I'm not saying that. Someone who wanted her piece of the pie or didn't get their money back. I don't see Novak getting upset over part of two million, or even all of it. Upset enough to kill, that is." She didn't mention his apparent ethical bent. Too hypothetical.

"All right," Eller said. "The junior detectives from Central arrived shortly after you left. Peabody sent one to grill Hank Payne's friends. There's something else. We just got a tip about Damijan Zupan being in Truro three times this past month. The detective will find out what he was doing there."

Bourque's mind buzzed. Zupan in Truro? She immediately thought of Hank and Nate. Were the three connected?

Eller moved on. "The youngest detective from Central, Carl Abbot, is handling the cellphone records. Evidently, he's a tech whiz." Eller raised an eyebrow. "These kids. They can hack a laptop, but I wonder if they can shoot straight or drive a hundred-and-twenty. Anyway, an hour ago, Abbot completed the Zupan file. Used algorithms, he explained." Eller chuckled. "Like I care about Al Gore's dance moves."

She managed a smile. Corny.

"So," Eller said, "our boy ran a program—wrote it himself, he claimed—to sort and group the phone numbers in and out, the call or text lengths, and tally the frequency of each number found. Zupan was called dozens of times by Novak, but never by Katrina Hayden, Melanya Novak, Atlas Novak, or Vega. There were no texts. No unlisted number incalls. Considering Zupan's outcalls, he only made forty-one and none to any of the names mentioned above. From what Abbot uncovered, they were all work-related. Deliveries, repairmen, etcetera. Nothing personal."

"No calls to or from his sister Snežana?"

"No."

That seemed strange. The siblings appeared to be close. "No calls to or from Slovenia?"

"No."

Bourque hiked her shoulders. *That doesn't prove anything.*

"I think Abbot agrees with you. Zupan doesn't have a social media footprint, but he has two email addresses. I requested the metadata from his recent e-correspondence, a six-month trail."

"Get Abbot to go deeper. Dark web." At the beginning of an investigation, she always threw a wide net. Speculation was as important as evidence when they had so little of the latter.

"Okay. By the way, Melanya Novak doesn't own a cellphone. She has a landline at her Boston apartment. I ordered metadata for that too."

"No cellphone? That's strange."

"Not that unusual," Eller replied. "Who needs to be available all the time? And don't get me going on messaging. It's for kids."

"And L is for Luddites." Bourque winked. According to most male cops she worked with, cellphones were okay, but texting? Why would someone with large thumbs want to text? She understood Eller's perspective. Her father had been the same way. He wanted to talk on his cellphone, not poke at a small keyboard. "The ex is under fifty," Bourque continued. "Almost everyone under that age has a cellphone. She's a very attractive woman. And she's single. Beyond that, women love to gossip. I know."

"You women, you're a mystery." Eller rolled on. "I've been talking to a profiler at Central."

Bourque didn't respond. Eller loved criminal profilers. The distant gods of crime scenes. While she admired their work, she found it too data-driven. She usually sniffed out exactly what the data crunchers reported. In the geography of the body, limbic paths predated neural networks. Humans were born to feel. Feelings fed thoughts, not vice versa—which was difficult for data systems to model.

"As you know," Eller related, "an angry or emotional murderer goes overboard and draws blood, lots of blood. A more bloodless CS speaks to a more dispassionate murderer. That's what we appear to have. The victims were garroted, which caused some neck bleeding, yet they weren't stabbed or otherwise mutilated. Speaks to perp self-control. Discipline over emotion. Admittedly, strangulation isn't exactly dispassionate but it's more controlled than a knife attack or blunt force beating."

She couldn't argue with that.

Eller carried on. "I assigned another of the junior detectives, Priya Patel, to investigate the May fourteenth camera footage from the castle security system. She reported the camera outside the back pool gate was disabled via a wire snip, like the gate alarm. She found zero human activity on the other outward-facing cameras until oh-eight-hundred-eighteen, when your local troopers arrived. She didn't discover any signs of a temporary pool-cam setup. It seems the perps couldn't see Novak from the outside and know he was post-coital."

Bourque was quiet as she digested the information. "What about a drone camera?"

"Possible. But I'd wager either they saw the semen on his penis when they entered and left him unsedated, or he wasn't meant to be sedated. The latter lends some credence to the idea he sedated and killed Hayden." Eller smiled. "I'm not sucking up to Peabody, but Novak's guilt is still in play. As for inside-the-castle footage, like Zupan told us, there isn't any. I'd bet the only witnesses were the killers."

She agreed. Unfortunately, that was often the case.

"In my opinion, Rob Landon's the best of the junior detectives. Why don't you oversee him? Assign him his tasks."

She could tell by Eller's collegial tone that he thought he was doing her a favor. However, she preferred working on her own.

"He's a go-getter," Eller noted.

She nodded. She knew Landon, ex-Boston police, early-thirties. He'd worked a few State cases with her. She supposed it would work. Personnel Management 101. Marty had warned her she'd have to be a bureaucrat to get ahead. He knew that game, and had walked away from the Navy Seals before it happened. In his view, if she ascended the career ladder, she'd end up as a female version of an old boy. "Okay," she told Eller, "I'll start Landon off with the two Novak wives."

He grinned. "Those two could be Stepford wives. That Melanya sometimes seems to be half there. Incidentally, the lab is pulling an all-nighter. Peabody wants us to work late. He's ordering takeout supper for the staff at twenty-hundred."

□ □ □

In the murder room, Bourque sat next to Landon. He shunned suits yet looked perfectly put together. At first glance, with his sandy hair and tanned face, he resembled a movie star—a bad look for a cop. But when you looked again, you saw hard, calculating eyes, the eyes of a man who could get what he wanted. She briefed him on Katrina and Nate Hayden, then filled him in on Hank Payne.

"A hood-in-the-making," Landon said when she was done. "You have to shake that type out of their stupidity."

She remained silent.

"Sorry, stupor."

"No, stupidity."

Landon shot her an evaluating look. *Good,* his eyes said, *we're on the same page.*

Maybe, she thought, maybe not.

"The thing you have to like about hoods-in-training is their consistency. They always think they're smarter than you. But the little fuckers always fuck up."

She coughed. She didn't care about the f-word, but others might. Detective Patel had glanced up.

"Pardon the language," he said. "I mean, *little felons.*"

Bourque nodded wryly. She could work with this guy. The hell with being politically correct. However, she motioned with her hand for him to keep the volume down. "I'd like you to do a full social media search on Katrina Hayden, then Melanya Novak. Sift through all the hits, sort out if anyone connected to either of them might be a POI."

"Roger that."

Roger that? She could do without the radio-speak. "You can debrief me after supper."

"Roger."

Bourque wondered if Nate Hayden was lying about his granddaughter. Apparently, Katrina Hayden didn't have much to do with her Truro relatives. Bourque wasn't so sure. She needed a peek into Hayden's calls, whether Abbot was busy or not. In a case like this, with no forensic breakthroughs and no apparent suspects, they had to learn as much as they could about the victims' families and hope something clicked.

Abbot proved to be fully cooperative. His partial trace revealed Katrina Hayden hadn't called any numbers linked to the Truro Hayden or Paynes in the last six years, and vice versa. Six years was enough to suggest Nate Hayden and Hank Payne weren't lying—about that.

◻ ◻ ◻

Bourque headed outside to take a breather. Afternoon had given way to evening. The sky was oyster grey. She sat at a picnic table under a maple tree. The "gloaming," as Cal Knowlton called it—the onset of darkness—was in full swing. She heard birds fidgeting above her head. Shutting out their rustling, she reviewed the case. What certainties did the team have?

Two garrottings. No definite suspects. No perp DNA. Currently, she reminded herself. What else? Eleven shoeprints. Three perps. Two red neckties. But she didn't know what the ties signified, if anything. Any other certainties?

She searched her mind. Nada. To be a detective was to be a question mark. How? When? Where? Especially who and why. Always questioning, always pushing. Never finishing. She felt like Sisyphus.

Chapter 14

Shifting at the picnic table, Bourque pulled out her personal phone to call Cal Knowlton. He brought to mind her maternal grandfather, Thomas Day, who'd run a dairy farm near Salem. Grandpa Thomas was an atypical Yankee, given to what he called "foolish extravagances" like beach cottages and sailboats. Bourque had loved being around him. If not for his *foolishness*, she wouldn't have grown up sailing on the Atlantic. Both Cal and Grandpa Thomas smelled a bit gamey. She knew Thomas had only bathed once a week. Anything more, he'd claimed, was a foolish extravagance. His smell hadn't bothered her. In fact, she missed it: hay mixed with cow manure. Reality.

She punched Cal's number, thinking that if perps smelled guilty, her job would be easy. *Did you catch a whiff of that?* one detective said to another. *Yeah, he's guilty as hell.*

"It's your neighbor," she said when Cal answered.

"I bet you're calling because you miss me."

"With all my heart, darling."

He chortled. "What have you been up to?"

"Shining my shoes," she kidded.

"Hang on, I need to grab a coffee."

She waited.

"Done. You know, the coffee bean was discovered in Ethiopia in the ninth century. It's an amazing story—"

"Sorry," Bourque interrupted, "can I ask you a few questions about the Novaks?"

"Sure, I'll tell you what old Hermes, the Messenger God, revealed to me. He's a cunning deity, if there ever was one. He's usually accompanied by a sacred hawk. A hawk has great—"

"Cal."

"Just ribbing you."

She chuckled. "What do you think? Did Novak build the castle in Falmouth because Katrina asked him to?"

"I'd say no. She had roots here, but she wasn't close to her family. And that's an understatement. To Katrina, the Cape was the past, Novak was the future. And the twain didn't meet."

"Was it that simple?"

"I have more. Nate Hayden never forgave Katrina for not telling him where his son was buried. Some say she didn't know, not exactly. But it was somewhere in Slovenia."

Slovenia again. Another coincidence? "Who told you that?" Bourque asked.

"She did. I knew her a bit. I know all the beauties on the South Cape, you included."

"Why, thank you," Bourque said, channeling Dolly Parton. "You'll give me a swollen head."

"Not you. Your head's on straight."

"Why, thank you." Bourque paused. "Pardon my pushiness. When did she tell you and where?"

"At Collard's Coffee House. Let me think when."

Bourque remained silent.

"Right, I remember. It was over a year ago, in late March. She was wearing one of those big coats, a faux fur. Looked smashing. Her and the coat. I've always thought, if she wore dresses, she'd look like Marilyn Monroe. But she wore tights—leggings, my granddaughters call 'em. And they were skintight, I can tell you that."

"Interesting, but back to the facts."

"Those are facts."

"Other facts. Was she alone?"

"Yes."

"How did the topic come up? You know, where her father was buried?"

"She was saying she and her hubby were going to Slovenia at Christmas, to see his family and all. And then she mentioned it was also her father's burial place. She didn't mention the exact place. Just the country."

"Why did she tell you?"

"I'm not sure. It's possible she wanted me to spread the news. People know I like to talk. I realize that's an understatement. My mother used to say Calder was the perfect name for me. It means 'stream,' and I'm a stream of words. But I'm not a gossip. That's a four-letter word."

"Six, Cal."

"Four to me. My dear mother warned me about gossip. It doesn't have a long shelf life. Someone claims breakfast is piping hot pancakes but, when you get there, it's cold porridge."

"Ah," Bourque commiserated. Beyond that, cold porridge was a sin. "By the way, did you spread the news?"

"If you're asking if I told a few people about the burial in Slovenia, the answer is 'Yes.' I'm sure Nate Hayden heard the news."

"Did Katrina tell you anything else about Nate or Nestor Hayden?"

"No."

"What did you two talk about?"

"The weather, the music she danced to, that sort of thing. She was quiet at first, but when she got going, she could talk the scales off a salmon. I'm sure she was lonely. She didn't have that many friends."

"Here, you mean?"

"No, everywhere. She often said she had a great online life, but no real life. Poor girl, she's not the only one. I pity the young ones. She'd lost touch with all her girlfriends after marrying Mr. Novak. She was wary of them. Thought they might steal him from her. That girl acted like a grand lady but, deep down, she wasn't very confident. Another Marilyn Munroe trait."

"Any idea why Katrina told you her feelings? You know, the revelations about loneliness and jealousy?"

"People talk to me. I'm non-threatening. Couldn't harm a flea."

"What else can you tell me about her?"

"She was a wonderful dancer, though I'm sure you know that. She could sing too. Did you see her on *The Tonight Show*?"

"No. Too late for me. I'm an early riser."

"So? I get up at six no matter when I go to bed. Stamina, my dear."

"You're a lion."

"And a tiger." He chuckled. "Anyway, Katrina joined the house band and belted out a blues standard, "Baby, Please Don't Go." She was magnificent. But you know what she told me? What she really wanted to do was become an actress."

"Marilyn Monroe again."

"Right. You're not just a pretty face. Somehow, I'm not surprised Katrina died young. She had a tragic aura."

"How so?"

"She didn't seem long for this world."

"Why?"

"Just a feeling. The first time we left the coffeeshop together, we stood talking outside. The sun seemed to shine right through her. She appeared to be made of nothing. It was strange, I tell you. Very strange. I know, that's an impression, but it's what I felt."

"Did she ever talk about death?"

"No. We never spoke about such things."

Enough for now, Bourque decided. A lot of the Old Guard thought female detectives were too invested in victims. And some were, she agreed. They believed you had to bond with victims, bring them back to life so you could know their hearts. Method sleuthing, the Old Guard scoffed. Bourque went with them on that one. While she always felt for victims, she didn't need to know absolutely everything about them. Instead, she wanted to know everything about their potential killers. "Thank you, Cal. I appreciate the help."

□ □ □

Bourque entered the murder room to find Donnelly doling out fried chicken, chips, gravy, and coleslaw. More health food, she jokingly thought. Marty didn't approve of her diet. Truth be told, neither did she. Chicken 'n' chips after a lunch of fish 'n' chips. Double jeopardy.

Donnelly was hamming it up, pretending he was Friar Tuck. "Fire and brimstone," he deadpanned, "that vile Nottingham!"

"What?" she asked in faux horror.

"He repossessed the roast beef."

She faked a swoon.

Donnelly winked and offered her food. "*Poulet*? *Pommes frites*?"

She bowed. "Thanks be, kind sir. Just a little chicken and some slaw."

"It's agonizingly delicious," he said. "Agonizing."

The slaw wasn't seasoned; it was sugared. The fried chicken was swimming in grease. Agonizing indeed. She knew Donnelly was ridiculing Peabody's cheapness, not his food selection. Donnelly usually loved fried chicken.

After the late supper, Bourque returned to her office. The *Angels or Devils* video files had been posted to the case database. She wanted to determine how often Novak had been a devil financier before she updated Eller on the wives. Hayden could have been involved with investment seekers who got deviled by her husband.

Bourque pulled on headphones and plugged her mind into the *A or D* footage. The series presented updates whenever angels became devils, first rerunning the original investments, apparent angel outlays, and then highlighting what had happened on the road to devil takeovers. Some were hostile, others benign, even welcome.

To Bourque, a murder investigation was like reverse-engineering an organic compound. It was a private notion, not something she talked about, not even with Marty or Gigi. Organic chemists studied atomic elements that formed compounds. What she needed to do now was take a compound called murder and search for its building blocks, its atomic elements and reactions—i.e., perps and their movements. Trouble was, like real atomic particles, perps were difficult to pinpoint in space and time. An hour later, she'd quickly run through the first year of the show. No building blocks. No devil takeovers. Evidently, they took time, even for a snake like Vega.

She continued scanning the footage. A lot transpired in year two. Six of the show's investment seekers were deviled, three by Karlos Vega. By the end of the footage, she'd determined all the financiers except Novak had deviled multiple seekers on their own. Vega had deviled ten. One of his takeovers had been done in partnership with Novak. Other than that, Novak had been a rare angel.

She opened a spreadsheet and entered the details of the Vega-Novak takeover. She'd get M&M to dig into it. She knew the footage hadn't shown all of Novak's potential business enemies. However, it was a start. It also gave her a reason to continue probing Vega. The man was a snake, a tempter from a corporate Garden of Eden. Plant an apple tree, take the whole garden. But she wasn't interested in his morality. Others would judge him on that. Tomorrow she'd look into the business he co-owned with Novak.

□ □ □

Dropping into the murder room, Bourque walked to Landon's hutch. The man was zoned in. She hated to bother him, but wanted an update on Novak's wives before midnight.

"Detective," she said, "how about we ditch the formalities? I call you Rob and you call me Ivy."

"Sure, Lieutenant." He grinned. "Just joshing you, Ivy."

She smiled. "What's the goods on the wives? Any hits?"

Landon whistled softly. "Plenty on Hayden. Thousands. An effin' avalanche. Might be good news, but who knows what's under all that snow. Dirt or gold?"

"What about Melanya?"

"Not much on her. A dozen or so hits. A divorce announcement, some pics of her out with Novak, all a few years old or older. That's it. She's not on Facebook, Pinterest, Instagram, Twitter, none of them. No profiles on dating sites either."

Bourque figured the ex was out there on a few of the exclusive sites. "Are you sure?"

"Ninety-five percent. I used name and background searches, plus photo recognition software."

"Tell me about Hayden."

"Now, there's a woman with a social media footprint, more like a giant boot print."

Bourque nodded. The boot print fit with what Cal had told her.

"Pics galore from all the major galas and award shows in Boston, New York, and L.A. A ton of Fb friends and Instagram followers." Landon referred to his notes. "Plus over eighty thousand Twitter followers. You can guess the type of tweets. What organic flaxseed she ate for breakfast. Where she got her yoga mat. Where she got her Botox."

"A girl's gotta have it," Bourque said.

Landon eyed her. He didn't realize she was joking. She could see his mental wheels turning. *Does she use Botox?* Let him wonder. Since leaving Boston behind, she'd shunned makeup. Surprisingly, her mother Sarah said she didn't need it. She had good bones. Nicest thing Sarah had ever said to her. Of course, Sarah insinuated the good bones came from her.

"Thousands of Instagram pics," Landon went on. "Everything from Hayden at a Balinese temple to pics of her big toe."

"Okay, she was a star. Any ideas on who to zero in on?"

"I'll use name, background, and photo recognition software again. First, I'll identify anyone who shows up more than five times. I expect that'll return a lot of POIs, possibly thousands, so I'll have to adjust for six times, then eight, then ten, and so on. I'll narrow the interview list down to a hundred or so. I figure we can handle that."

Bourque nodded. The team had next to nothing on Katrina Hayden. Her relatives didn't seem to know anything, or weren't saying anything. Landon had to go ahead with a social media generated list. Of course, he'd have to sit on his behind for hours, but what did Peabody expect? The alternative was to knock on hundreds of doors. That was Peabody for you: Don't spend any money but solve the case by sundown. "So," she asked Landon, "how long?"

"I'll probably have to run twenty batches. Maybe more. I'd say tomorrow afternoon. It's not rocket science but it is time consuming."

"Right." If they had a few weeks, they'd set a trap. Create fake accounts, friend all of Hayden's friends, wait for some to friend back, then message them, try to milk them for info. Subtly, of course. You couldn't milk too hard.

□ □ □

Well after midnight, Bourque left the unit and took in the sky. The spring constellations were arcing across the heavens, spinning westerly, heading for the Berkshires. The moon was waxing, casting long shadows. The oaks bordering the unit looked like eerie wraiths. She hurried to her car. The best way to serve the case was to get home. Sleep would clear her mind. And before sleep? There was Marty. He'd clear her mind too. Better yet, her body. Was it too soon to sneak naked into his house again? Not a chance.

Chapter 15

DAY FOUR: *Barnstable, May 17th*

The next morning, the temperature had dropped twenty degrees Fahrenheit. Walking from her car to the unit, Bourque tracked an armada of steel-grey clouds sailing across the Cape from the northeast. The sky was the color of pewter. It felt like March again.

When she entered her office, Eller was at his desk.

"Morning, Bourque. Peabody had to go to Boston. We're running the meeting."

□   □   □

In the murder room, Eller called the meeting to order and motioned Abbot to the front.

The junior detective looked like a racoon caught in the headlights. He faltered and coughed, then started again. He'd completed cellphone traces for Novak's son. Atlas had communicated frequently with unlisted numbers. He'd also communicated with Karlos Vega forty-eight times in the past three months. With metadata, Abbot noted, all he could do was look at it. If the team wanted to access actual call transcripts or text messages, such as Atlas's, they'd have to subpoena them.

Eller took over, addressing the team from his chair. "Just got some interesting news." He paused for effect. "Novak gave Katrina Hayden two million dollars by automatic e-deposit on May fifteenth last year, and the year before as well. May fifteenth happens to be a day after they were both killed. It also happens to be their wedding anniversary. I looked that up. A real sweetheart, is our Mr. Novak, a sentimental sort. Maybe. As it happens, the two million dollar 'gift' didn't occur this year. The e-deposit was cancelled on May twelfth—by Novak himself. Is it possible he didn't have the funds on hand? Not likely. His net worth is estimated to be nine-point-seven billion. Maybe he didn't want to pay his wife two million dollars. You'll note I said 'pay.' To Novak, his gift might seem like a big bill. If so, did he have her killed or kill her himself?"

No one replied.

"Maybe you're like me. Maybe you're wondering *why wouldn't he want to pay her? What's two million bucks to him?* Captain Peabody asked M and M to dig deeper. They just got back to us." Eller had everyone's attention. "Novak's average monthly expenditure for the last two years is under five thousand dollars."

A few gasps.

"I know. A trifling sum for a billionaire. A bit like you or me spending two cents a month. You might think his business paid for most things, but that figure includes both his business and personal expenditures. Although he and his wife entertained in East Falmouth and Boston, and elsewhere, and not cheaply, it appears she paid for that. Her credit card statements show numerous bills for gourmet caterers. His statements don't show any. On his personal side, we see bills for books, haberdashery, and toiletries. That's it. On the business side, there are infrequent bills for airline tickets and hotels. M and M will establish when his stinginess started. And what are we going to do?" Eller held his fire.

The room leaned forward.

Bourque admired his technique. He knew how to hold an audience.

"Look into the *why*," Eller disclosed. "Why was Novak a spendthrift? Patel and I will take that up." Eller sat back. "Let's consider a bigger question. 'Is it possible Novak had Hayden killed, or killed her himself?' The short answer? Yes."

Bourque glanced around the room. A few looks of doubt. A few of outright disagreement.

"Allow me to elaborate," Eller said. "Novak's cancelled payout suggests he was planning to get rid of her. As you'll recall from yesterday's meeting, a needle was used to sedate Hayden, but not Novak. He could be the person who used the needle. He sedated her first, and then strangled her. Seeing as she was young and fit, it'd be easier to strangle her if he sedated her." Eller raised a cautionary hand. "I know what you're thinking. Then why was Novak murdered? He disposed of Hayden, then he got killed? Why?"

The room was silent.

"Let that percolate. Captain Peabody sent an update from Boston Homicide. Four Metro detectives have been assigned to the case full-time. They searched Novak's Avon Hill house. The usual trappings of the wealthy: high-end furniture, art, and electronics.

Clothes galore, mostly Hayden's. The detectives found plenty of Slovenian documents and mementos but, curiously, very little in English. No paperwork with Hayden's handwriting or name. It's almost as if she had no past."

Or, Bourque speculated, she was hiding it.

"The Metro detectives also investigated Novak's extended family in Boston. There's only one relative, the maid at Atlas's condo. Her alibi checks out. As for other POIs in Boston, Metro is working a list of Novak's business contacts. I have more information," he went on, "about the one known strangulation case in Massachusetts where neckties were used. One of the killers was connected to the family. The murder was an inside job. We need to look into that case. Patel will take that up as well."

Hmm, Bourque thought, Patel on the rise. It appeared Eller was grooming the junior detective, helping her climb the career ladder. Bourque was pleased. The State Police needed more high-ranking female detectives. Things weren't much different than they were two decades ago. It wasn't enough for a policewoman to be talented. She had to be more talented than her male colleagues. Of course, she also had to be feminine: supportive and self-effacing.

Eller regarded the whole team. "Good work so far. But, unfortunately, not good enough." He morosely shook his head. "I realize the enormity of our task. The case might seem impenetrable at this point. Remember, though, there is only one sin when working a case. Not stupidity, not mistakes. Giving up is the sin. Letting your side down."

□ □ □

After the meeting, Eller joined Bourque in her office. He was in a pensive mood. He sighed as they sat. "I meant it when I said 'not good enough.' We're dragging our heels. The more hours pass, the farther away the killers get. Figuratively, if not literally too."

She nodded. If progress stalled, inertia would sap the team's willpower. Like Eller, she felt frustrated. They were swimmers caught in an undertow, flailing their arms but barely moving.

A moment later, Eller pointed at his laptop. "More news from Peabody. Karlos Vega opened his own tip line. He's going to offer a five-million-dollar reward for information leading to the Novak killers. He doesn't believe the Novaks killed themselves."

Bourque whistled. *Five million.* Rewards had a habit of getting in the way. The bigger the reward, the bigger the barrier.

Eller shook his head ruefully. "Our tip line is officially dead. Vega's reward will be broadcast at fifteen-hundred today, on TV, radio, Twitter, the whole shebang. He said we're, I quote, 'pursuing false leads and wasting time.' He's also going to let the killer angle out of the bag. Central wants to let the cat out of the bag before Vega does. What do you think?"

"Sounds good."

"No concerns?"

"None." She winked. "For a change."

Eller grinned. "They'll announce we have a double-murder on our hands, not a double suicide. They'll dangle a few choice tidbits, such as we have plenty of DNA from the scene."

"I like it," she said. "Let the perps think we're on to them. Might flush them out."

"Two out of two for Bourque. What's the world coming to?" Eller grinned again and rolled on. "Vega and Atlas are well acquainted. The forty-eight calls. M and M is digging into their financial connections. In addition, Metro is putting a tail on Atlas. Central had to defer to them. Territorial conflict."

Bourque had seen plenty of them in her undercover years. They could get ugly, especially when State detectives got overruled by Boston Metro, whose top dogs occasionally referred to the State Police as the *KK*, the Kountry Kops.

"We can't bug Atlas or his property," Eller said, "but we can watch him. We'll see where he goes and who he meets. Vega's another matter. He's out of the country a lot and has a raft of security people around him. We wouldn't likely get anywhere."

She nodded.

"I'd like to interview Zupan again. We can't let him leave the U.S. like his sister did. Then there's Melanya. A woman like her attracts men. She and Zupan are almost the same age. He appears to be as offended by Katrina Hayden as she is." Eller paused. "Maybe the butler and the ex are collaborators. He helps her, he gets a share of her windfall."

Bourque waved Eller on.

"Her knockout body makes me think sexual liaison, not just partners-in-crime. Coincidentally, she and Zupan grew up in the same town: Jesenice, Slovenia. The population was about six thousand in the mid-eighties, when Melanya and Zupan were youngsters. I expect they saw each other around town then, if not knew each other. Let's look into that. I know, it's a long way to Slovenia and we don't speak Slovenian, but both he and Melanya have lived in Boston for at least three years. We can probe them and anyone who knows them." Eller stood up. "I need a walk."

□ □ □

Thirty minutes later, Eller returned.

"What were you thinking about?" Bourque asked as he sat.

He shrugged.

"I noticed something about you on an earlier case. You go for a walk when you want to think."

"You're right. Good eye. By the way, let's give M and M another day to dig into the money trail. You know what the TV detectives say: 'Follow the money!'"

"They only say it once?"

Eller chuckled. "Seriously, when we know more, can you go at Zupan and Melanya? I'm too invested in Zupan."

She nodded. "You don't like him, do you?"

"That's not it. I don't trust him."

"Listen, I have a question for you. Do we know if Hayden had any money before she married Novak? I mean serious money."

"Doesn't look like it. M and M examined her tax records. Before she met him, she reported roughly forty G a year."

That discounted another investigative angle. Bourque had wondered if Novak appropriated Hayden's wealth and gave it to someone, and if that person killed him to keep the money. Now that appeared unlikely, unless Hayden had a money hoard somewhere. It also appeared unlikely she'd invested in Bluefin Bay Campground. Forty G a year didn't provide much venture capital. It seemed she wasn't murdered for money. Why was she killed then?

Eller coughed, interrupting her thoughts. "Are you following hunches?"

"No such luck. More like dead-ends."

"Let's consider Vega. His net worth is twenty-two-point-seven billion. He's probably gunning for thirty."

She nodded. To make a million dollars was a tremendous feat; to make a billion seemed impossible. However, she admired brains in a person, not wealth. In her view, money was a necessary evil. The Pilgrims and others had left England to escape religious persecution and economic hardship, to establish a society of equals—hence the Commonwealth of Massachusetts. Look at it now. There wasn't enough "common" wealth. She had nothing against billionaires per se, yet a lot of hard-working people made under $30,000 a year. It seemed her maternal ancestors had left one Kingdom of Inequality only to set up another. New England was supposedly a bastion of fairness, a place where the *little-guy-was-as-good-as-the-big-one*, but the little guy was sinking.

Eller kept going. "Crime psychologists say humans usually kill for money. If you subscribe to that view, Vega is a prime suspect."

She agreed. "I reviewed the *Angels or Devils* footage. Vega executed ten hostile takeovers. One of them was done in partnership with Novak. That's at least one to fully investigate. Vega arrives back in Boston this evening. I want to see him ASAP."

Eller held up a stop sign hand. "Patience, Grasshopper. We'll get more out of Vega if you go in with some ammo. Let's decide by seventeen-hundred."

□ □ □

Bourque grabbed her laptop, walked to the murder room, and sat next to Landon. "How goes the battle?" she asked.

Landon didn't look happy. "Damn list is going to take forever."

"I'm going to help you, Rob. Let me do a little background research."

She booted up her laptop and examined Hayden's social media profiles. She wasn't sure about the dancer's profile numbers. A hundred bucks could buy 5,000 "real" Twitter followers, some who occasionally commented, as opposed to bots who just followed you and never said a word. You bought followers at the start, to seed your profile so you never looked like someone with ten friends. From what Bourque saw of Hayden's sites, the dancer was trying to be a Nouveau Royal, one of the social media glitterati. She was obsessed with her looks as well as her posts.

Bourque turned to Landon. "Okay, Rob. Let's go."

"I'll set you up to run batches with eight, nine, and ten likes or comments. I'll do eleven to fifteen-plus."

Chapter 16

Late that afternoon, Bourque and Landon finished the Katrina Hayden social media friends-of-interest list. They'd whittled it down to ninety-two names. Bourque liked casting wide nets but ninety-two POIs was triple-wide. She turned the next phase, scheduling interviews, over to Landon. Seniority had its benefits. She wanted to return to Novak's castle before leaving for Boston the next morning. M&M had come through. She had good reason to visit Vega. While he and Novak had no traceable history of financial transactions, they had a fiduciary connection involving their devil takeover of an American company called BioCell LLC, valued at $15.2 million.

Vega was the beneficiary of Novak's shares, not Hayden, Atlas, or any family member. The two billionaires each owned thirty-three percent of the company. The original owner, Gene Cantor, had sued Vega and Novak for breach of contract and lost. Cantor had then sold his shares to ZelleMed, a DNA sequencing firm based in Zurich.

Bourque walked outside, pulled out her duty phone and punched Vega's direct number.

He answered on the fifth ring. "Vega speaking."

"Hello Mr. Vega. It's Detective Lieutenant Bourque, State Police."

"Yes?"

"I'd like to see you tomorrow. How's eight a.m.?"

"Eight a.m.? That's not much notice."

"I don't have time to waste."

"Touché. All right, Lieutenant, come to my downtown condo. Make it nine."

With Vega lined up, Bourque called Zupan and arranged to meet him at 1400. Two birds with one stone. Two jailbirds?

□ □ □

Bourque roared out of the detective unit and sped toward East Falmouth. Given her long work days—a never-ending string of interviews, meetings, and travel—she hadn't gotten around to examining Novak's castle again. As she drove up the umbrella pine corridor, the sun started sinking. Upon arrival, the castle walls appeared to be skull-grey, not white. The windows were as empty as a dead man's eyes. When she stepped out of her car, a chill wind bit into her. An unseasonably cold day was due to be followed by a colder night. The weather channel had warned the Cape to expect frost. She could feel it already.

In the open yard, the reflecting pool looked forlorn and lifeless. The red oaks loomed eerily. Three days after the murders, the lawn was already in decline. The impending dusk spoke of a lost world. A man was gone, and his dreams as well. She gave herself a shake. A woman too.

Though the white coats were finished, police tape was still in place. After signing in with Trooper Walsh, Bourque pulled on CS gloves and headed to the master suite. She knew there were twin walk-in closets. The ninjas had catalogued their contents. Miller had videotaped them. While their job was to record dots—facts and details—Bourque's job was to connect them.

She stepped into Katrina's lair. The closet smelled of expensive perfume: rose petals and ambergris. Thankfully, unlike with Melanya, the scent wasn't cloying. There were hundreds of outfits. Bourque flicked through the hangers. All top designers: Dior, Fendi, Versace, D&G, Prada. She imagined a life of exclusive dinners, soirees, and premieres. It made her head spin. Uncharacteristically, it also made her envious. She'd never seen such extravagance. And this was only one Novak house, one walk-in closet.

Forget it, Bourque ordered herself. It's not your world. She breathed deeply and exhaled, calming her mind. Other than the obvious wealth, the outfits didn't tell her much. A dancing girl had hit the jackpot. However, was she happy? Did she love her hubby? Did she enjoy the castle?

Bourque kept searching, digging into pockets, opening drawers, sounding for hidden compartments—looking for notes, letters, receipts, clues of any kind. In the end, she found nothing of interest. She hated to admit it: the team knew very little about Katrina Hayden's past.

Bourque walked across a hall hung with mirrors and stepped into Novak's clothes cave.

Half an hour later, she walked out. The closet held twenty or so elegant suits, all beautifully tailored, but of an older vintage. There were dozens of work pants and shirts, also expensive but older, and many exclusive ties, all of them silk. Nothing plain or solid-colored. Nothing red. As with Hayden, Bourque hadn't discovered anything new. Nor had she come closer to understanding Novak's past.

Leaving the master suite, she felt a sudden urge to talk to her old friend Gigi Lambert. She couldn't discuss the details of the case. They were classified. She just wanted to know how Gigi was doing. *Now*? Bourque asked herself. Yes, now. It had been far too long.

She called Gigi. "Hi Gee, it's your State Police buddy. Can you talk?"

"To you Borky, always! Where are you?"

"East Falmouth. And you?"

"DC, spying on the CIA."

Bourque laughed. "One thing I always wanted to know. Do the female agents eat Special K for breakfast?"

"Of course, with skim milk and three grapes. The outliers eat four." She chuckled. "What's on your plate?"

"Can't say much. A double murder."

"The Novaks?"

"Yep." Of course, Gigi knew. Wherever she was, she always had an eye on Massachusetts.

"Any progress?" Gigi asked.

"Plenty of POIs, yet does that help?"

"Nope. Confuses the picture. Through a glass darkly."

"Oh yeah. We see, we think, we rethink. It takes forever."

"Slowly doesn't matter in the end."

"To the politicos it does."

"Screw them. Although I wouldn't, even if one of them had a ten-foot pole."

"Speaking of, how's your night life?"

"The same. Still trying to land a hunk with a heart and a soul. As if they exist. I don't learn."

"*They* have to learn," Bourque said.

"I don't think there's time."

Gigi was lucky in everything except love. In her view, finding a good man took forever, finding the father of your children took longer. "There's time," Bourque reminded her.

"For you. You have Marty."

"No guarantee. Men can be so clueless. Tell them forty's a special birthday and they think you want special jewelry."

"Spell it out for him. He's a good man. Tell him you want a baby. Tell him you don't need marriage. One less hurdle for him. You can look after yourself and the baby. And be there for him—if he's there for you."

"I suppose."

"Don't *I suppose* me, Ivy Bourque. Do it. Tell him."

"I will."

"Promise me."

"I will."

"I'm thinking of leaving the FBI," Gigi briskly said.

"What? Why?"

"I'm going to apply to the Mass State Police."

"Why would you do that?"

"You enjoy your job," Gigi countered.

"I do. I love it, most of the time. But don't forget the Old Guard and the hours."

"Same as every cop job."

True. "Really? You want to join the Staties?"

"If they'll have me."

"Oh, they'll have you."

"I don't know, you're real cops. Me, I chase scumbags who launder money and lie to their wives and their girlfriends. Narcissistic assholes who never confess. Sorry, gotta go. Call coming in."

Bourque sighed. Gigi. The Amazon of the FBI. How would she fit into the State Police? The same as Bourque did. In her own way.

Bourque pocketed her phone, stepped toward the stairwell to the foyer, and stopped. Something told her to revisit the library. Before bed last night, she'd googled Confucius. Among other tidbits, she'd learned the Sage of Zhou considered merchants guilty of profiteering and ostentation, not doers of good deeds. In the Tang Dynasty, regarded as the zenith of Chinese civilization, he was a voice of integrity, of reform and ethics.

Inside the library, she strode to the far-right corner and reread the framed Confucian quote on the wall: "The gentleman is conversant with righteousness; the small man is conversant with profit." It had a Biblical echo. She'd spent many a Sunday in bible school. *The righteous shall inherit the land.*

Turning away, she took in the whole library. The room possessed an aura of rigor. The silence was expectant. The books weren't for show. She felt humbled. It was as if everything that could be known was here. It was waiting for you to learn it.

She approached the first bookshelf. From what she could tell, nothing had been moved for days, if not far longer. Systematically, she pulled each volume down, looked for handwriting within it, then held it spine up and shook it. Afterward, she searched the shelf itself, probing and sounding. Nothing. Having examined all seven shelving units, she walked toward the door, still empty-handed. That was life as a detective. You dug, you deliberated, you formed new theories, you dug again—and you got nowhere.

In the doorway, she halted abruptly and turned back.

Pacing slowly, she circled the library, trying to experience it as Novak had. What was it to him? A collection of knowledge? A place to relax, to be himself? Would could the room tell her?

She finished her circuit, but had no revelations. Her mind seemed to be stretched as thin as a strand of silk. If only walls had ears. However, even if the old saying were true, the library walls were covered with thick, opulent wallpaper, a textured mahogany red.

She resumed her walk, re-examining every nook. Her senses felt muted. She noted a clock on the wall: quarter after eight. No wonder she was fading. She hadn't eaten since noon. Yet something told her to circle the library again. Focus on the room's structure, she ordered herself. While the contents were important, the structure itself often provided a key.

Near the far-right corner of the room, Bourque spotted an anomaly she hadn't noticed before. With the setting sun coming in low and straight, she detected a tiny indentation above the Confucian quote. It revealed the faint outline of a lintel, masked by the thick wallpaper.

She strode up to it. On each side, there were slight recesses, straight lines all the way to the floor. They seemed to mark a door. She leaned against the wall. No movement. She pushed harder. Nothing budged. She stepped back. No obvious means of entry. No sign of a door handle. All she saw was the framed quote. You idiot! She reached up and lifted the plaque. Exactly. A blue metal lever was built into the wall. She'd walked by the wall half a dozen times over two visits, with her eyes on high alert. Was there a level below idiot? Yes. Super-moron. She pulled the lever.

A door opened. She entered a room the size of a large broom closet. As expected, there was no window. Feeling inside, she switched on a light. The room was illuminated by overhead LEDs. Nothing was dusty, nothing smelled musty. It seemed the room was frequently used. A purpose-built wooden desk spanned the far wall. Despite its sleek lines, it had capacious drawers, painted lacquer red. The hardware was polished steel. The overall effect was Art Deco meets Chinese Antique. She pulled on the main drawer. Locked. She tried each of the six side drawers. Again, locked.

Unshouldering her crime scene bag, she fished out a set of lock picks. The main drawer yielded immediately. No need for deep security here, she reasoned. If Novak's house was a castle, this was its secret keep.

The drawer held nothing of interest. No papers, photos, scribblings, or bills. Only office supplies.

She picked five more drawer locks. Supplies.

In side drawer six, she found a pile of posters, cards, and snapshots. She unrolled the top poster. It featured a skier with Mount Everest in the background and the words *Slovenian Daredevil DAVO KARNICAR, Descent of Everest, Year 2000*. The poster was signed by Karnicar, followed by an inscription that included the name "Rollo." Guessing the inscription was Slovenian, she used her phone to translate the words. "My dear friend Rollo, I couldn't do it without your support. Next time, join me."

There were two more Karnicar posters, the first with the skier posing on Mount Kilimanjaro in 2001. She translated the inscription. "Dear Rollo, your support is immense. You missed a great ride." The third poster presented Mount Elbrus in 2002. "Dear friend, I treasure your support. Next time."

Bourque placed the posters on the desktop and examined the cards and photos. Mainly notices of society events. The material could be useful to Landon. She'd take the drawer's full contents.

In drawer six, she uncovered a mass of correspondence, most with business letterheads. Sifting through the letters and documents, she found two from Vega and four from Atlas, and set them aside.

Atlas's letters were very stilted—which revealed something of the relationship with his father—but were otherwise innocuous, a son thanking his father for business opportunities.

She skimmed the first Vega letter. A thank you for a gala invitation. She skimmed the second. Her pulse quickened. It was a formal document setting out Vega's promise to "shepherd" BioCell LLC, the company he co-owned with Novak. In the event of death, he'd inherit Novak's shares but divest them within a month and give the proceeds to charity. The document was notarized by two witnesses. Paydirt! She snapped pics of the "shepherd" document, drew a large evidence sack from her crime scene bag, and carefully packed all the paperwork.

It was almost midnight when she left the library. On the way downstairs, she glimpsed the outdoor pool through a window. The water looked white, not blue. It seemed to be frozen over, like a skating rink. The ninjas had set up motion-cameras around the pool; the property was no longer being guarded 24/7.

Outside, she found that Walsh was gone. A nocturnal sea breeze filtered through the pine trees. The grounds were doubly dark, like a night within the night. She walked slowly, breathing in cool air tinged with pine sap, lulled by her favorite essence. As she opened her car, her neck hairs bristled. Someone was watching her. The feeling intensified. She heard a sharp sound close by.

Kneeling low, staying next to her car, she scanned the grounds on both sides. No signs of movement. Overhead, thick clouds eclipsed a salting of distant stars. She scrutinized the pine forest, looking and listening. Again, nothing.

She studied the darkness behind her. Empty. Nonetheless, her heart raced, triggered by adrenaline, fueled by a primeval urge: flight or fight. But there was nothing to fight and no reason to flee.

Keep looking, she ordered herself. She slowly scanned the darkness in all directions. No movements, no sounds. However, she'd heard something. She was sure she had. *Something* had created sound waves; they'd reached her inner ear and sent a message to her auditory cortex. She kept listening. It could have been a human footstep. Or a falling pinecone hitting a stone. Or an animal.

She got in her car, but didn't turn the ignition key. Window down, she sat in the driver's seat, watching and listening, waiting for whoever was there to break cover. *If* someone was there. Her eyes adjusted to the dark. The silence deepened. All she could hear was her own breathing. The seconds stretched to minutes.

Enough, she finally told herself. She felt foolish. An animal had been watching her, maybe a coyote or fox or a wary deer.

She started her car and drove off. The pine corridor seemed to stretch endlessly into the gloom, the way ahead only dimly visible in her headlights. The gloom intensified. All she heard were her tires chittering the road and pine boughs stirring in the wind.

After turning onto Route 28, her mood lifted. She'd been imagining things. She buried the incident. No one had been watching her.

While she drove, her brain replayed the shepherd document. It was legally binding unless superseded by more recent communications.

She entered the detective unit to find Eller gone for the day. The murder room was empty. After securing the Novak desk exhibits in the evidence locker, she updated her case notes and uploaded the shepherd document photos to the Novaks Case database. It was a good haul, an inroad into Novak's life. However, they still had none into Hayden's.

Marty's house was dark when Bourque arrived home, cold and exhausted. It was too late to eat. She drank a glass of milk and crawled into bed.

Chapter 17

DAY FIVE: *Boston, May 18th*

The next morning Bourque rose at 0630 and quietly left Marty's house. Crossing the road to Bristol Beach, she saw it had been torn up by the recent nor'easter. The sand was strewn with seaweed. A line of breakers rushed ashore. Nonetheless, she donned her swim gear, waded in, and got knocked over. The ocean raced crazily sideways, angrily bucking and foaming. She dove under and swam out past the breakers. It didn't help. The Atlantic was churned up for miles. She turned back ten minutes later.

After a quick shower at Marty's, she stood naked in front of the bathroom mirror. Her hazel eyes were bright and clear; her face, bronzed by sailing. A few errant pounds had attached themselves to her hips. She dismissed the baggage. Nothing a weekend hiking trip in the Berkshires wouldn't dislodge.

She had to move it to get to Vega's condo by 0900. These days, downtown Boston traffic was horrendous, and she wanted to stop for a big breakfast. Having toweled herself dry, she put on her best outfit, a sleek Italian indigo pantsuit, and twisted her hair in a bun. According to her mother Sarah, men liked that. It said she was professional, but there was a chance she'd let her hair down. After the cleavage and the eyes, men looked at your hair. Sarah was always pressuring her to use her looks. Though Bourque didn't care about appearances, they could be useful. They were mutable. Like any profession, the police needed people who didn't fit the profession's stereotype. She'd proven it as an undercover operative. Give her a blonde dye job, makeup, and black leather and she looked like a gangster's moll. Today she wanted a different look: refined yet knowing, a society belle with a hooker undertow. What was the best way to catch the eye of an ultra-wealthy man? Make yourself look expensive yet available. She left the top three buttons of her pantsuit undone and strung a necklace of white gold and diamonds around her neck, a gift from a grandaunt. It winked softly, resting on her skin with the weight of expectation.

□ □ □

Bourque arrived at Vega's condo with minutes to spare, tossed her car keys to the valet, and strode into the foyer. Vega's security manager awaited her.

As did Eller. *What the hell?* Why was he here? She wanted to interview Vega solo, with no partner to distract or irritate him.

Mr. Security pointed to the elevator and left the detectives alone.

Eller looked at her cleavage and quickly looked away. She could tell he was itching to say something. Lucky for him, he kept his opinions to himself. She was in no mood. She'd cranked up Blondie on her drive to the city: "Heart of Glass."

Eller adopted a chatty disposition as they set off for the elevator. "Drove home to Holyoke last night," he said. "Made great time. Well under two hours."

Christ, she thought, that's fast. She was envious; on the other hand, she wished he'd gotten a ticket. *Hey*, she wanted to say, *you should have told me you'd be here!*

He seemed to read her mind. "I was thinking of phoning you. But it was oh-seven-hundred when I decided to hit Boston. I thought it was too early to call." He winked. "Cancelled my Days Inn reservation in Barnstable. That'll make Peabody happy."

"Don't count on it."

"I read your case notes and the BioCell document," he soothingly said. "I want to watch how Vega handles it."

As they entered the elevator, Eller dropped the conversation. Walls had ears, especially private elevator walls.

Vega was waiting when the doors opened. His presence stated *I don't care if you like me, I like me.* He wore a bespoke suit, charcoal-grey this time, and the same accoutrements: white shirt, charcoal tie, gold cufflinks, and crocodile-skin shoes. His long dark hair was loose. Although not a big man, he was striking. With his flowing hair, he resembled Samson, albeit a half-Samson. Silently, he led them to the alcove near the foyer. No gold-liveried waiter attended them. The silence deepened, casting a cold shadow on the room. Like four days ago, the alcove had a single piece of decor, a gold vase with fresh tiger lilies. The petals glowed.

Bourque spoke to break the ice. "Thank you for meeting with us, Mr. Vega."

"I thought I was meeting you." He took in her low neckline. His lips curved slowly upward, into an affable smile.

"Lieutenant Eller was in Boston," she said. "Two heads are better than one."

"Sometimes," Vega replied. "And sometimes not."

True, she thought.

"Coffee?" Vega asked.

She declined. Eller shook his head.

Vega sat back. "What do you want to know?"

She grinned mischievously. "Everything, Mr. Vega. By the way, I saw something recently. A document linking you and Mr. Novak to a company named BioCell." She pulled out her phone, navigated to the document, and showed it to Vega. "Is that your signature at the bottom?"

"Yes. Let's not prevaricate. I agreed to divest Rollo's shares. Yesterday, I sold them all. And mine as well."

"You sold all of yours?"

"Correct. To the highest bidder."

"ZelleMed?"

"How did you know?"

It was a guess—ZelleMed would be a likely bidder—but she didn't tell him.

"I see you've done your research." He eyed her with respect. "ZelleMed will do good things."

"Would Gene Cantor agree with you?"

"Yes. He admired ZelleMed."

Eller leaned forward. "But not you. He sued you."

Vega regarded him superciliously. "I was speaking to Lieutenant Bourque. Where are your manners?"

Eller smiled. "When it comes to criminal investigations, I don't give a fig about manners."

"Are you saying I'm a criminal?"

Eller didn't reply.

"Back to Cantor then. He *attempted* to sue Rollo and me. He failed."

"Why?" Eller asked.

"Because he tried to run BioCell like a majority stakeholder. He owned one-third." Vega shook his head. "Some people are wonderful inventors, but can't do simple math. You'd think a scientist could do division."

Eller ignored him. "You told us Mr. Novak had many female friends. What kind of 'friends'?"

"Exactly what the word connotes: *friends*. Not whores, not escorts. Let me be clear, Rollo didn't 'entertain' call girls. Incidentally, neither do I."

Eller nodded dubiously. "You sell shares worth five million dollars and then offer a five-million-dollar reward. That seems convenient."

"The shares have nothing to do with the reward."

"Some might think you offered it to get us off your tail. To a wealthy man like you, five mill is chump change."

Vega bristled. "My finances have nothing to do with Rollo's death."

"We'll be the judge of that."

"Incorrect. If the matter went to a court—*if*, I repeat—a judge would be the judge of that. Or a jury. Not you," Vega emphasized.

Eller smiled again. "It appears you've spent a lot of time in courts. You know a lot about them."

"You have to these days. What with the incompetence of the police. Not to mention the time wasting."

"Let's get to the crux then. What did you do with your share money?"

"I gave it to charity. In fact, I gave over a hundred million last year. I expect your forensic squad didn't tell you that."

Eller said nothing.

"Here's another thing you may not know. I added five more million, for a total gift of fifteen million."

"I'll take your word for it. Did your tax accountants recommend that figure?"

Vega shook his head. "Beating a dead horse? Is that your strategy?"

Eller stood. "Pardon my hasty departure." He grinned at Vega. "No time to waste."

□ □ □

When Eller left, Vega pulled out his phone. He spoke in a low voice that brooked no argument.

Afterward, he turned to Bourque. "My lawyers will email you copies of the BioCell divestments. Perhaps you'd like a drink? You're not in uniform."

"But I'm on duty."

His voice got more honeyed. "Just one."

She gave him a Mona Lisa smile. Maybe yes, maybe no. Why was he turning on the charm? Until now, he'd been formal, which had been beneficial. Formality imparted predictability.

"Lieutenant Eller won't know. Such a *cabrón*. *Un viejo cabrón*."

"I speak Spanish, Mr. Vega." She'd learned it for undercover stings connected to Latin American gangs.

"He's an old goat."

"*Cabrón* means bastard."

Vega grinned. "Okay, how about an old dog? And how about that drink? It's almost eleven. I have the finest condiments. Coconuts from Costa Rica. Especial limes from Venezuela, my birthplace." He grinned again. "And rum from Guyana. Twenty-five years old. El Dorado Demerara."

Play along. "What kind of drink?"

"A Karlos Special. My version of a mojito but sweeter, given the coconut and demerara rum."

"All right." One way into a suspect's mind was through the bottle. As an undercover agent, she'd done anything to get people talking. Talkers were a gift. They could reveal body language that indicated when they were lying. Not that there were universal tells, just tells for individuals an observant cop could pick up.

□ □ □

Sipping a mojito, Bourque slipped into flirt mode—*I love beach holidays* (she didn't), *Costa Rica is the absolute best* (she'd only been there once, for three days)—then slowly shifted gears. "You're quite the philanthropist, Mr. Vega."

He shrugged. His eyes wandered to her neckline.

"Very few people know that. Why?"

"I prefer it. Most people see me as a financial bulldog, the Bulldog of Wall Street. I'm a money-thirsty Vandal. I want to keep it that way." He released a short smile. "What the world knows of you diminishes you. Mystery gives you power. But I know you're digging. I'll speak off the record. I assume your phone recorder is on. Please turn it off."

She did so and showed him.

"What do you want to know about?" He smiled like a naughty Buddha. "Rollo's excessive cravings? He had none. He was an unpretentious man. His secret hates? None that I know of. His enemies? Ditto. He didn't cheat people."

She scrutinized Vega as he spoke. Some people could control their eyes. However, most couldn't manipulate their mouths for long. She'd watched Vega's mouth in the past. From the set of his lips, he was telling the truth.

"A top up?" He reached for the mojito pitcher.

"Thank you." She raised her glass. "*Saludos.*" She knew she was stepping over the line. It was illegal to drink on duty. Yet ex-agents like her knew how to stay sober—not that the State Police brass would care. You let a mixed drink sit, let the ice melt and dilute the alcohol. You feigned imbibing, holding the glass to your mouth for an extended period, but only sipping a little. You held each sip in your mouth, further diluting the alcohol with as much saliva as possible. You "accidentally" spilled some if you had to. It was a science. Well, a pseudo-science.

"I'll tell you a story," he said, "about a beach with no name."

"Another time."

Vega sighed. "Is your recess over, Lieutenant?"

She laughed. "Who were the lucky charities?"

"Charities?" he asked.

"The ones you and Rollo Novak donated to yesterday."

"Oh, that. To be honest, they were Rollo's. Mountain village schools in Nepal. Rollo was a mountain skier. A very good one."

"I see." Maybe that explained the Davo Karnicar connection. "Did Rollo give to other charities?"

"Dozens. He gave away hundreds of millions annually." Vega shook his head. "About three years ago, he decided to emulate Bill Gates, to give almost everything to charity. Gates says it's meaningful. He says it's fun." Vega huffed. "Not to me. I don't mind admitting it. I'm a Vandal."

"With a heart."

"Maybe. Okay, a small one." He chuckled. "That's really off the record."

She nodded. "You said Rollo began giving a lot three years ago. Did he make large donations before then?"

"None that he spoke of. And he didn't just hand his money over. You had to roll up your sleeves to get Rollo's money. He didn't become a billionaire by being a patsy. Anyway, I noticed him starting to change. He started acting more, let's say, concerned about others. How they were affected by his actions. By my actions. By everyone's actions. It got a bit tiresome."

"How so?"

"He was always talking about Confucius. Confucius this, Confucius that. He even had a framed Confucian quote."

Bourque pretended Vega had told her something new. *Tell me more*, her eyes said.

"I gave him a Confucius wall hanging about a year ago. A joke one." Vega chortled. "It said: *I Didn't Say Any of That Shit*. He laughed when I gave it to him, but he didn't hang it on the wall. In fact, he got sanctimonious. Prattled on about the Confucian Golden Rule. Treat others as you want to be treated. That's when I prattled back. I studied philosophy when I was younger. I'm aware of Confucius. He wasn't an egalitarian. In fact, he was a social conservative. He had nothing against wealth."

The usual, she reflected. Everyone saw ethics or politics from their side of the fence.

Vega kept going. "In the end—these last few months, that is—Rollo was usually serious. You couldn't joke about ethics. You couldn't joke about much. He was still kind, but he'd become humorless." Vega sighed. "He was living a dichotomy. He'd embarked on a renunciation of money, but not of fame. He believed fame could be used to ethical effect. In his mind, greed was problematic, not money." Vega nodded thoughtfully. "I agree. But you can go too far the other way. He used to be judicious in everything. That was his strength—in life as well as in business. He could bring two corporate sides together like no one I knew, sometimes two sides that had been warring or stalling for months. He could seal a difficult deal in an afternoon. Well, he once could. Then he went off-kilter and didn't come back."

"What threw him off?"

"I don't know." Vega's eyes misted over. He stood. "I have to get back to work."

"Of course. One more question, if I may."

"One."

"Why did he appoint you to divest his shares in BioCell? Why not his son or his wife?"

"That's two."

"Sorry. Why?"

"Because he trusted me," Vega replied.

"And he didn't trust his own family?"

"Not fully."

"Please elaborate."

Vega sighed and sat. "You're lucky, Lieutenant. I have a weakness for you."

That's good, she thought.

"Of course, this is all off the record. Power off your phone."

"The recording button is off."

"Regardless, power off your phone. You know what Rollo told me? 'Never trust technology.'"

"Some truth in that."

"Another Rolloism: 'Always disable the location function.'"

She nodded and turned off her phone. She didn't tell him the only way to ensure privacy was to remove the battery. The less the public knew, the better. A phone could be tracked even when it was powered off.

His eyes returned to her neckline. This time they stayed there. "Do you have a recording device on your person?"

She laughed. "*On my person?*"

"That's what they say in the movies. Well?"

"No. *Categorically no.*" She grinned. "That's what they say in the movies."

"I'll have to verify your assertion." He smiled. "Take off your clothes."

She laughed again. Maybe it was time to leave. No, she told herself. *Talkers are a gift.*

"Did you notice my guitars?" He pointed to a trio of instruments resting on their stands.

She nodded. The guitars were beautiful, their bodies made of honey-golden wood, each inlaid with a gilded rosette. A continuation, she noted, of Vegas' Midas theme.

"I'd like to play you a little piece, if I may."

He strode to the guitars, picked the middle one, and sat across from her. Not looking at her, he began playing.

She observed him intently. What a strange morning. A yard from her, a billionaire was strumming a guitar with gusto and talent—not that he looked like a billionaire. With his long loose hair and soulful expression, he resembled a flamenco artist. His impromptu concert seemed the most natural thing in the world. She knew the piece.

When he stopped, she applauded. "*Bravo*! 'Romance of the Guitar.'"

He smiled widely. "Most police officers wouldn't know that."

"You underestimate us."

"Not you."

"Good. Trust me then. Everything you've said since I turned off my phone recorder is anonymous."

"I see your recess is over. Again."

She grinned. "Yes. By the way, anything you say might be used to help solve the case, but it won't ever be used in court. It will never be attributed to you."

"All right. If you ever mention my name, I'll reveal that a certain Massachusetts detective, a very beautiful one, was drinking on duty."

She nodded.

"Velvet fist," he said.

"The best kind."

Chapter 18

"Just so you understand," Vega began, "the formal silence isn't about me. I have nothing to hide. I'm looking out for Rollo. He can't protect himself."

Bourque nodded.

"We were a good team. The Yin and the Yang, he called us. He brought gallantry to the table. I brought discipline. I was bluster and chaos. He was brotherhood and peace."

She remained silent.

"I'll give you an insight into his relationship with Kat. In the eyes of the world, he was thrilled with her. Kat was everything he wanted: a smart, sexy, hard-working young woman."

"I notice you call her Kat," Bourque interrupted. "Did Mr. Novak?"

"No."

"Did anyone else?"

"No one I know of."

"Why did you?"

"To me, she was a 'Kat'. Feline. A beautiful tiger. Alluring yet unpredictable. But don't think salacious. Kat was a friend, nothing more. Contrary to what the media says, not all wealthy men are womanizers. I might be a hard-hitting businessman but I'm honorable in affairs of the heart. I believe Rollo was as well."

"Tell me about him and Katrina."

"He was enamored with her. He used to teasingly call her his *Dancing Queen*." Vega grinned. "However, in truth, he wasn't completely thrilled. I don't think many people knew that, or even sensed it. 'Who knew?' I ask myself now." Vega pondered for a moment. "Me, his son, probably his butler. Rollo talked to that man about everything."

"What about Katrina herself? Did she know?"

"I'm sure she did. She and Rollo showed great passion for each other. They were like teenage lovers. On the other hand, there was a friction between them. A sense of loss." He eyed Bourque. "Are you married?"

She didn't respond. She felt Vega looking into her head and seeing all of her past.

"A lot of cops are divorced," he said.

"Nature of the job."

He nodded. "With Rollo and Kat, you sensed disappointment. Unfulfilled expectations. Do you know what I mean?"

"Yes. Why was he disappointed in her?"

"A few reasons. The main one being Kat wasn't, let's say, very intellectual. She was smart, sharp as a whip. Mentally tough too. But she wasn't the studious type."

"And Mr. Novak was?"

"Oh yes. Another hidden trait. Over the past few years, he spent most of his time in his libraries. They were all well-stocked, but the main one was in Falmouth. Come to think of it, that was also a bone of contention." Vega stopped. "Funny how things crystalize after the fact. Rollo wanted to be in Falmouth, not Boston, not Paris, Milan, or London, not the villa he had near Dubrovnik, or the beach house in Mexico. But those were the places Kat wanted to be. To be seen, to dine, to dance. To show off her clothes and jewels."

"Are you saying she was shallow and ostentatious?"

Vega chuckled. "Are you dissing my friends?"

"Oh no. Just trying to paint a picture, to find the murderers. Was she an ambitious woman?"

"Of course. In my experience, most beautiful women are. They want to maximize their assets. I don't mean that crudely."

"Did Mr. Novak know Katrina wanted to be an actress?"

"Yes, and he approved. He had no problem with her or anyone pursuing their own dreams. *Dreams* being the salient word. If you wanted money—if you held it above all else—Rollo wasn't in your corner." Vega smiled. "He was in my corner. I didn't want any of his money."

Bourque nodded. "Why did he run his enterprises out of Boston?"

"He didn't like New York. New Englanders are his type: shrewd yet fair-minded. He wanted Boston to be Silicon Valley East." Vega shook his head. "I don't see that, but I'm not Rollo."

"I can see Mr. Novak and Katrina weren't absolute lovebirds, yet surely he could count on her to divest some shares."

Vega studied Bourque intensely, but not for long. "I think I know why Rollo didn't fully trust her. And I think I can tell you."

She made an *it's your choice* gesture.

"As I mentioned, he'd embarked on a mission to give his money away. All of it, with the exception of two gifts. Twenty-five million each for his son and his wife. Oh, and his ex was going to get two million. He'd already bought her a large condo. The rest was going to his causes. The mountain villages, the rivers of the world, deforestation, climate change. The usual."

Bourque snorted quietly.

"Don't think me dismissive. They *are* the usual causes. I'm not saying useless, just usual. And I'm not saying Kat disagreed with his choices. However, she didn't like the fact she was getting so little."

"Relatively speaking."

"Yes."

"How do you know?"

"She said it. Not so bluntly, but her meaning was clear. She also joked she wanted Rollo to be more like me. A harder man. It was one of those serious jokes." Vega paused. "This is just speculation. Recently, I sensed their relationship was, shall I say, *evolving*. It's something I've witnessed before. Personally, in fact. The impending end of a relationship, especially of a marriage, is not all doom and gloom. The person who wants out gets a new lease on life. They know they'll soon be free."

"You're talking about Mr. Novak?"

Vega shook his head emphatically. "I'm talking about Kat."

Bourque shot him a measuring look. How could that be? Why would Hayden want to end the marriage? "You're suggesting Katrina was going to pull the plug, not Mr. Novak?"

"That's the sense I got. She'd started acting more independent. You do that when you think the end is near. In your mind, you're already gone."

"But you said he was disappointed with her. More disappointed than she was with him?"

"I'd say it was equal. However, she seemed to be preparing for the end, not him."

"Please elaborate."

"Not helping much, am I?"

"Everything helps." She smiled. "Every little bit."

"Well, from what I know, no one was surprised by the marriage. Which is surprising. Wealthy, somewhat older man marries poorer, younger beauty. Recipe for discord. Very few people understand marriage. In a sense, it's a mathematical phenomenon. Marriage doesn't create one-in-two, it creates two larger twos. It expands egos. You get four people: two new people, plus the two original celebrants. All four are distinct. They share constituent elements, of course, but they're unique."

Bourque didn't respond.

"I admit, I'm divorced, but don't think me pessimistic. We all hope for the one in two. Even men like me." He grinned self-deprecatingly. "Rollo was a complex man. He often said he was a typical Slav, both an intellectual and incredibly naive. Self-awareness. I value it highly. Rollo had a saying about it. *Stupidity isn't lack of knowledge, it's lack of self-knowledge.* He always said lack of knowledge was nothing to be ashamed of. There's so much to know, so much to forget. On the other hand, self-knowledge is paramount. Everyone should know themselves by the time they're forty."

"Did you?" she asked.

Vega smiled modestly. "No. I'm still trying."

"When did Kat suggest she wasn't happy with the twenty-five million?"

"A few times." Vega held up a finger. "Let me think." He eventually spoke. "Twice. The first time was about eight months ago. The second, a month or so ago."

"What about the day before she and Rollo were killed?"

"There was no talk of money or causes that night. We had a great time."

"What about Atlas? Does he know about the twenty-five million?"

"Yes. Rollo told him. He wasn't pleased."

"Would he have divested shares and kept the money?"

"I don't know with certainty, but I think he's capable of it. That's my opinion, of course. Look at the matter as a whole. Rollo didn't park his wealth offshore. He always paid his fair share of tax, and on time. He didn't agree with tax breaks and trickle-down economics. In his view, if you paid all workers a decent wage, they'd have disposable income to spend, which would trickle up from the lower and middle classes to the wealthy." Vega shrugged. "Not a bad idea at heart. I may sound like an unfettered capitalist but I'm not. In principle, I agree with trickle-up economics. The more the common man can spend, the better—not just for my betterment, but also for theirs." He smiled. "Of course, that's a private observation. In the end," he continued, "in Rollo's case, about nine billion will go to charity. Atlas wanted a good chunk of that.

He expected to get at least a third. I know others who would say the same thing. In private," Vega added. "I'll tell you another thing, a personal observation. If anyone was prepared to die, it was Rollo. He'd done everything he wanted to. It could be why he was killed. He'd arranged to distribute all his wealth. Not everyone agreed with that. I'm not pointing fingers at anyone, Lieutenant, but you've heard my opinion."

Bourque nodded. "Was Katrina disappointed by Mr. Novak?"

"Yes. I'd say she expected more of a freewheeling lifestyle. Rollo had that side, of course, and right to the end. However, it was often suppressed. What's that Bowie song? *Ch-ch-changes. Turn and face the strange.* Rollo got stranger. She had to adjust to that. I felt sorry for her. Him too." Vega sat back with a sigh. "I like talking with you. It's honest, it's refreshing. And they say you shouldn't speak honestly to a police officer." He grinned broadly. "They're wrong. Well, in this case."

"Good." Days ago, in their first encounter, Vega had seemed vulgar. Now he seemed civil, possibly even gallant.

"Work can wait. Let's have another pitcher."

She gave him her Mona Lisa smile and consulted her watch. "I'm sorry. *My* work can't wait."

"Ah. Next time."

"Yes."

"I can't read your mood."

"I don't have moods." She laughed. "Thank you, Mr. Vega. You've been very helpful."

"I'm not a bad person." He regarded her seriously. "I want to help."

As she stood, Vega rose and kissed her cheek.

She smiled and quickly turned away. Maybe she was a tease. But there were times to tease and run. This was one of them.

Chapter 19

Waiting for the valet to fetch her car, Bourque fastened her pantsuit's third button and stepped away from Vega's tower. The late morning sun was a crimson ball. Its rays glinted off the building's glass walls, igniting a neighboring tower. The surrounding perennials were in full bloom, unlike in Falmouth. The condo groundskeepers had probably force-fed the gardens with fertilizer. If money couldn't buy love, it could certainly buy greenery.

She pulled out her phone and quietly dictated the main points Vega had related into her case notes app, not mentioning where the info had come from. Novak had been divesting his entire fortune; his main heirs were to get twenty-five million each, a small bequest considering his fortune; one was dead, which put the other one, Atlas Novak, in the crosshairs. That was convenient for Vega, she knew. He could be setting her up: he wanted her to believe Atlas was the prime suspect when it should be him.

She pocketed her phone. Could she believe the Bulldog of Wall Street? Deviousness was often the brother of charm. The thing about people like Vega—charming, self-important—was that even if you were confident they'd told you the truth, you couldn't trust them fully. They'd revealed truths, yes, but the whole truth? That was another matter.

Eyeing a nearby lily pond, she wondered what Vega had left underwater. Was he being charming to get in her pants? If so, why? Or forthcoming to help with the investigation? Did he have another motive? His elusiveness brought to mind the detective's uncertainty principle: the closer you got to a suspect, the farther you got from the objective truth.

She exhaled. Forget the principles. Sometimes you had to dance with the devil to get what you needed—dance close but keep your clothes on. She felt sure the "mutual silence" pact she'd made with Vega would stand. Then again, perhaps she'd made a deal with the devil, a devil who happened to look like a Biblical hero.

□ □ □

When the valet delivered her car, Bourque tipped him too much. He'd pretended her Mazda-3 wasn't a junk box. She drove a few blocks, pulled into a parking spot, and called Eller.

"Bourque here. I'm out."

"That was a long meeting. I tried your phone ten minutes ago. Dead."

"Huh." She couldn't tell Eller she'd turned off her phone. It was against regulations in a POI meeting, especially if you were solo.

"I was worried. I tried you a second time. Dead too."

"Must have got powered off by mistake." While she didn't like lying, she hadn't been unethical. She wasn't a straight arrow with regard to regulations, but she was a stickler when it came to ethics.

"I almost headed back there," Eller disclosed. "What kept you so long?"

"Vega was a windbag." It was best to tell Eller the truth—well, most of it. "Got some good stuff from him. He agreed to talk if we spoke off-the-record. I can give you a two-minute synopsis." She told him about Novak emulating Bill Gates, the charities, and the twenty-five-million-dollar gifts. "Oh, there's another thing. Apparently, Novak and Hayden had a crack in their love boat. It wasn't sinking, but—let me put it this way—they weren't intellectual partners. According to Vega, Novak was a bookworm, she was a goodtime girl. Don't shoot me, I know goodtime girls read. Just not the kind of books he read."

"Which were?"

"Philosophy and religion. Not business books."

Eller shut down his questioning mode. "I'm stuck at Metro HQ. By the way, two more Metro detectives have been assigned to the case. Due to Branka Novak's family ties, they just interviewed her again. She could be involved. However, I see her as the family conscience."

"Family consciences can do ugly things," Bourque noted.

"Be that as it may, Metro is now scheduling interviews with Amber Luu as well as Novak's main business associates. His umbrella corporation had thirteen board members. Made me wonder, so I checked it out. Thirteen's not unlucky in Slovenia."

Bourque didn't reply. She knew that.

"Incidentally," Eller continued, "M and M delivered a report on Gene Cantor, the biotechie who got devilled. He lost in court to Vega and Novak a few months ago. Shortly thereafter, he went down the tubes. He gambled away his assets. His girlfriend left him. There's a man who has potential motive. Two Metro detectives did a preliminary search. Didn't take them long to find out he lays more blame on Novak than Vega. According to the biotech community, Cantor didn't expect much from Vega except money. However, he expected Novak, a fellow techie, to support him. Supposedly, Novak understood R and D. Research now, profit later. But that didn't happen. And now Cantor's living in a converted garage in Revere. He used to own a Brookline mansion. That's a long fall. And you know the saying: 'Long falls trigger large paybacks.' Metro's going to call on him this afternoon." Eller paused. "I won't make the Zupan interview. You'll have to see him alone."

"Okay," Bourque replied. In fact, better than okay. As with Eller and Vega, she didn't want Eller and Zupan in the same room. The butler had been fed enough bad cop shtick. When interviews got too adversarial, pissed-off POIs didn't tell you anything.

"Join me with Atlas," Eller said. "Fifteen-hundred. Make sure your phone's working."

"Roger that." She grimaced. Maybe Eller knew. Fortunately, he wasn't a straight arrow either. In any case, his dig deserved a "Roger that."

◻   ◻   ◻

Pulling out of her parking spot, Bourque decided to have lunch. Although she'd eaten a stack of pancakes for breakfast, it was over five hours ago. She headed toward downtown Boston, to a Jamaican takeout she knew.

Golden Patty was busy yet she didn't mind standing in line. The decor was all Jamaican: green, yellow, and black national flags; the same color curtains; framed photographs of Kingston Town. She picked up two spicy patties, sat in a nearby park and quickly ate both. She couldn't stop. The pastry was that good. She kicked herself for not eating any salad, but who ate salad with patties?

By 1400 she was sitting in a different park, this time at a picnic table. She had a coffee in hand, as did her table mate, Damijan Zupan. The butler was facing her, looking out over the ocean at Nahant Beach near Boston. At Eller's insistence, she'd arranged to meet Zupan away from the Novak mansion on Avon Hill. Badge or not, gun or not, Eller didn't want her alone with Zupan in a big house on a large private lot. While they could ask Metro Homicide to assign her a sidekick, Bourque knew them. They'd be giving her the gears behind her back. *What, little lady, you scared of a butler?*

Zupan seemed ill at ease. With his burning eyes and slick-backed hair, he didn't look like a man to mess with. Her undercover training was in full effect: expect the worst. She'd readied her Smith & Wesson for quick access. The table she'd selected was in open sight of a parked State Police cruiser. She'd seen the troopers inside chowing down on pizza, not donuts. As Donnelly joked, pizza and donuts were cop superfoods. How could she shun them?

A sharp wind crested the ocean with blue-white waves. "A beach day," she said, watching two windsurfers in wetsuits enter the water.

Zupan grunted. "Is not. In my country, we await twenty-five Celsius. Seventy-five Fahrenheit. Then beach."

"We'd be waiting until July."

"Why not?" His voice softened. "You are Crazy New Englanders. I am still amaze by this state. I first see downtown Boston in August. Is business area, is rich area, but many men are wearing shorts." He smiled. "Mr. Rollo is always teaching me new words. He explain to me that New England people are 'egalitarian.'"

"Well, we like to think so."

"I think you are, Lieutenant. I miss Mr. Rollo. He was very good man."

Bourque let the moment linger. Zupan looked despondent. After watching a windsurfer execute a few somersaults, she leaned forward. Loose the sympathetic sister look. It was fine to be polite, but Zupan was a POI. "We know," she firmly began, "that you and Melanya Novak grew up in Jesenice. Yet you said you didn't know her."

"We did not grow together. I did not know her."

"Jesenice is a relatively small place, Mr. Zupan. I believe she was a beautiful young woman. Surely you saw her or noticed her?"

"No, her, I did not see. She was not in my school."

"I'm sure you saw her elsewhere, such as at dances or clubs."

"Is incorrect."

Strange, Bourque reasoned. They'd have to check when Melanya left Jesenice or if she was schooled elsewhere. "Is your phone turned off?" she asked.

He seemed taken aback. "No."

"Is the ringer low?" Ironic, she knew, grilling someone about their phone. "I called you three times before you answered."

"I do not keep with me always, not now. I do not need. Mr. Rollo, he is gone." Zupan shook his head sadly. "People here, they are always holding phone." He snorted. "Like baby holding doll."

True. "Do you call home often? Slovenia, I mean."

"No. Is not home now. Mother and father are dead. This country is home." He seemed to feel the need to explain himself. "I am content here."

"Did you help Snežana find an apartment near Avon Hill?"

"Yes. Her job is close by. She can walk there. That is Old Country way. Not drive all the time."

"Do you help her pay rent?"

"No. Why you ask this? She can afford. She is paid well."

"When will she be back?"

"Tonight. She arrive at 11:40 p.m."

To be seen, Bourque thought. If true, she'd interview Snežana tomorrow. "Are you picking her up?"

"No. I must go to Falmouth. Atlas Novak call me yesterday. He is soon moving into Avon Hill house. I must vacate immediately. Atlas allow me to stay in Falmouth suite for one month. After that, I am needing new job. He give me notice too."

"I see." Hasty, but not surprising.

"I will rent apartment in Boston."

"Why don't you stay with Snežana?"

"Her place is very small. And I prefer downtown."

"Why did Mr. Novak leave Yugoslavia?" Bourque asked.

"To be free."

"To make money?"

"No. He does not care about money. I hear some people say he is 'Adriatic Oligarch' but they are barking. If such people meet Mr. Rollo, they see he is not oligarch. He is humble. I can tell you, he steal nothing from people of Slovenia. He leave Old Country with nothing."

"How do you know?"

"My army friends inform me. I ask them before I decide to work for him. When I think to join Mr. Rollo, friends back home find out about him. High friends. They report nothing bad or unusual about Mr. Rollo. He is opposite of oligarch. When he leave former

Yugoslavia, he is just village boy. He take no money with him. He make all money in USA. In Slovenia, after USSR falls there are some oligarchs, of course, but they are junior oligarchs, you can say, very junior. They are not like big Russian crooks."

"Did Mr. Novak have enemies in Yugoslavia?"

"No."

"How can you be sure?"

"He told me."

"Maybe he lied."

Zupan's eyes flashed black lightning. "Mr. Rollo does not lie."

"Everyone lies."

"You are police, I understand, but you can still believe in good of people. Some people," he qualified.

"Like you?"

"Yes. I am honest man. I serve in Serbian Army. It knows a lot about all of population." His voice hardened. "Knows more than police here. What people say to neighbor, when butcher pig or cow, when drink too much. I tell you, Mr. Rollo is good person. When he leave Old Country, he is also poor person."

If true, that countered another one of Bourque's suppositions: that Novak had smuggled money out. "Didn't he become an enemy of the state when he defected?"

"He is defector, but 'non-political' one. Freedom seeker. You think Communists try to kill everyone who defect? First, is impossible. Second, even if they want to, they are too busy trying to survive. Which they fail at."

She didn't respond.

"You cannot know," Zupan asserted. "In Yugoslavia, they watch everyone, of course, but most people are left alone."

"What about the red neckties? The last time we spoke you said the color red was 'most important' in Yugoslavia."

"Of course. Was Communist country. Flag has red band, flag has red star."

"Do you think Mr. Novak's killers came from the former Yugoslavia?"

Zupan stared at her. "You think this?"

"It's a possibility."

"Why you think this? You are barking up wrong tree. In wrong forest, too. You think many ex-Soviets are bad men. We are heartless, we are big gangsters."

She couldn't deny that a lot of police officers thought that, Tom Gronski included. In his arena, Chechen gangs were trouble, run by cagey men with nothing to lose. It'd been comrade eat comrade in much of the USSR; now, in the west, it was ex-comrade eat Westerner. These days, the Chechens were among the top dogs in Boston, having superseded earlier mobs, foremost among them the Irish and Italians. It was a palimpsest of sorts, layer upon layer of criminality, with tendrils reaching back to the past, clear enough for anyone in law enforcement to see. "Was Mr. Novak working with any Chechens?" she asked.

"He never mention Chechens. He never meet with them."

"What about you?"

"I spit on Chechens. No finesse. I do not trust them. They are not Slavs. They are Turkic peoples, tied to Central Asia, not Europe."

"Did you ever have any dealings with them?"

"No. In Old Country, I deal with Russians. They come to former Yugoslavia to help Tito. But they do not help. Leninists know nothing about running a country."

"Let's return to Mr. Novak's killers."

"Yes, let us."

"Could Chechens be involved?"

Zupan shook his head forcefully. "They butcher with knives, they shoot, they do not hang. I do not see foreign killers, not Chechen, not Yugoslav. Point of fact, Old Country killers would take silverware, wine, what they could carry. But no one steal anything from Falmouth house. In addition, I talk to Old Country people in Boston. There is no news Šef's killers were from Yugoslavia. I am thinking killers were American."

"But you said Šef—I mean, Mr. Novak—had no enemies, American or otherwise."

Zupan sighed. "Is puzzle."

"Did you hear any *hints* about American killers?"

"No." He raised a hand apologetically. "I understand. You are doubtful. But American killers is my belief. If I hear more, I will tell you."

She handed him her State Police card.

Chapter 20

As Bourque walked away from Zupan, she glanced at her watch. Christ! Twenty minutes to get to Atlas's condo. She ran to her car, fixed the detachable siren to the roof, and sped to Salem Turnpike channeling Mad Max.

She was lucky. For a change, drivers pulled off to the side. She reached the condo at 1502. Eller was waiting in the foyer, pointing at his watch.

"I heard you coming, Bourque. Traffic a little uncooperative?"

"You could say that."

"Any revelations from the butler?" Eller asked as they walked to the penthouse elevator.

She shook her head.

Branka Novak greeted them when the elevator doors opened. She led them immediately to the study. Her whole face looked flushed, as if she were nervous. Bourque looked again. It could be the maid's natural skin tone. In quick order, she delivered a silver coffee service. Two cups of coffee later, the detectives were still waiting for Atlas.

"Pulling a Vega on us," Eller muttered. "The usual bullshit."

Bourque nodded. Her partner seemed to be easily riled today. She drew out her phone. Her "doll." Well, when dolls talked to Google, they had a place in her world. She spoke quietly into the phone. "How many Slovenes live in the USA?"

There are approximately 300,000 Slovene-Americans. Most live in the Great Lakes region.

"How many Slovene-Americans live in Massachusetts?"

In the last census, 0.54% of Massachusetts residents reported Eastern European ethnicity.

She couldn't find a precise figure for Slovenes in Massachusetts, but did some quick math. Given the state's population, 0.54% meant roughly 35,000 people. Seeing as Slovenia was a small country amongst many larger Eastern European nations, she guessed the Slovene figure might be 1,000 at most. Perhaps Zupan's network knew a lot of them. As she considered ways to question his Old Country grapevine, Atlas strode into the room. "How can I help you?"

"You can be on time," Eller pointedly said.

Atlas smiled impishly. "I heard you're rather time crunched. But I was on the phone with India. Couldn't just hang up."

Bourque scrutinized him. He seemed pleased with himself. In the looks department, admittedly, he had a right to be pleased. He wore the finest suit she'd seen in years, a midnight-blue number that appeared to be made of silk but was more structured, ephemeral and substantial at the same time.

"We have some questions about your whereabouts," Eller sternly began. "Specifically, on the day of your parents' murder, and the day before it."

"Katrina Hayden is not my parent."

"She's your stepmother," Eller said. "You told us you ate dinner at Strega on Sunday, May thirteenth, but there was no reservation in your name."

"I didn't make a reservation. They know me. They always find me a table."

"I showed your photo to the owner and the staff," Eller related. "They do indeed know you."

Atlas smiled.

"But none of them saw you on May thirteenth."

"That's strange. I ate dinner there. I arrived about nine o'clock."

"No staff saw you."

"I called Amber from the restaurant. She can verify where I was."

Eller's look said *I wouldn't believe her for a second.* "Let's help each other, Mr. Novak. Let's not waste time. I want the truth."

"That's what I'm giving you."

Eller glanced at Bourque. "What do you think?"

"First time for everything."

Atlas shook his head. "I do the decent thing and agree to talk to you people again, no lawyers present, and look what I get in return. The third degree. Believe me, I had a nice table, near the fountain. And I know why they didn't recognize me. I was wearing a ballcap and sweats. I had no clean suits."

"That seems convenient. Can Branka corroborate your dinner attire?"

"She didn't see me. Sunday is her day off."

"That's convenient. Again. And I'm not even talking about the fact you were alone that day. No one to verify your whereabouts until the next morning, when Miss Luu entered the bedroom. The picture, I should say. What time did she arrive here Monday?"

"I don't remember."

Bourque made a mental note to requisition the condo security footage.

"Strega can't verify your presence," Eller went on. "Branka didn't see you Sunday. Miss Luu didn't see you Sunday. Except on video phone. However, we all know how easy it is for a techie to alter video. And you're in the tech game."

"The phone call generated AT&T data, not personal data."

"I'm sure that wouldn't stop you," Eller noted. "You could have been anywhere when you made that call, with a photographic facsimile of your bedroom behind you."

Atlas laughed. *"Photographic facsimile?* Image, you mean."

Eller seemed about to retaliate but let the jibe slide. "I'm sure the doorman saw you leave for dinner on Sunday. Or return."

"Perhaps, but he wouldn't likely have recognized me. I rarely wear sweats."

"Do you exercise, Mr. Novak?"

"Yes."

"Then the doormen here have seen you in sweats."

"I exercise in my condo. Do you want to see my gym? I caution you, it smells. Like your line of questioning."

Eller grinned aggressively. *You jab me, I jab back.* "You weren't close to your father, were you?"

"Who says so?" Atlas shifted uncomfortably.

"We know more than you think we know," Eller stated. "For example, we know your father left you twenty-five million dollars. A far cry from three billion. You didn't like that, did you?"

Atlas appeared flummoxed. "Okay, I disagreed with my father on some things, but I respected him. I loved him."

"That's easy to say. And hard to prove."

"I don't need to prove it. To you or anyone." Atlas raised his hands in frustration. "I've told you where I ate, when, what I wore, when I got home. Everything."

Eller's expression said *I doubt that.* "You know what's as troubling as your whereabouts on May thirteenth? Your phone calls over the past few months. They're being requisitioned as we speak. The full transcripts. And Miss Luu can't do a thing. A Judge agreed with our subpoena."

Good lie, Bourque thought. You just couldn't trust cops—not when they didn't trust you. A judge had rejected Eller's request, citing lack of evidence against Atlas.

"You have a tendency to call unlisted numbers," Eller continued. "Or be called by them." He pulled out a sheet and showed Atlas a list of the numbers Abbot had found. "Who were you calling?"

"I don't have to answer you."

"No, you don't. But you do need to listen to me, for your own good. I can help you. I want to help you. I'm trying my best to be *understanding*. That can all change."

Atlas didn't respond.

Bourque considered his body language. No jumpiness, no wince-smiles or flinch-grins, sure signs of an unreliable POI. Then again, these days, people knew body language tricks. Someone like Atlas, who spent a lot of time in business meetings—prevaricating or posturing—would know all the tricks.

"Fine," Eller said. "You don't want to talk. I'll tell you what happens when you clam up. I get doubly motivated. I use every trick in my arsenal. All legal, of course. The criminal system is like a tight rope. I know how to walk it. You don't."

"The *criminal* system," Atlas mocked. "What happened to the *criminal justice* system? You know the problem with you? You have no class."

Eller pretended to be overjoyed. "That's quite a compliment. But perhaps you're unaware. The police are supposed to be classless. It ensures fairness." He leaned forward. "Let me ask you something. Did you really think you'd get away with murder?"

"Get lost."

"Did you really think?"

"Enough! Talk to my lawyers."

"Are you saying you're guilty?"

Atlas's face went red. "Get out!"

Eller didn't budge.

"Get the fuck out!"

Eller grinned. "I heard you the first time."

☐ ☐ ☐

The two detectives didn't speak on the elevator ride down to street level. Standing next to Bourque's car, Eller looked wound up. He fizzed with anticipation. "We have enough to order Atlas in for questioning."

Cool your jets, Bourque thought. "We should subpoena the security footage at his condo," she said.

"We don't need the footage to question him. You know the line that separates POI from suspect? That *fuck* pushed him across it. I don't care about the language. I mean the whole story. He thinks he's above the law."

She didn't reply. Why was Eller so jumpy? She wasn't sure about Atlas. Unlike Zupan or Vega, he didn't know how to control his temper. They had no unequivocal evidence against him.

"I have some information from M and M I didn't use today." Eller's voice quickened. "They got Novak's will just before noon. Atlas's going to inherit more than twenty-five million. A lot more. He's the named beneficiary for forty-three percent of Novak's holdings."

"Who's the will's executor?"

"Katrina Hayden, but Atlas is the backup. He kills his father and the first executor. The will falls into his hands."

Not inconceivable, she thought. Kill the gander and the goose, get the golden egg. She thought again. "Vega said most of Novak's assets are going to charity."

"That's correct. Fifty-seven percent is earmarked for charity. Atlas is supposed to divest the rest and give it away. In theory. It's a complex will. M and M passed it on to Legal. We have to wait. I got Central to book us into the Sheraton again."

Back to the high life, she thought. "I'm sure Peabody will be happy."

"Forget him. Let's meet in my room at twenty-one-hundred for a team debrief. All right, other avenues. What did Zupan say about Novak and Yugoslavia?"

"Nothing we can easily corroborate. According to Zupan—that is, according to his sources in the Old Country—Novak left Yugoslavia with no money. I doubt we can find those sources and question them."

Eller rolled on. "I want to see Vega again. He's flying to Hong Kong tomorrow morning. We better see him now. We have to question him about those shares."

"His lawyers emailed me the paperwork. It appears they were all sold."

"I didn't see the paperwork. Did you email it to me or M and M?"

Bourque winced. She'd forgotten. She reached for her phone, navigated to the lawyers' email, and forwarded it, chastising herself inwardly. She'd been so chummy with Vega she'd gotten off track. Lesson learned. "I checked the documents. They look good."

"I get the impression you're willing to give Vega a break."

"Not at all. He can be charming, but where there's a charmer, there's often a lie spinner. Regardless, I don't think he was involved in the murders. He doesn't need to kill for money. He makes a *lot* of money. And I think he's truly fond of Novak."

"You've done your part. Let me go back at him. I'll be playing bad cop," Eller forcefully said. "We won't need a good cop. Trust me."

Bourque shrugged. Mild-mannered Eller had left the building. Something was up. Had Atlas or Vega suddenly got to him?

□ □ □

Eller and Bourque arrived at Vega's condo unannounced. Inside, there was no sign of Wideneck. Good cop, bad cop, or no cop, she didn't want to see Vega. It was too soon. Besides, she wouldn't be much use at detecting his lies. She'd allowed herself to fall a little bit under his spell. Bad for the investigation, and possibly bad for her career.

The concierge informed them Vega was at home. Luckily, she reflected, then immediately changed her mind. Vega was temperamental. If angered, he might turn vengeful and out her little mojito intake.

While she and Eller rode up the elevator to the penthouse, she calmed herself. What was a drink? One drink was nothing. She'd known plenty of undercover officers who'd literally slept with the enemy. She was one of them. Her past had taught her to tell the truth to any police tribunal. Always, no exceptions. If Vega outed her, she'd plead pragmatism and face the music.

Vega was waiting at the elevator door, wearing a silk shirt and trousers. Without his suitcoat on, he looked diminished, like Samson shorn of his locks. For the first time, she saw he had a pigeon chest. His eyes were red and bleary. He appeared to have had a hard day.

"I'm about to eat," he truculently said. "Could you come back later?" His normally smooth voice sounded ragged. "Let's say in half an hour?"

Eller shook his head. "We're very *busy*. Strange as it may seem, we serve society, not you."

Vega turned his glance to Bourque. His look was unmistakable. *Get this cabrón to come back.*

She looked away.

Eller harrumphed and pointed toward the meeting alcove. "Sit down, Mr. Vega. I have some questions for you."

"You can ask them here."

"No, I can't. We're going to sit down."

Bourque silently applauded Eller. They were serving the people, the common good, not billionaires. As Eller strode to the alcove, Vega grudgingly followed.

"Earlier today," Eller began, "you claimed you divested Rollo Novak's shares in BioCell. I haven't been able to confirm that."

"My lawyers sent the paperwork to Lieutenant Bourque."

"I didn't get it."

"Not my problem. I repeat, it was sent to Lieutenant Bourque."

Said with displeasure, Bourque noted.

"You also claimed you gave the money to charity," Eller stated. "Yet you haven't provided proof of the charitable donations. Like the IRS, I need receipts."

"Some of Rollo's charities take months to issue receipts. He often donated directly to village councils. My lawyers will send copies to you as soon as they arrive, not Lieutenant Bourque."

Bourque read his tone. He didn't trust her. She'd failed to do her job. Or maybe she'd failed to keep the investigation at bay. Perhaps he *was* trying to use her. If so, he'd soon learn he couldn't.

"Send them to Lieutenant Bourque," Eller ordered.

"You, Lieutenant Eller."

Good, Bourque surmised. Regardless of motive, it appeared Vega had lost his weakness for her. As for his insights, she had what she wanted. Now they needed to be corroborated.

"Where and when did you set up the share divestment with Mr. Novak?" Eller asked.

"Here, just before Christmas."

"Who was present?" Eller inquired.

"Rollo and I. Let me impart some wisdom to you. Free of charge. The secret to doing business is to keep things as private as possible. No prying eyes or ears. Beyond that, no endless discussions. You get to the crux. You get things done."

"Same as in policing, Mr. Vega."

"Then why are you taking so long?"

Eller ignored him. "What other investments did you have with Mr. Novak?"

"None. Let me impart something else to you. If you're looking into Rollo's background for financial misconduct of any kind, you're wasting your time. Rollo was fairer than anyone I've known. He acquired his money by hard work. And he acquired it here, not behind the Iron Curtain. He wasn't an autocrat or oligarch. He was the epitome of a decent man."

Eller moved on. "Your phone records indicate you had many conversations with Atlas Novak. What about?"

"I mentor him."

"How?"

"By *mentoring*, Lieutenant. Surely you know the concept."

"Tell us your version."

"Atlas is aggressive. He often jumps when he should wait."

"Meaning what?"

"He's twitchy. I try to moderate his buying habits. A wise investor waits for the market to show its future colors. The timing is always different. Sometimes it only takes hours. Sometimes you have to wait for weeks, even months. But enough. In the end, you have to lose and learn. I assume you have a pension. I'll give you two pieces of advice. One, cash it out now and invest in the market. Two, lose it all. You have to lose it. It teaches you to make wiser investments next time." Vega sat back. "Any more questions? Final questions."

"You claim no one was present when you and Mr. Novak met to discuss the charity shares. You're lying. The divestment document was notarized by a pair of witnesses, partners in a law firm you often use."

"They weren't part of the meeting. They came in, witnessed the document, and left."

"They may have heard things we want to know."

"Let me assure you, they didn't hear anything. When they were in the room, Rollo and I didn't speak. Standard procedure."

"I'll take your word for it."

"That's a change. My cooperation clock is ticking down. Let's wrap this up."

Eller switched topics. "Did you and Atlas make any investments together?"

"Not by design. However, we may own shares in the same corporations or own the same bonds. But that's meaningless. You and I might own the same shares, although that's highly unlikely. You're not an investor. You're a saver, not a risk-taker."

Eller remained silent.

"I thought so." Vega gestured at Bourque. "Lieutenant Bourque, however, is a risk-taker."

She didn't respond.

"We're done here, detectives."

"We're done when *we* say we're done," Eller replied. "However, we are done for today."

"You're persistent, Lieutenant Eller, I'll grant you that. But there's a big difference between persistence and intelligence, not to mention between persistence and influence."

"Are you saying you can buy influence?"

"Not at all. I don't have to. I have nothing to hide. *Adios*, detectives."

Eller glared at him. "You're on public time. Do I make myself clear? When we want you, make yourself available." He stood. "Otherwise I'll send a bailiff."

Vega grinned. "To Hong Kong?"

"To the ends of the earth."

Chapter 21

Standing in the street, Eller consulted his watch and looked up at Bourque. "I think we should revisit Melanya. I have a meeting at Metro. Can you handle her?"

"Sure."

"I know what you think of her," Eller said.

Bourque eyed him. *You do?*

"She's a hedonist."

"Pretty close."

□ □ □

Having inhaled a chicken-salad sandwich, Bourque left a nearby Dunkin'. Her phone started pealing. "Watching the detectives ..."

"Lieutenant Bourque," she answered, "State Police."

"Is Damijan Zupan."

"Good evening, Mr. Zupan."

"Old Country people tell me something. It is, you say, *interesting.*"

"Please, go ahead."

"Two immigrants arrive recently from Ljubljana. They are couple, man and woman, maybe thirty. They are living with Albanians. That is very strange. We are Christian, many Albanians are Muslim. Old Country people do not trust the couple. They do not go out in daytime. It is like they are hiding." He paused. "I know, I say killers are American people. But these two arrive five days before Šef's murder. They are young and strong."

"Do you know their names?"

"I do not have. I will get."

□ □ □

Bourque drove toward Boston's Inner Harbor. While mornings were her favorite time in Falmouth, in Boston she preferred evenings. The city seemed smaller. It was a web of cozy neighborhoods. People were strolling or heading out to eat. Normal indulgences.

Melanya Novak lived in a new condo tower steps from the harbor. Bourque parked in the visitor's lot and walked to the main entrance. A ship horn hooted from across the harbor, followed by the plaintive honking of geese, as if the birds were answering the ship.

The condo grounds were immaculate; the high-end trees and shrubs perfectly coifed. However, the Javex-like smell of the harbor overrode the floral notes. The water might look beautiful, but all the overflow from nearby rivers and streams funneled into Boston Harbor. She picked up her pace, musing that upward mobility wasn't what it used to be. Pricey neighborhoods didn't guarantee clean air and swimmable water.

Inside the tower, she showed her badge to the security guard, ascended the elevator without notice, and knocked at Unit 2212. The occupant didn't keep her waiting.

Not you, Melanya's eyes said when she opened the door. She wore a body-hugging leisure suit, obviously expensive. It was dark blue, the color of kingfisher wings. Despite the hour, her big hair was flawlessly styled.

Bourque smiled. *Yes, me.* "I need to ask you a few questions."

"Now?"

"That's why I'm here." That's why you need to lose the attitude.

Even fully clothed, Melanya looked half-naked. Bourque guessed the ex had been "entertaining." The contours of her large nipples were visible. Yet she wasn't flaunting them. They were simply and visibly her's, like another woman's eyes. The scent of Mitteleuropa permeated the air. Like Cleopatra, the ex wore so much perfume you could smell her before you saw her. Her hair was Byzantine in its complexity—curls and swirls and crossovers—a beehive made by a mad hatter. She rolled her eyes and let Bourque enter.

The apartment was a two-story affair. Descending a spiral staircase to an expansive living room, Bourque took in the surroundings. Cluttered and spacious at the same time. Nothing was cheap, but, to her mind, nothing was desirable. Two suede sofas, a rococo buffet table with silver decanters and goblets, dozens of glass ornaments and crystals. She recognized the brand. Swarovski. Expensive kitsch, but kitsch nonetheless. From what she'd seen in movies, the decor was the height of Iron Curtain chic. Heavy furniture, shiny baubles. A home that echoed its owner's past.

Melanya pointed curtly to an oversized armchair. She didn't offer refreshments.

As Bourque sat, she noticed a photo of Melanya in a graduation dress: a young, unsmiling knockout, the stern Slavic face a contrast to the voluptuous figure. Despite the Soviet-style dress, her perfect body was evident.

"Is that you at your high school graduation?" Bourque asked.

"I didn't go to high school." Judging by the size of Melanya's chest, her lungs weren't small, yet she had a small voice, low and breathy. "I went to a gymnasium."

Same difference, Bourque thought, but smiled. "You were beautiful. You still are."

Melanya shrugged.

Her skin was radiant. Her high cheekbones, surgically-enhanced or not, were perfectly symmetrical. Her lips—pouty and bee-kissed—were almost as pronounced as her cheekbones. Bourque felt a rare pang of envy. Her own cheekbones, shaped by French blood, weren't bad. Her hair, on the other hand, was nowhere near as elaborate as Melanya's.

"Were you a good student?" she asked Big-Hair.

"Yes. Very good."

"In what?"

"Mathematics."

"I loved math too." A lie, but Bourque wanted to draw Melanya out.

"It's the best field. A theorem is always true. Unlike a story."

Bourque grinned. "Or a man."

"You are correct."

No grin, Bourque noted. "Did you study hard?"

"Of course. It's the only way."

Bourque agreed. Again, a serious reply. From what Vega had told her, Novak had become serious too. She wondered why Novak ditched Melanya. Her intensity should be a good match for an ethical philanthropist. With her silky skin and air of sadness, she was the embodiment of beauty and loss—someone Bourque could pity but, like Zupan, not completely trust. "What else did you study?"

"Science," Melanya softly replied.

"What fields did you like?"

"Some."

"Physics?"

"No."

"Chemistry?"

"No."

Bourque persisted. It was like pulling teeth. "Biology?"

"No. Computer science."

"Math and computers, a good combination."

"True," Melanya said. "I first saw a personal computer in Ljubljana, an IBM 386. Not a clone. A real IBM. You know it?"

Bourque nodded and kept quiet. The ex was opening up.

"It had a DOS system. Very powerful." She smiled. "Then."

Bourque nodded again. Ah, Melanya could smile. Her eyes were intelligent. Her mouth wasn't the mouth of a helpless dependent. It was the mouth of somebody who was on the ball.

"In Jesenice," Melanya explained, "at home and in school, there were no computers. Eventually, at the Ljubljana gymnasium, there were many. I liked that."

"When did you start there?"

"I began pre-gymnasium in nineteen eighty."

"In Ljubljana?"

"Yes. Jesenice was too small. I left at age five."

Perhaps that explained why Zupan hadn't known her in Jesenice. "Where did you meet Rollo Novak?"

"Ljubljana."

"Where?"

"At school."

Bourque smiled genially, hoping to get past Melanya's reticence. "I bet you fell in love at first sight."

She tsked. "He fell. Not me. Or so he said. What does it matter?"

Dour and sour, Bourque thought. Slavic severity was supposedly a cliché. In Melanya's case, Bourque figured it was merited. She changed tack. "How did you and your husband escape?"

"We took a little boat to Italy, across the Golfo de Trieste. It was a long trip at night. The engine failed. We paddled." Her small voice took on strength and depth, as if she were reliving a triumph. "Rollo worked the oars for many hours. Finally, we arrived after sunrise. The dawn light blazed but no one stopped us."

"Good fortune. Was Rollo anti-communist?"

"No."

"Were you?"

"No. I was in the Yugoslav Army Cadet Corp," Melanya proudly said. "I was a member of Ljubljana's Young Communist brigade. They supported my education."

"Why did you leave?"

"Rollo wanted to go. Slovenia, Yugoslavia, was too minor for him. He was intelligent. I went."

Bourque nodded. *Who's your lover now?* she almost asked, but perhaps Melanya didn't have one. It was puzzling. From the look of her, men should be falling over her. Bourque adjusted her thinking. From the look of Melanya's *body*. Her unreceptive eyes were another matter. Bourque moved on. "Rollo must have had money."

"Phh. He had nothing."

"Did he go to the West to make money?"

Melanya shook her head emphatically. "He did not care about money."

"Do you?"

"Look where I live," Melanya snapped. "Do you see a lot of money?"

Bourque noted the snideness.

"I'm comfortable," Melanya immediately added, "but not wealthy."

Bourque said nothing, filing away the ex's short-lived outburst. It was as if she'd momentarily lost control, opened a veil hiding her true self, and quickly shut it. In any case, she lived in a showy condo and was about to get two million dollars. She was more than comfortable. Bourque had a final avenue. "Did you make government enemies when you left Yugoslavia?"

Melanya waved a hand dismissively. "We were nothings. Young and poor."

"What about after you became rich? Did anyone from your homeland bother you in the U.S.? As in try to extort you or Mr. Novak?"

"Never. Ex-communists can't do anything. They are no longer powerful."

Bourque took that with a grain. In her undercover days, she'd come across many powerful ex-Communists. They ran shady enterprises everywhere, including New England. She'd contact Gronski to get the goods on Melanya Novak, née Kemet. Bourque switched topics. "One last question." It wasn't her last question but POIs often dropped their guard when they thought an interview was ending. "What enemies did Rollo make in Boston?"

"Enemies? Always you are talking enemies."

"Someone killed your husband."

"Yes, someone did this. But I don't know of any enemies."

Another broken record, Bourque reflected. According to everyone she'd interviewed, Novak had no enemies. If that were the case, he'd still be alive. "When did you last visit Slovenia?"

"Four years ago."

"Do you know if your husband lent money to anyone in Slovenia?"

"Not that I know of." Melanya gestured helplessly. "I wasn't involved in his businesses."

"Did you meet anyone who was angry with your husband?"

"No."

"Did he mention any arguments with people in Slovenia?"

"No."

"Thank you, Mrs. Novak." Bourque stood and left her State Police card on the buffet. "Call me if you think of anything."

□ □ □

Bourque knocked on Eller's room door at the Sheraton. He ushered her in with his phone to his ear, holding a finger up for quiet. A minute later, he signed off.

"M and M," he explained as he gestured Bourque to a chair and sat. "Legal just got back to them about Novak's will. If Atlas wants to keep Novak's houses and condos, he doesn't have to divest them. Being the new CEO of Novak Enterprises, he's entitled to 'living quarters' wherever he does business. That's almost the whole planet." Eller shook his head. "He's also allowed to keep the Novak office tower in Boston. He can rent out any Novak property, but can't sell them. M and M determined he could make as much as eighty million a year on rent."

The rich getting richer, she thought.

Eller moved on. "Anything new on the ex?"

"Everything and nothing."

"More wise words for Peabody?"

She winked. "In truth, I can't say yet. Perhaps she's happy to swim and dance. A woman disappointed by her ex-husband, yet getting on with life. You know, she may well be a Stepford wife. She's a bit of an automaton."

Eller grinned. "Did that hurt so much? Agreeing with Lieutenant

Eller?"

"Very painful."

He laughed. "Okay, time for the team debrief."

Eller initiated a teleconference and turned the line over to Landon, who reported on the Hayden social media friends file. He'd prioritized the ninety-two POIs by number of hits. The twelve highest hitters—those with over 300 likes—were in New England. All twelve were scheduled for interviews. Fortunately, due to Central's budget, the remaining POIs would be questioned within four days, even the European ones. There were eight in the former Yugoslavia.

Munro spoke next, relating M&M didn't uncover any evidence of illegal financing connected to Bluefin Bay. Nate Hayden had bought it for $411,000 in 2004. A steal considering its current value. He owned one hundred percent of it. Munro noted no suspicious prints were found inside Novak's castle, which supported the supposition that the perps accessed the pool from outside.

Wolf followed Munro, reporting Zupan had gone to Crystal Fishery in Truro three times in May to buy halibut for his boss. Apparently, Novak loved halibut. Two junior detectives had canvassed the area, including the Bluefin Bay neighborhood. Zupan hadn't been spotted anywhere in the area other than Crystal Fishery, which seemed to refute a possible Zupan-Hayden/Payne connection.

Eller took over, relaying that Novak and Katrina Hayden had a simple prenup with one clause: Hayden agreed to abide by Novak's will. Full stop. To date, Metro hadn't uncovered any extramarital affairs or call girl assignations involving Novak.

Bourque considered that intel. Vega seemed to have told the truth about Novak's female friends. She felt discouraged. Despite their progress, they had no suspects, whether in Boston, Falmouth, or Truro. Their radar was sweeping across an empty sky.

Eller ended the meeting with one of his "don't-give-up" pep talks.

When Bourque stood to leave, he waved her down. "I'd like to run something by you."

She almost glanced at her watch. *Now*?

"I have a little news for you," Eller rolled on, "not the entire team. Central plans to expand the soil analysis. They're going to analyze all the watercraft access points around East Falmouth, including beaches and boat ramps. The perps may have used various watercraft to get to the path to the house, possibly kayaks, even paddleboards. In which case, they could have used multiple entry points."

Bourque whistled. This was getting expensive. Those kinds of craft could be launched from almost anywhere.

"Central is invested in the case." Eller smiled. "We're moving along."

Really? she thought. The investigation was stalled, like the worst kind of hockey game: one with no offensive forays. She was a forward; she played to score goals. The investigation's score was still zero: no suspects.

"Central," he continued, "is going to release the details about Novak's philanthropy to the media. That'll engage the public."

"True." She changed tack. "Is Novak off your radar?"

Eller blew out his cheeks. "Fair question. No. However, for now he's a blip on the outer screen. We can't prove motive for the Hayden murder. There's no indication he would gain financially. There are no reports of abusive behavior or heated arguments. I'm leaning toward Atlas," Eller announced.

She nodded. Of the four POIs she'd seen that day—Vega, Zupan, Atlas, and Melanya—Atlas had the most to gain.

"He could have driven to East Falmouth with accomplices on May fourteenth, or met them there, killed the Novaks and drove back."

"Possible," she allowed. "However, the drive from Boston takes at least an hour and a half. The murder window was between oh-six-hundred and oh-seven-thirty. Atlas supposedly ate breakfast in the city that day at oh-seven-thirty. How did he get home for breakfast?"

"You can drive it in an hour," Eller countered. "Atlas drives a V12 Benz AMG."

"A what?" Men and their cars.

Eller shook his head, feigning despair. "A fast Mercedes. Alternatively, he may have done his part earlier. What if he opened the pool gate and left his accomplices to do the actual strangulations? I'm suggesting he had time to be at the murder scene and get back to Boston by oh-seven-thirty. What do we do when we don't have solid probable cause?" Eller flashed a quick smile. "Pressure the main POI until we do. We've waited long enough. I'm ordering Atlas into Boston District A-1 tomorrow, oh-six-hundred. We need to stir things up."

She didn't respond. She wanted to let the investigation unfold. On the other hand, Eller was right.

"I'll hand him a cold coffee," Eller announced. "You blow him a kiss. Then we'll leave and let him cure for an hour. When he thinks he's on Easy Street, we'll return and dissect him."

Chapter 22

DAY SIX: *May 19th*

Early next morning Bourque and Eller breakfasted at a Dunkin' near District A-1. As Eller finished a cream cheese bagel, his phone blared. A few moments later, he gestured to Bourque: *Meet me outside.*

She followed him to a quiet spot and waited while he talked into his phone. It was a long talk. The back of her neck tingled. She felt a sense of foreboding. After disconnecting, he glanced around. They were still alone. "The butler got jumped," he said. "Attacked in his suite at the castle."

Jesus. "When?"

"About forty minutes ago. That was Patel. She's on scene with Donnelly and the ninjas."

"Is Zupan all right?" she asked.

"Yes. He called in the attack. Fought off his assailant. Apparently, a man tried to strangle him. Same MO as the murderers."

She nodded.

"Zupan IDed the assailant as a tall male with brush-cut hair and a big forehead. Thirty-something. According to Zupan, he elbowed his attacker's head multiple times and also bit him on both hands. From what we know, the assailant wasn't armed, but we can't be sure. He may be a threat to the public. HQ deployed extra cruisers to secure the area and put out an APB describing the attacker and his possible injuries."

"Tell them to get Donnelly to assist the hunt," she advised. "He knows the region inside out."

Eller nodded.

Bourque hoped for the best but, like Donnelly, she knew the Cape. While the State Police could cover main roads, marinas, and airfields, there were many escape hatches: dozens of backroads, dune-buggy tracks, wharves, small plane strips, and floatplane takeoff spots. A resourceful perp could easily slip away.

"Zupan was taken to Falmouth hospital," Eller continued. "They're putting a guard on his room. Central received a Massachusetts property inventory from Novak's lawyers last night. According to Patel, besides Zupan, Atlas is the only one with keys to the castle. Of course, someone could have copied the keys."

"Did Patel say anything about a B and E?"

"The opposite. No forced entry. Might be a little more ammo against Atlas. He hasn't left Boston for days—so he has an alibi for the assault, but he could have passed the keys to an accomplice."

"There could be more ammo," she said. "In my interview with Zupan yesterday, he told me Atlas is moving into the Avon Hill house. He said Zupan could live in the castle suite temporarily. Atlas knew Zupan was going to be there. Beyond that, Zupan called me last night. Said he had some interesting news. I didn't think much of it then, but I do now. A young Slovenian couple arrived in Boston ten days ago. They've been keeping to themselves. They have immigrant status but haven't started working. Maybe they came here to do a murder hit. Zupan didn't know their names but he was going to get them and let me know."

"Good. HQ ordered full lockdown for him. No visitors at all." Eller paused thoughtfully. "I got a report his sister returned last night. That might be a coincidence, or it might not. It seems someone thinks the butler knows things, perhaps someone like his sister. To be safe, she should be on the no-go list. She could be involved in the murders without him knowing. In which case, maybe she hired someone to silence him."

"Conversely," Bourque said, "she might be an accomplice. Then again, she might be completely clean."

"For some reason, I doubt that. Call me suspicious."

More suspicious than her, Bourque realized.

Eller seemed to read her mind "I may be overly cautious but remember his phone file? Not one call to or from his sister. I'd say they weren't that close."

"Valid point," Bourque conceded.

"We'll make sure she doesn't enter his room or pass any food to him. Working in a pharma lab, she has access to numerous poisons. By the way, HQ is posting troopers at Falmouth hospital, twenty-four/seven. They'll add a local trooper to the mix. That'll put a blanket over Zupan."

Bourque nodded. They might need a lot more blankets. She sensed an Old Country connection could be rearing its head.

She pulled out her phone and called Zupan.

"Hello?" he replied. He sounded groggy.

"It's Lieutenant Bourque. How are you?"

"Okay."

"Are you in pain?"

"Some. They give me medicine. I have broken elbow and neck lesions, doctor calls them."

She wanted to check his self-defense story. "Sounds like you scared off your attacker."

"Yes. He run away. I elbow him in head and face and kick him in 'nuts,' you say. I also bite him on hands."

"Did you get a good look at him?"

"Not so good. He is younger than me, tall, short hair. Big forehead. Funny thing, he look like people in Old Country."

Ah. Were some ships finally crossing? "I have some questions for you, if you're up to it."

"Yes, yes."

"Would you be able to recognize him if we showed you a photo?"

"Maybe. It is dark. I do not see one hundred percent."

"Did he speak?"

"No. He grunt with pain. I kick him hard," Zupan impassively said. "He does not know correct man-to-man. Does not protect groin. I am older but I beat him quickly. Is easy fight."

"Did you hear any cars?"

"No."

"Did you tell Detective Patel about him?"

"Yes, I tell. They are searching grounds. I hear her say into phone to examine path to beach. They think attacker took boat to wharf near house and walk to house."

Bourque changed tack. "Did you find the names of the Slovenian couple who just arrived in the country?"

"No. I am waiting for news."

"Let me know as soon as you hear. In the meantime, get some rest."

"Snežana is coming. She will bring good food."

"Okay. Sleep well." Bourque didn't tell him his sister would be barred from his hospital room, as would her food.

Walking to District A-1 with Eller, Bourque tried to think things through. Was Zupan clean, or had he staged his assault, broken his elbow and attacked his own neck? She couldn't set her mind. *Always*, she ruefully reflected, *always*. There were two sides to every POI until a case was closed. Assumptions of innocence were as useless as assumptions of guilt. She switched to Snežana. Was she clean, was she involved without Zupan's knowledge, or was she working with him? Bourque shook her head. She couldn't nail anything down. Nothing could be taken at face value. The detective's curse. On top of that, the assault had opened a new front. HQ would have their hands full safeguarding the Cape and executing an APB. Their support for the murder investigation would be on the back burner.

□ □ □

Two hours later, Bourque and Eller were back at Dunkin', Atlas's cold coffee on the table between them. His lawyer and girlfriend, Amber Luu, had succeeded in releasing him, claiming her client had been cooperative and didn't warrant detainment. He was discharged with the proviso the State Police could question him at Luu's office. The interview would be conducted at 0800 that day.

Bourque took a sip of coffee. They'd submitted an updated warrant for Atlas's phone conversations with enhanced probable cause: the castle keys, the foreknowledge of the butler's location, and the assault. The Judge had thrown the warrant out: too speculative. Ditto for one requesting access to Atlas's condo security footage.

Re Atlas's tail, the surveillance team hadn't turned up anything. Other than eating dinner alone at Strega, Atlas hadn't gone anywhere the last two days. It was almost as if he knew they were watching him. Their ammo contained as many duds as live rounds. Atlas stood to gain financially. Hence, there was potential motive. Opportunity was another matter. They couldn't place him at the crime scene. They had no footage of him on May 13th or 14th. Amber Luu had just claimed Atlas was present when she'd arrived at his condo at 0700 on May 14th.

If her assertion stood, Atlas would have had to leave the crime scene well before 0600 to be in Boston at 0700. Conceivably, a man who didn't want to bring attention to himself wouldn't be speeding.

Bourque's mind buzzed. Hadn't the ninjas noted a castle alarm breach? Pulling out her phone, she opened the case notes app and saw an alarm wire had been cut at 0622 on the day of the murders. If Atlas was at his Boston condo at 0700, the Falmouth alarm couldn't have been breached by him. It wasn't possible to get from

Falmouth to Boston in thirty-eight minutes. Of course, he might still be in the picture—a distant accomplice, a planner not a doer.

She glanced at Eller. His back was rigid. He looked out of sorts, definitely more on edge than yesterday. It was standard practice to push suspicious POIs, but if you pushed with bad ammo, they could shut down and jeopardize an investigation.

She exhaled loudly. *Clean the slate.* To be a good detective, she needed to see everything, but overlook the unimportant. A short break would be good. She and Marty, a one-night camping trip. Somewhere close. The Berkshires: fresh air and starry skies.

Eller interrupted her thoughts. "Bourque, are you with us?"

She glanced at her watch. Time to go. Time for Atlas to face the music. Or for them to face it. She couldn't shake her pessimism.

□ □ □

The plaque on the door said *Amber Luu and Associates*. Luu's Boylston Street office sat two blocks from the hallowed core of Boston: Old South Church. As the detectives followed Luu down a wide corridor, Bourque counted six suites, high-ceilinged rooms of gleaming wood and exposed brick. The principal partner was dressed in a dark blue power suit with matching pumps. Bourque pegged her at thirty, older than Atlas. Her raven-black hair was impeccably cut. Her face was expressive; her eyes, perceptive. Entering Luu's suite, the detectives found Atlas Novak sitting in a deep leather armchair. He didn't stand.

"Take a seat," Luu told the detectives and sat behind a smoked-glass desk, crossing one well-muscled leg over the other. "Let me make something clear, officers. I'm a trial lawyer. I may be young," she casually said, "but I know all the tricks. By the way, I'm Vietnamese, not Chinese. I find most police officers don't spend a lot of time parsing the difference. They should. Let me make something else clear. As befitting my racial stereotype—" She stopped and smiled evenly. "—away from court, I'm usually polite and accommodating, even shy. But not in this case. You've been railroading my client. If you play any more games, among other things, I'll bring in the press. I'll make the State Police look like *buffoons*."

When she emphasized the word, Bourque recalled Eller's jab at Atlas about law buffoons. Luu had done her homework. Her threat wasn't empty. Amber Luu and Associates had a fiery reputation. Although Central had controlled the press so far, Luu could blow that wide open.

"My client is very busy," Luu continued. "You have fifteen minutes to question him."

Eller shook his head. "We have as long as we need."

"No, Lieutenant, you don't." She slid a document across her desk. "I lodged a protest. Judge Emerson Cameron agreed with it. You've ignored *praesumptio innocentiae*. Unless you have a case against my client—that is, unless you charge him for the murders of Rollo Novak and/or Katrina Novak, or actions related to said murders— you do not have a right to interrogate him further about that case. He already spoke with you willingly. Twice."

Eller nodded grudgingly.

"I'm allowing you fifteen minutes. After that, you'll need a warrant." She waved officiously. "Time starts *now*."

"Fifteen minutes?"

"*Now*," she repeated.

Bourque glanced at Eller. He was about to challenge Luu. However, he thought better of it. Good, Bourque said to herself. Time was ticking.

"I have a question for you, Counsel Luu. You claim you arrived at Mr. Atlas Novak's condo at seven a.m. on Monday, May fourteenth. Do you have proof?"

"Of course. I anticipated your question." She gestured to a large screen on the near wall. "In a moment, you'll view a security footage tape. I understand you haven't seen it." She smiled insincerely. "Sorry to hear your subpoena fell short. Again."

Eller's jaw muscles bulged. Bourque had observed it on other cases. He was struggling to keep his mouth shut.

Luu pointed at the screen. "Momentarily, you'll see me arriving at just after seven a.m. Time stamp is in the lower right corner."

Eller viewed the tape. "Can you verify the location?"

Luu pushed two sheets of paper across her desk.

While Eller examined the documents, Bourque skimmed them. The first was a signed deposition from the Management Office at Atlas's condo stating the security tape was valid. The second was an enlarged still of the image on the screen. The timestamp was easily readable: 0701.

"I have something else to show you," Luu stated. "Footage of my client coming down in the elevator to greet me that morning. At exactly three minutes after seven. Would you like to see it?"

"Yes," Eller blithely replied.

The clock, Bourque thought. They had eight minutes left.

Luu took her time finding the footage in question and displaying it on the screen. It verified her assertion.

"Very good," Eller said and smiled. "How much did you pay the Management Office?"

"I'll pretend I didn't hear that."

"Just like the Management Office is pretending that's an official tape."

Atlas seemed to suddenly awaken. "That's tantamount to libel," he cried. "You're saying they doctored the tape."

Luu eyed him sternly. *Sit back.* Atlas did so. "You're wrong, Lieutenant. However, you're welcome to speak to Judge Cameron. My documents are unassailable."

"If you say so." Eller turned to Atlas. "I understand you inherited all of your father's properties. That's why you killed him."

"Lieutenant," Luu warned. *"Praesumptio innocentiae."*

Eller smiled. *Game on.* "Admit it," he prodded Atlas.

Luu cleared her throat and addressed Eller. "Another remark like that and this interview will be terminated. Furthermore, you'll be charged." Luu turned to her client. "Ignore him."

Atlas hung his head.

Eller regarded Luu. "I suggest you let Mr. Novak speak for himself."

Luu appeared to be considering the request.

Eller didn't wait. "Mr. Novak, you'll make approximately eighty million dollars a year if you rent your properties. Is that your intention?"

When Atlas opened his mouth to reply, Luu cut him off. "That's immaterial."

Bourque studied Luu. She obviously wore the pants. Was she the mind behind the murders? Had she used Atlas to get at Novak's money? Maybe she was the queen bee and Atlas the worker. He knew the castle and he had keys.

Eller shook his head. "Incorrect, Counsel Luu, it is anything but immaterial. Eighty million is, let's say, a tidy sum. Extremely useful capital to launch other enterprises."

Luu examined Eller as if he were an alien lifeform. "Let me see if I can read your mind, or whatever you might call it." She glanced at the clock and smiled tartly. "But that could take years. We only have minutes. For your benefit, Lieutenant, I'll be succinct. I take it you're suggesting someone—*not* my client—killed his beloved father to get eighty million a year and a one-time bequest of twenty-five million."

"No. I'm suggesting someone killed his father for *two billion* dollars. Multiply eighty million by twenty-five, as in twenty-five years, and you get two billion."

"Your math is correct, but not your logic. Why would someone wait for things to materialize over twenty-five years when they can work, honestly and hard, and make over three hundred million a year, which is what someone's ventures will realize this year. In other words, why kill for eighty million a year when you already make three hundred million? Let's dispense with the charades. My client, Atlas Novak, is hard-working and ambitious, not greedy. Now, consider your psychological premise. How can you say my client expected anything? As I'm sure a judge would rule, you don't know his state of mind."

"Is that right?" Eller turned to Bourque. "Any questions?"

She regarded Atlas serenely. "Mr. Novak, let's start again. Perhaps you can tell us exactly when you were inside your condo on Sunday, May thirteenth."

Atlas glanced at Luu.

Luu signaled to her client. *Go ahead.*

"I was there all day," Atlas said, "except for when I went out to dinner, from nine p.m. until eleven-fifteen p.m. Give or take five minutes."

"What about Monday, May fourteenth?"

"All day with the exception of about half an hour. After breakfast Amber and I went for a walk. We left about nine-thirty and were back before ten a.m."

"Did you ever leave the condo after you returned with Counsel Luu?"

"No, I didn't. We didn't. Branka served us lunch and provided us with dinner. We heated it up about eight p.m."

"Can Branka verify that?"

"Yes. The food, but not when we ate dinner. She finishes work at four."

Bourque scrutinized him. She'd pegged him as an over-confident silver-spooner. She could be wrong. He looked tired and dispirited. She turned to Luu. "Were you with Atlas Novak all day Monday, May fourteenth?"

"Yes." Luu pointed at the clock. "By the way, your time is almost up."

"Agreed. Just a few more questions, Counsel."

Luu nodded graciously. "Continue."

"What about your work?" Bourque asked.

"I worked from Mr. Novak's condo. I was preparing a case."

"For him?" *As in a murder defense.*

"No. A *pro bono* client. The Trillium Cancer Hospice. I help organize their charity events."

"Did you meet with anyone from the hospice that day?"

"I don't book anyone on Mondays." She glanced at Atlas and beamed. "It's our day."

Real love birds? Bourque wondered. Time to switch gears. "Did you know Atlas Novak was going to inherit twenty-five million dollars?"

"Yes. I helped Rollo Novak shape his will."

"Did you *shape* the codicil that allows your client to keep the Novak properties and rent them if he chooses?"

"No. I wasn't involved in that. I'm not a property lawyer."

"Did you shape the corporate motion that now makes your client the CEO of Novak Enterprises?"

"No. Rollo Novak did."

"When?"

"Ask my client."

Bourque turned to Atlas. "When did your father appoint you to succeed him?"

"Three years ago. When I turned twenty-one."

Eller butted in. "We need proof." He sneered. "*Unassailable* proof."

Luu paid him no heed. She addressed Bourque. "I'll provide the documents you require."

Bourque nodded. "Do you have footage of you and your client leaving his condo at nine-thirty a.m. on May fourteenth and returning at roughly ten a.m.?"

"No, but I can provide it."

"Email it to me," Bourque said, "plus the two videos you showed us."

"Of course. One more thing, officers, a personal thing. Rollo Novak was a guiding light to me. He knew what was right, and he did what was right." Luu's eyes softened. "He'd wanted a Slovenian daughter-in-law but he accepted me even though I was Vietnamese, the last daughter of lowly boat people. Among other things, he showed me that money wasn't everything. He didn't want it for the sake of having it. He wanted it to help other people."

"How so?" Eller abruptly asked.

"In many ways, Lieutenant." She smiled coolly. "Ways even you could see. He used money to make lives better, although it wasn't what made his life better. To him, that was the paradox of money. It was powerful but secondary."

Saint Rollo, Bourque thought. She stood. "We'll show ourselves out."

Chapter 23

As Eller left Luu's building, he slammed the door. Bourque didn't flinch. She'd seen the outrage in his face, something she hadn't witnessed before. In retrospect, however, she had seen a change coming. For the last day or so, Eller had seemed to be fighting a growing internal pressure.

Now he strode along Boylston Street, marching past Old South Church like an avenging angel. She had a hard time keeping up to him. He stopped a block later. She could tell he was still fuming.

"They paid the management office," he ranted. "I know it."

She said nothing. There was nothing to be said.

"They paid, didn't they?"

She started walking again.

Eller easily matched her stride. "*Speak to Judge Cameron,*" he mimicked Luu. "*My documents are unassailable.* Unassailable, my ass. More like underhanded."

Bourque didn't look at him. Let him vent.

"Useless subpoena system," he seethed. "Effin' molasses moves faster. Can't get a fuckin' warrant unless you have a smoking gun. And when a case doesn't involve firearms, they don't know what to do."

She swallowed her retort. Eller had jumped the gun—and smoked *them*. They shouldn't have gone after Atlas without first examining his phone conversations and the security camera footage. Sometimes you prevailed, sometimes you failed. In any case, in the grand scheme of things, Eller's move was a small setback. It wouldn't derail the case.

She slowed her pace and let him rage ahead. As she strolled, her heartbeat stabilized. She'd watched Atlas during the whole interview, rigorously assessing what she was witnessing. She had to trust what she saw, not what she hoped to see. While Atlas might be guilty of greed or the expectation of a huge inheritance, she'd seen no indication he had any part in the killings. There was no doubt Luu was tough, yet it didn't mean she was predatory. She was straightforward. Even discounting her admiration for Novak, Bourque could see why he'd dealt with her. Just as he'd dealt with and trusted Vega. Which left Zupan and possibly his sister. It was easy to fake an attack, but not successfully. Bourque would scrutinize Zupan's wounds at Falmouth Hospital.

She caught a glimpse of Eller two blocks ahead. Still furious. She suspected his internal pressure could be due to a family matter—not something he usually talked about. Then again, it could stem from his sense of self. He had a high solve rate to maintain and the case was currently stalled. Regardless, in her view, the team's position wasn't all bad. Although they hadn't found the building blocks of the murders, they'd dropped three POIs to the bottom of the suspect pile. Atlas looked clean, as did Luu and Vega.

A few minutes later, Bourque reached Eller. He was standing next to a mailbox, looking sheepish.

"I broke a few eggs back there," he said.

She shrugged.

"And didn't make an omelet," he added. "I was wrong to push Atlas."

She played it down. "You tried."

"No, I failed. It's embarrassing."

"You saw something, you went for it." He shouldn't be embarrassed. In time, she might have done the same thing herself.

"How do you keep your cool, Bourque? You never boil over."

"I boil inside."

"No, really, how do you do it?"

"Well."

"Tell me."

This could get tricky. Some people didn't really want to know. She wasn't sure about Eller. "I try to stay on an even keel," she began. "No expectations, no preconceptions."

He nodded, his eyes saying *keep going*.

She felt she'd said enough. Besides, there was little more to say. He was still eyeing her.

"Don't let POIs get to you."

"I don't." He shrugged. "Usually."

"Cut out the sneers." She smiled to soften the blow, to show she was on his side.

"Understood."

"You want to talk about anything?"

He shook his head. "Listen, I just got a call about Gene Cantor.

He's at home in Revere. I'll be at Metro HQ all day. Can you re-interview Biotech Boy?"

□ □ □

Cantor's "home" was a repurposed two-car garage. The attached house, a 1960's bungalow, hadn't been painted in decades. The lawn hadn't been mowed since last fall. However, the property was pleasant enough, a large lot with shade trees and tall hedges. The morning was indolent, with enough heat in the air to make summer feel imminent. The sky looked like old denim: deep blue faded to white. Bourque had barely driven ten miles, yet Revere seemed a long way from downtown Boston.

Cantor had been deemed low-risk for violence but she had backup across the street—two State Police detectives in a ghost car. Per procedure, she parked behind Cantor's BMW SUV and boxed him in. Despite his money problems, he still had a high-end vehicle.

Cantor answered the garage-side door on the first knock. He looked like an athlete, not a down in the dumps lab scientist. Late thirties, over six-feet tall, broad shoulders, a chin cleft from central casting. His skin was deeply tanned, like someone who'd recently returned from a beach holiday. Poor wouldn't keep women away from this guy. Those shoulders, that chin cleft. He wore cargo shorts and a sleeveless T-shirt. Not what she was expecting. Ditch the preconceptions, she told herself.

"Detective Lieutenant Bourque, State Police," she said.

"Come in, Lieutenant. Nice to meet you." He sounded overly sincere, as if he were trying to snow her.

She stepped inside. Cantor waved her to one of two kitchen chairs. Though he was tall and dark-haired, he didn't have any head injuries or hand bites. He wasn't likely Zupan's assailant. The unit had a kitchenette, desk, TV, and bed—and nothing more. It was excessively neat, as boats and cramped spaces often were. It smelled of bleach. Wrong, she decided, a stronger cleanser, the sort used to sterilize labs or remove bloodstains.

Although there hadn't been much blood at the crime scene, her antennae went up. There was another possible red flag: *excessively neat*. Hayden's strangler had twisted the ends of the wire around her neck with extreme neatness. Bourque surreptitiously shifted her holster, making her handgun easier to access. "I have a few questions about BioCell," she said and turned on her phone recorder.

"What do you want to know?"

"The whole truth, and nothing but the truth. Why did you sue Karlos Vega and Rollo Novak?"

Cantor looked away.

"Why?" she repeated.

"It was a mistake." He sounded both resigned and annoyed. "I won't ever seek venture capital again. You can't trust the bastards."

"Bastards?"

"Pardon me, the *Paragons of Capital*."

She scrutinized him, allowing the seconds to slowly tick past before speaking. "You haven't told me why you did it."

"Did what?"

"Sued Vega and Novak."

"I told a detective yesterday."

"But not me."

Cantor had started sweating. Two trickles ran down his neck. It was partly the overheated garage and partly, Bourque knew, because she made him nervous.

"It's all in the past," he said. "I made some bad decisions. Both business and personal. I lost everything."

"You're avoiding my question. Why did you sue?"

"I was angry," he eventually admitted.

"Was?"

"Yes, *was*. I don't hold grudges. I'm not a fighter."

She took that with a grain. He'd started a legal battle. "What about a killer?" she asked.

"Lieutenant."

"Answer the question."

"I'm not a killer."

"Do you know any killers?"

He shook his head.

Lies didn't come out at first blush. "How many hitmen do you know?"

"Lieutenant."

Most people couldn't maintain a lie. On the third or fourth prod, they often broke. She figured Cantor might. "How many?"

"None." He stared her in the eye.

She still didn't trust him. She'd noted his thick, muscular fingers.

Although he was a lab scientist, he didn't have refined, lab-scientist hands. Or shoulders. His body spoke of power, not dexterity. She looked down to make a note on her phone.

A second later, Cantor shot past her.

She jumped up and lunged for him. Too late. He was gone. The door slammed shut.

"POI running!" she barked into her two-way radio.

Pulling out her gun, she raced to the door and yanked on the knob. It was stuck. After fiddling with it, it finally gave. She stepped into the driveway. No sign of Cantor. The two backup detectives were running her way, one pointing to an alley leading toward North Shore Road.

Bourque signaled for the other detective to follow him, ran across the lawn and crashed through a hedge. Hoping to catch Cantor in a pincer, she sprinted to the sidewalk.

A car was barreling down the street. She held her hand up to stop it—I said *stop, you fool*—crossed the street and sped south, scanning the area as she ran. A low-rise neighborhood, mostly bungalows. Good visibility. No high fences. With luck, she'd intercept Cantor before he slipped away or reached North Shore Road, a busy thoroughfare.

When she hit the pincer's east-west street, she raced to the corner of the alley, knelt, and peered around an old garage. All she saw was two detectives running her way, no Cantor caught in a pincer. She stood, motioned for one of the detectives to head west and waved the other one to her. When he reached her, she spoke calmly. "Cantor could ram my car and drive off. Get to the house. Call for assistance and APB him. Consider him dangerous," she added.

Running east, she scanned left and right. Her head was pounding more than her heart. She'd let a POI escape, a POI in a homicide case. She ran as fast as she could, fit from years of playing ice hockey. At the next intersection, there was no POI in sight. Keep running, she told herself, close the pincer.

Two minutes later, she heard the first squad-car siren, then two more in short order. Revere was doing its part. She reached the next intersection. Still no Cantor.

□   □   □

Just before 1000, Bourque was sitting in her car in Cantor's driveway. She hadn't done enough. In fact, she'd failed. While Cantor's vehicle was still there, he'd eluded them. She felt terrible. Due to her failure, the team had another APB on the books. In comparison, Eller pushing Atlas was a minor mistake. She'd let a high-profile POI get away, possibly a murderer.

She exhaled slowly. It was unforgiveable. Admittedly, Cantor was fast and he'd caught her off guard, but that was no excuse. You didn't let POIs catch you off guard, especially in a homicide case. Then there was the doorknob. It had taken her far too long to open it.

To add insult to injury, on top of the blow to her pride, she'd cut her face going through the hedge near Cantor's garage. Tilting her rearview mirror down, she examined the cut, a two-inch gash across her right cheek. It didn't need stitches, but it looked angry. As she was dabbing antiseptic cream on it, she heard boots approaching her open car window.

"You run into Jack?" a male Revere officer asked.

"Jack?" she said.

"The Ripper." He snorted and stood back to let his buddies see her face.

Smiling sweetly, she pitched a two-day-old muffin bottom at his nose—the hockey puck variety, harder than frozen lard. Still smiling, she started her car and tore out of the driveway. So much for keeping an even keel. She knew not to give cretin-cops any satisfaction, but she couldn't help herself. It was that kind of morning.

"Say hello to *Jack*," the cop called.

She zipped her lips and kept driving. The gash on her left cheek was stinging now. She figured it'd throb for a day or so, which was good. It was a reminder not to let any POI surprise her.

Chapter 24

Barnstable

Bourque stopped at her favorite takeout in Bourne for chicken Kung Pao. Under the noonday sun, couples were strolling in a nearby park. The grass was emerald green. A stiff breeze chased spinnakering clouds across the sky. Two sailboats were heading offshore. The whiteness of their sails deepened the blue of the sky.

She immediately felt better. The Revere cretin-cop was history. Her mistakes were history too. HQ had issued a top-tier APB for Cantor. She'd let the manhunters handle him and focus on the case. In her eyes, she was like a hockey player who'd missed the net on a penalty shot. She had to forget it and move on.

Sitting at a picnic table, she dug into her Kung Pao. It was a beautiful day: seventy degrees, the sun strengthening by the minute. The park's lilacs were blooming, presaging the promise of real heat, instead of the hoped-for-heat New Englanders cultivated in their dreams all winter. The warmth was welcome; the spicy chicken, more welcome. But she wasn't really savoring it. Her mind kept turning the case over. Thinking of Atlas's security footage videos, she checked her duty phone. Luu had delivered.

Chicken finished, Bourque called E-Forensics in Maynard.

"Lieutenant Connie Dagleish," a gruff voice answered.

"Morning, Dagleish." AKA Lieutenant Daggers. "Detective Bourque, Cape & Islands."

"Yes?"

"Got three videos. I need to know if they've been doctored."

"Send 'em in," Daggers curtly ordered.

"When will they be done?"

"I'll call you."

"When?"

"A day or two."

"Thanks."

"Glad to be of service."

Glad? Service? That wasn't Dagleish. *You're lucky you're working with Captain Peabody* was closer to the truth.

□ □ □

Despite her stop, Bourque arrived in Falmouth before 1300. When the roads were clear, she overlooked speed limits. There were so many other protocols she had to follow. Driving like an old maid shouldn't be one of them. She knew her undercover work had affected her. She was critical of rigid authority, believing people should make their own decisions, not always, but most of the time—the exact opposite of what the Old Guard wanted. In their view, uncontrolled decisions resulted in chaos, which made her appreciate her undercover boss all the more. When she'd started in the narc squad, he gave her one simple rule: You can buy drugs, you can use them to play a part, but you can't ever sell them. An easy rule to follow.

Upon returning from Boston to her place on Fox Lane in West Falmouth, Bourque often felt she was far from "civilization," as if she'd travelled to Cuttyhunk Island, population fifty-four, the outermost of the Elizabeth Islands. In the city, the air had been humid. As Marty told anyone who'd listen, the planet's city dwellers now outnumbered the non-urbanites. Though Boston was a benign city, it was too urban for his taste. Her's too. In Falmouth, the air was clean and refreshing. Driving past Old Silver Beach, she saw the sun shimmering on the water, which was shimmering back at the sun. Fox Lane was exactly what she wanted. It was out-of-the-way without being isolated. She savored the slow rotation of the seasons. She appreciated neighbors like Cal. They actually liked cops. She stopped just long enough to water two freshly planted dogwoods and change into clean clothes.

Leaving her house behind, Bourque drove to Falmouth Hospital. In the parking lot, she spotted a ghost van nearby, one of HQ's fleet. Civilians wouldn't recognize it, but she did.

Zupan's room was in the hospital's quietest area, a small side wing. A pair of fully armed troopers from Special Tactics and Operations, aka the STOP SWAT unit, secured the wing. Donnelly stood sentinel outside the butler's room. She gestured inside. "He all right?"

"Oh yeah." Donnelly winked. "A butler in bed is better than a butler dead."

She smiled wryly. As usual, Donnelly couldn't contain his

witticisms.

"The sister's waiting in the cafeteria. She's quite the charmer. Don't worry, no one let her in."

Bourque nodded. She'd received an update on Zupan and Snežana. The siblings had clean local sheets: no speeding, no traffic violations, no misdemeanors. Gronski hadn't found any international anomalies. Before coming to Boston, Snežana had worked for a pharma multinational in South England.

Donnelly spoke softly. "You know what her name means in English? She told me. *Snow White*." He chuckled. "If we need more guards, you can call the seven dwarfs."

"We could always use another Happy."

"At least one." Donnelly gestured at her cheek. "Rogue fencing lesson?"

"Ran into a fence. Well, a hedge."

"They grow fast."

"Sure do."

She signed in and entered Zupan's room. It smelled of sour milk.

"How's things?" she asked, carefully evaluating his injuries. Other than a cast on his right arm and a deep mark around his neck below his Adam's apple, he looked the same. His hair was perfectly combed.

"Fine." He grinned broadly.

"Are you in pain?"

"Some. Neck is stiff. More pain there now."

Always true, she knew. After the adrenaline rush wore off and the body took an inventory of its injuries, the pain intensified. Good thing. It shut people down and allowed them to heal. "Are they giving you enough medication?"

He smiled and pointed to an IV drip.

She saw he'd taken note of her cheek gash. Being reticent, or polite, he didn't comment. "Do you need anything?" she asked.

"Yes, please. Rye bread. They won't let my sister in. They say I am under witness protection. Protection from my sister?"

"From everyone."

"You are barking up wrong tree again."

"That's the system."

"It barks a lot."

"Only when we're not sure."

"Can you get dark rye? They sell at big food store in Falmouth."

"Of course."

□ □ □

Entering the hospital cafeteria, Bourque immediately saw a woman who had Zupan's eyes. Her hair was long, black, and lustrous; her skin, porcelain smooth. She wore a belted powder-blue coat cinched at the waist, which accentuated her bust.

Bourque approached her table. "Snežana Zupan?"

"Yes."

"Detective Bourque, State Police."

"Can I see my brother?"

"Not yet," Bourque replied. "However, I assure you, he's safe."

"Who attacked him?"

"The investigation is ongoing. Don't worry, he's fine."

Snežana nodded. "My brother's a strong man." Her accent was noticeably British.

To Bourque's ear, she sounded like Nigella Lawson. Come to think of it, she looked like her too. Bourque sat across from Snežana. She didn't own a car but Bourque wanted to see if she'd rented one. "How was your drive here?"

"A friend drove me. Jonathan Clarke."

"Tell me about him."

"He's handsome, he's single." Snežana's eyes sparkled. "He's a Boston banker. I got my license last year but I don't like driving. Men want to drive." She unleashed a radiant smile. "I let them."

"Where's Mr. Clarke?"

"Gone to get some wine."

"How was your holiday?"

"Wonderful. Time flew. It felt like one day, not five."

"Do you have a man over there?"

Snežana winked conspiratorially. "One or two."

"Where were you last night?"

Snežana's demeanor didn't change. Her face remained open. "At Jonathan's house in Melrose."

"Where were you on Monday May fourteenth at seven a.m.?"

She thought for a moment. "My apartment in Cambridge."

"Can someone verify that?"

"Yes, Jonathan."

"When did you leave for Logan Airport that day?"

"Eight-thirty."

"Was anyone with you from seven to eight-thirty?"

"Jonathan was. He drove me to the airport. My friend Miroslav picked me up at the other end, in Ljubljana." She smiled coyly. "Like I said, I don't like driving."

"Did Miroslav drive you back to Ljubljana airport?"

"Oh no. Tristan did."

"How many 'drivers' do you have?"

She grinned. "Many, but not enough."

"Did you go 'driving' with Rollo Novak?"

"Of course not!" She shook her head. "I should be offended but I'm not. You're a police officer. You have to ask."

"Do you have any insights for us about the Novaks?"

"Maybe. Rollo was much more serious than Katrina. I didn't see them fight but they disagreed a lot, mostly about money." She sighed. "He said the world was becoming too prosperous. In his view, humans consume far too much. We're succumbing to prosperity. Katrina didn't agree."

"What do you think?"

"I see what Rollo meant. But," she acknowledged, "I love good company, I love parties."

"You're like Katrina."

"In some ways."

"How do you get to work?"

"I walk. It's perfect. It only takes ten minutes."

Bourque recalled what Zupan had told her about walking. The siblings were in accord on that. "Who pays your rent?"

"I do. However, I admit, men pay for many things. If they want to, as I said, I let them—if I like them."

Bourque nodded. Why not? To each, her own. "What else can you tell us about the Novaks?"

Snežana sighed again. "Katrina was very beautiful, and far more driven than I am." She shook her head sadly. "More troubled too. She wanted to be with Rollo, and yet she didn't. After a few months, I could see that. After a year, she didn't try to hide it from me. To her, Rollo's houses were like prisons, dead even in the heat of a party, even when full of life. He was obsessed with ideas. She wanted to be more than an idea." Snežana held Bourque's gaze. "I don't know if this makes sense to you. They were cheerful together, but unhappy."

Shades of Vega's story. "Do you think Rollo killed her?"

"Killed her? Not a chance. They had an imperfect love, but it was a love."

"Please, continue."

"In a sense, they were doomed. They seemed to be very close at times but you could see they wouldn't be a long-lived couple. In Slovenia, the Old Ones would say their end was fated."

□   □   □

After leaving the cafeteria, Bourque walked quickly to Zupan's room. In her estimation, Snežana was off the hook. If Bourque was wrong, she'd wear it. That was the job. You made snap decisions and you lived with them.

"Back already," Donnelly noted.

"Got some alibis to check but Snow White looks clean."

"As pure as driven snow?"

"You could say that. However, she's still on the no-go list."

"Her?"

"For now." It appeared many men, even policemen, were susceptible to Snežana's charms.

Sitting next to Zupan, Bourque faced the butler directly. "Does your sister have a lot of men friends?"

"I think so. She likes men."

"Did she flirt—do you know the word?"

"I know word."

"Did she flirt with Mr. Novak?"

"Never! Snežana is friends with Šef and wife. Friends, that is it."

"Tell me about the attack in your suite."

"I am usually light sleeper. I do not hear door open, but suddenly I hear steps next to me. Floor, it creaks. Then I feel cord around neck."

She scrutinized his neck mark as he spoke. It was a deep imprint, very excessive if self-inflicted. "What did you do then?" she asked.

"I pull cord away with both hands and bite attacker's hands. When he let go cord, I elbow him three or four times. Then I kick him. He back away, then run. Even after kicking him, he is fast."

"Did you follow him?"

"Yes, but I am not good runner. He escape."

She decided to trust Zupan. In her view, he wasn't faking the attack. She'd recently learned the possibility of him sedating Novak was zero. Although the date-rape drug ketamine was found in Katrina Hayden's body, no tranquillizer was found in Novak's. "I'm glad you're okay," she said. "It could have been bad for you."

"Bad for attack man, not me."

"This time. You could have been killed."

Zupan shrugged nonchalantly. "No, not possible. Most people, they do not know how to fight."

"But."

"I am survivor. In Sarajevo, I am close to death many times."

She nodded. She didn't fear death itself—carbon to carbon—but she wasn't looking forward to facing it. Though the end rarely took more than minutes, they were long, long minutes. To fight death. To grudgingly accept it, or not. Her cover had been blown twice during her years as an undercover agent. Blown identities were usually fatal, but she'd escaped. Feeling she had two strikes against her, she'd made peace with death. When the third strike came, she didn't want any theatrics, just her ashes sprinkled off the Aquinnah Cliffs on Martha's Vineyard. From blue sky to blue water.

"Do not worry, Lieutenant. I am fine."

"Good." Some days, like today, she felt the fragility of life. She hadn't felt it in her twenties working dangerous assignments undercover, but now, in her late thirties, death was starting to roost. She'd seen too many murder victims to slough it off.

"You will catch attacker," Zupan confidently stated.

She nodded assuredly, although she was far from sure. Unfortunately, an APB didn't guarantee quick results; it didn't even guarantee results. These days, perps knew how to disappear. So far, the APB for Zupan's assailant had drawn blanks. To date, all the roadblocks and surveillance points were unsuccessful. She switched gears. "Can you talk about the young Slovenian couple who recently arrived in Boston?"

"Yes, yes. I just get news. I think couple are, you say, pertinent to case."

She gestured for him to continue.

"It is said they leave Slovenia with help of Albanian gang."

"Who said that?"

"Many Old Country people say this."

"And you?"

"I have not talked to couple. I cannot say."

She nodded. She'd get Tom Gronski to check them out. She'd

always sensed the case had an Old Country connection. This could be it. "Do you know their names?"

"Yes. Tomaz and Marta Ravlic. Be aware, spelling is not American. I send you email."

"Thank you."

"Lieutenant, my feeling is different now. I think maybe Old Country people kill Mr. and Mrs. Rollo."

Mrs., Bourque noted. The butler had promoted Hayden.

"When I leave from hospital, I will help you."

She shook her head gently. "It's a police issue, Mr. Zupan. I'm sure you understand. No civilians."

He nodded with acceptance. "Please call me for anything."

"We certainly will. We appreciate your help."

Chapter 25

Outside the hospital, Bourque considered going to Marty's place. La dolce vita. She wanted to see him so badly. His dolphin grin, his tousled hair. His long, strong arms. Starting her car, she told herself to forget it. Not a chance. Peabody had charged her with overseeing the scheduling of the Hayden POI interviews.

In lieu of a "visit," she called Marty.

"It's your long-lost detective," she said when he answered.

"Hey, you back from Gotham North?"

"Finally. What's up?"

"Got a four-thousand-word article on the burner. The history of lumbering in Massachusetts."

"Four thousand? Try six. They came, they cut, they overcut."

He laughed. "I have a surprise for you. A whopping sea trout. Went out early this morning with Ken. I hear there'll be a party tonight. You and me and a baked ichthus."

"A what?"

"Fish."

She grinned inwardly. Good thing she liked wordy guys. "And how will that be prepared, chef?"

"With two exotic New England spices."

"Salt and pepper?"

"*Oui, exactement.* Ah, just for the hell-of-it, I'll add fresh thyme, lemon, and capers, and dish *ichthus* with rosemary-roasted potatoes."

"Chill the wine."

"Already done."

When the case was over, when she got home before dark for a change, she'd cook for him. Maybe a cioppino, maybe a fettucine alfredo, definitely a bottle of wine.

□ □ □

At Barnstable Unit, Bourque found Landon's eyeballs "chained to a screen," as he frequently said. She nodded hello. "How's the list that keeps giving?"

"Giving me a headache," he said.

No surprise. "How're you doing with the bookings?"

"About ninety percent done."

"Excellent," she enthused. She could move on. She hadn't yet worked her way through the material from Novak's secret desk. She needed to clone herself. As usual, interviews and meetings had been taking precedence over research.

Landon eyed her appraisingly. "I heard a POI got away. No biggie. It happens."

She nodded. Damn, who didn't know? The State Police grapevine was bigger than Jack's beanstalk. Jack again, she realized. Damn Jack. "Any interviews complete?" she asked.

"Twenty-four. No useful leads yet. All that work and not a sniff."

She nodded. Par for the course. POI Number Ninety-two would probably be the best lead. Murphy's Law of Detection: *Whatever's really useful will remain hidden until the end.*

"We did have one sighting," Landon admitted.

"Share."

"Hayden was spotted at Boston's Faneuil Hall the day before she was murdered. She was wearing pink tights. They looked great. That's the best intel I have."

Bourque shrugged. "They say the worst thing you can have is early success."

He looked at her dubiously.

"You get lazy. You have no persistence."

"Really?"

"You don't learn anything new."

"Are you done?"

She chuckled to herself and navigated to the Novaks Case notes. Only one entry since 0830, an update from Abbot. None of Atlas's unlisted numbers were connected to criminality. It would have been good to know that before they went at him.

Walking to the evidence locker, she checked her personal messages, saw one from Cal Knowlton and phoned her neighbor. "Lieutenant Bourque here. How's my old friend?"

"You calling me old?"

"No. I'm calling you a friend."

"Okay then. I might have a break for you. Can you meet me at my office?"

"Sure." She signed off and sighed. Another meeting. Research interruptus. The backlog that never died, yet she couldn't complain about it. There were three Ds: ditch it, delegate it, do it yourself. If she didn't use the first two, it was her fault. She wanted to dig into the desk material herself.

□ □ □

Bourque located Cal sitting at his usual table in Collard's Coffee House. She took a quick glance around. Being mid-afternoon, the place was almost empty. Cal looked particularly dapper. He wore a blue captain's blazer and navy-and-gold ascot. His white hair was short and spiky. "Looking good," she said.

"Just got a buzzcut. The Buzz Aldrin, aka the *Moonwalk Special.*" He patted his head. "Bristly and virile. I feel like a randy boar."

"You lucky man."

"My default mode." He grinned. "Nasty cut," he noted, assessing her cheek gash.

She shrugged.

He nodded considerately and moved on. "I wanted to speak face-to-face, like old-timers. You know I love to talk," he said, underlying the obvious with a droll smile. His eyes were like Sean Connery's—playful and merry.

She chuckled. Her cheek hurt, but she kept chuckling.

He leaned closer. "I may have a lead for you. I just thought of it, but it's an impression, not a fact."

"No problem."

"Well, Katrina once mentioned she knew her predecessor, Novak's first wife. I got the impression they were more than passing acquaintances."

"How did they meet?"

"She didn't say. But she said they met about three years ago. Before Katrina was married to Novak."

Bourque nodded. That could be important. There could be a connection to the case, although she wasn't sure what it was.

"Is it helpful information?" he asked.

"Could be."

He grinned. "You need me."

She nodded amicably. "Is that a twinkle in your eye?"

"Must be my glass eye." He chortled, then regarded her seriously. "Let me join the team. Put my skills to work."

"Sorry, Cal, no can do."

"Why not?"

Another civilian wanting in. "I really appreciate your help, but that's not how the State Police does things. I apologize."

He waved her off. "Fair's fair."

"You're a good man."

"And easy to find." He winked.

Chapter 26

Back at the detective unit, Bourque strode into her office. There was a sticky note from Donnelly on her laptop: *Nate Hayden called. Wouldn't talk to anyone but you. Wants you to phone him ASAP.*

"Good afternoon," she said when Nate Hayden answered her call. "It's Lieutenant Bourque."

"Lieutenant, I'm a little worried. Hank seems to have been in a bad fight." Nate sounded more than a little worried. "His hands are cut up, his face is real bruised."

Bourque immediately thought of Zupan's assailant. Could it be Hank? "When did you notice the injuries?" she asked.

"First thing this morning."

Her pulse quickened. That synched with the timeline of Zupan's assault. Hank was younger than the assailant's reported age, but he could pass for thirty in the dark.

"He's been in plenty of scraps," Nate admitted. "He'll heal. That's not it. He's in trouble. I can tell by the way he's acting. I don't want him in more trouble. The youngster's been down the shore for two days, at an old cabin about half a mile from here."

"Alone?"

"As far as I know. I called out three times as he slunk by this morning but he didn't answer. His face told me his answer. To be polite, it was 'Get lost.' He needs to turn himself around. After you left a few days ago, he said you talk straight. Maybe he'll listen to you."

"I'll come and talk to him. But don't tell him. He might take it the wrong way. If he leaves, call this number. If you see anyone approaching him, take note of them."

"I'll do more than that," Nate vowed.

"No, sir. Don't."

"What if he's being attacked?"

If Hank was Zupan's assailant, she thought that unlikely. She considered Nate's tone. He sounded genuinely protective. "Call me immediately if that happens. Warn the attackers off."

"Shoot to injure, you're saying, not kill."

"No, Mr. Hayden, I'm not saying that. Don't shoot anyone, under any circumstances."

"No disrespect, this isn't Kansas. That might not work out here. There's an old twenty-two in the cabin. What if Hank starts firing at them?"

The gun changed things, but she wouldn't mention it to Nate. "I assure you, there'll be no cause to shoot anyone."

"I won't start anything but I'm no pacifist."

"Restraint, sir. We'll be there in less than half an hour."

□ □ □

Bourque checked out a cruiser and roared along Route 6, siren blaring. Three more cruisers were on the way, one carrying Donnelly and Zupan's two sentries, who were trained snipers.

Patel and a trooper had temporarily assumed Zupan's watch. The team wouldn't leave Zupan unguarded. There was a possibility Nate Hayden's call was a ruse to draw the State Police away from the butler. Although Nate sounded genuine, Bourque didn't trust him fully.

Concentrating on the road, she topped 100 mph. In the event that Hank did a runner, Peabody had alerted the APB units already covering Cape Cod. Central was readying a second search helicopter.

Well before reaching the lane to Bluefin Bay, Bourque turned off her siren so as not to alert Hank. The cruisers behind her followed suit. She exited Route 6 doing 35 mph. She would have cornered faster but squealing tires could be heard a long way off. The lane was bordered by thick cedars. Hank wouldn't see the cavalry coming. Ten more troopers were on the way, five each from South Yarmouth and Bourne.

After she'd mentioned the .22 rifle to Peabody—the complication of an armed suspect—he went into overdrive. She realized the brass had to err on the side of caution. Still, the extra troopers seemed excessive. Over the decades, the State Police had been forced into big policing: backup cars and blazing guns. She preferred one officer at a time. De-escalation, thinking on your feet.

Pulling into Bluefin Bay, she parked thirty yards from the campground office and methodically surveyed the area. All clear, from what she could tell. She saw no campers or seasonal RVers.

Her Kevlar vest was already on. She pulled her hair into a tight ponytail, donned a helmet, and readied her Smith & Wesson

M&P45, accurate to 120 yards. Easing out of her cruiser, she kept low, maintaining cover. The afternoon was sliding toward evening. There were no clouds in the sky. For a change on the Outer Cape, she didn't hear the roar of the sea.

Nate emerged from the office, looking ornery. His hair was plastered to his head; his face, beet red. To counter the weight of his stomach, he walked like a sumo wrestler: shoulders back, head held high. A shotgun was crooked in his left elbow. Not what she wanted to see. Another armed civilian, potentially a resister. If push came to shove, Bourque knew where Nate's allegiances lay: with Hank, not the police.

Still keeping cover, she waited for Nate to reach her. His shotgun, a Maverick 88, was well-maintained. They had to disarm him. "Good afternoon," she calmly said. "Hank still in the cabin?"

Nate nodded gravely. "I didn't see him leave. There's a path along there." He pointed to the Atlantic shore. "He didn't come out of it."

"Any other ways out?"

"One. He could bushwalk an old dune trail to the highway, although it'd take an hour. There aren't any boats at the cabin and he can't swim."

Seven officers stepped from the cruisers following her.

Nate regarded them uneasily. "That's a lot of cops."

And that's less than half of them, she thought. "Just a precaution, Mr. Hayden."

Nate didn't respond at first. "I suppose," he grudgingly said.

"Fact is," she relayed, "they're to Hank's benefit. If he thinks about running, he'll soon see he's surrounded. We'll keep him out of trouble."

Bourque signaled for the officers to stay back. Despite her misgivings, she had to work with Nate. He provided the best route to apprehending Hank. She felt like she always did when the path wasn't clear: like a sailor up a mast in a storm, with the sea crashing around her. Drawing out her phone, she pulled up a local Google map. "Can you show me where the trail meets the highway?"

Nate leaned closer to her. He smelled of aftershave. It didn't mask his BO. "There," he pointed, "about two miles before the turnoff to our lane."

She switched the map to Street View and zoomed in on Nate's property. "Can you identify Hank's cabin?"

Nate pointed to a small one-story building about 800 yards away, next to the ocean. The cabin had a single door centered between two front windows, which looked to be broken. "There's trouble brewing," Nate asserted, "the windows are smashed."

"Are you sure Hank's alone?"

"Yep. I've been watching the path ever since he took it today. If any of his friends went through the dunes, I'll eat a stinkin' squid."

"What about Jim McVey and Randy Connors?" she asked.

"Huh. Those two? They're lazier than sea cows."

"What about Hank's father?"

"He's washed his hands of him."

"Does Hank have night vision goggles?"

"Nope. Nothing like that here."

"You said the twenty-two was old. Is it a long rifle?"

"Nope, it's a twenty-two short."

She returned to her cruiser, unsure if Nate had told her the whole truth. You couldn't fully accept what relatives of suspects told you. After relaying the cabin's description and coordinates to the team, she dispatched two troopers to cover the dune trail. Next, to eliminate possible meddling from Hank's family or friends, she directed the South Yarmouth troopers to round up McVey and Connors as well as Hank's father, Jeb, and his uncle Tobias. If they lodged any complaints, she'd deal with that later.

Motioning for Donnelly to stay where he was, she walked over to him. "Get Mr. Hayden to surrender his shotgun," she quietly said, "or take it. We don't want him interfering."

"Consider it done."

She smiled. In her view, she'd given Donnelly the most difficult task. "When you've done that little deed, keep him 'occupied'—or forcefully detained if you have to. You're our backup for now. The Bourne troopers will join you. If Hank gets by us, he might head this way. Be ready for a runner."

□ □ □

While Bourque prepared her small backpack—adding a compact megaphone and night vision goggles to a comprehensive first-aid kit, energy bars, and water—her phone vibrated. She'd muted the ringer. She checked the name on call display: Peabody. The last person she wanted to talk to.

"Captain Peabody," he hastily said when she answered.

She got into her cruiser to talk in private.

"I called HQ," he went on. "They're sending a quick-deploy STOP unit, four men."

"They'll crowd the field," she objected. Too much firepower was often worse than none. "I already have two STOP snipers. I'm sending one to the dune side of Hank's cabin; the other, to the rear." As Peabody knew, their rifles were accurate to over 400 yards. They'd position themselves 150 yards from the cabin, ready to move closer if they needed a better sightline. The accuracy of a .22 short rifle degraded steeply after fifty yards. In the event that Nate was lying or mistaken about the .22, a .22 long was only good to 140 yards.

"Dispatch HQ's men as backup," Peabody said.

"Could cause crossfire," she replied. She wanted to approach Hank with as few officers as possible in as few places as possible. Given her years undercover, when it came to ops, she had more experience than Peabody. In addition, he hadn't been on the ground in decades. What did he think this was? The Battle of Berlin? "I need a small footprint," she said. "You can call them off."

"No, I can't. You may not see it but I'm following my instincts. My intuition, if you like."

She sighed inwardly. Instinct wasn't the same as intuition. To most men, instinct was the primeval hunting brain at work. Darwinism in action. Survival of the biggest and fastest. Intuition was understanding, not hunting. You needed to give your subconscious time to work. It grasped so much more than you realized. "The four are overkill," she insisted. "Nate Hayden is already spooked. If Hank Payne gets a sniff of them, it could make things worse."

"It's not only me," Peabody said. "HQ's masters want them on board."

Christ. Political football. "This got anything to do with Cantor getting away?"

"No. Don't beat yourself up on that. After Cantor's first interview, he was ruled low danger. You carry no blame. One suggestion," Peabody added. "Don't approach Hank until dark."

She didn't respond. Exactly her plan. The team had night goggles. If Nate was right, Hank didn't.

"Keep me posted," Peabody said.

"Roger that." She wouldn't call him until it was over. If too many chefs spoiled a soup pot, too many cops could kick it over.

She exhaled after disconnecting. In truth, Peabody was just trying to help. His job, like hers, was to mitigate danger. With a possible armed suspect in the mix, going overboard wasn't a bad thing. She checked the dashboard clock: 1922. She'd assign HQ's STOP unit to fan out 400 yards from the cabin. If needed, she'd call them in.

When she exited her cruiser, Nate stepped forward. "I'm coming with you," he quietly announced.

She shook her head. "Not necessary. I'll talk to Hank." She acknowledged the trio accompanying her, a veteran Bourne trooper named Hosken and the two STOP snipers. "These officers will stay back. Hank won't see them."

"Yes, he will. Hank's smart, you know."

"They're fully-trained, sir. Hank won't hear them or see them. It'll be dark when I approach him."

Nate shrugged. "I'm warning you, Hank's a woodsman. He tracks deer in the dark."

"It's going to be okay, Mr. Hayden. He's safe now."

Bourque felt a tinge of disquiet. *Deer in the dark*. She recalled the night she'd left Novak's house with the shepherd letter. She was sure someone had been watching her. Had it been Hank? She could envision him doing it. Or perhaps one of his buddies, despite Nate's low opinion of them.

"I'm coming," Nate repeated.

"Makes more sense if you stay here," she replied. "Hank probably knows you're angry with him. You might rile him up more."

"He's already cantankerous."

She nodded but didn't change her calculus. "Why don't you wait inside? Trooper Donnelly here will wait with you. He used to play football. You two can talk gridiron. He played with a few former Patriots."

"More than a few," Donnelly confided, channeling the Friendly Giant.

□ □ □

Bourque and the approach team switched to night-op gear and blackened their faces, then ran their hands over their guns and ammo, double-checking everything. Finally, knowing there'd be sandflies, they applied bug repellent. Swatting at bugs had ruined more than one op.

With dusk falling, she led the three men forward, thinking *deer in the dark*. If Hank had been watching her, he was good. Vigilance was the key. She reasoned she could get close enough to the cabin to begin a parley with him. He probably intended to stay holed up until his injuries healed or he could hide them.

The STOP duo vanished into the dunes. The light dwindled by the minute. The gloaming slowly dissolved. The wind died down. The only sound she heard was the slow roll of the Atlantic to her left, breaking rhythmically onshore. To her right, dunes and seagrass reached inland, interspersed with bayberry, scrub oak, and pitch pine. The trees offered little cover. She could see the sky through them. The dunes were another matter. From Nate's office, they'd looked inconsequential. Now she saw their true magnitude. They loomed above her, some as tall as three-story buildings.

In the near distance, she saw a rare large rock, almost ten feet high, and waved for Hosken to stop at it. Nightfall was still an hour away. Reaching the rock, she ran a hand along it: warm to the touch, still holding the day's heat, a hunk of granite abiding where a glacier had dropped it 23,000 years ago. She slipped behind it and squatted with her back against its warmth, situated to intercept Hank if he came out. Hosken stood placidly nearby. However, she knew he was on full alert. His head was cocked toward the cabin, like a pointer in the woods in hunting season.

She felt a sudden weariness, more physical than mental. She'd been up since 0500. Pulling two energy bars from her pack, she ate them slowly and drank a few slugs of water. Better.

She didn't bother checking the time. It didn't matter. Op time wasn't measured in terms of minutes but of events. She had no idea when her day would be done. The sun sank further, falling below the dunes. Then the pine trees stood still, signaling a change in the Cape's diurnal rhythm, the day giving way to night, the world reversing itself. The two STOP men messaged they were in place. The quartet from HQ checked in.

She turned her mind to Hank. He appeared to be a local thug on the road to big trouble. Few murderers were caught red-handed. Usually, they couldn't hide out long enough or didn't think things through. They got impatient, or stupid, or both—which could be Hank's fate.

Bourque's aim was to talk him in. She'd done it before. You started out magnanimously—almost defensively—then gradually, inevitably, let the suspect know they had no choice but to surrender. She always relied on a strategy, not a script. Her plan was simple. Listen carefully to Hank's words, and only then reply. And hope Hank kept his cool. She didn't try to guess what he'd do or what he thought. The human brain was a labyrinth. Anything could get inside it. The question was: What would get out? In Hank's case, she couldn't say. However, one thing was certain. In the event of a firefight, he was at a distinct disadvantage. If Nate was right about the .22, Hank's odds were low: one person with an old .22 and no night goggles against two high-powered handguns and two expert snipers, all with night vision, not to mention a raft of backup troopers.

Breathing deeply, she focused on the parley. It could take hours. It could end in a shootout or success, guts or glory. She'd seen both.

Chapter 27

When darkness fell, Bourque and Hosken set off wearing night goggles, maintaining an even pace, moving silently, like fog rolling in from the Atlantic. They'd disabled their phones' screen brightness. A lit screen was a target. In the fading light, Bourque's sense of smell rose to the fore. The air was saturated with ocean brine. The path smelled of decaying pine needles. There were no rocks underfoot that could echo footsteps. The area seemed to have closed in on itself, shutting out the rest of the National Seashore. As they walked, a gibbous halfmoon climbed into the southern sky. Fortunately, it wouldn't reach its zenith for hours. The dunes didn't reflect its wan light. Instead, they absorbed it like a black hole. She'd entered full undercover mode, ready for a feedback loop that could keep changing.

She and Hosken stopped about seventy-five paces from the cabin. They could see its outline in the distance. She scanned the surroundings, internalizing the terrain: the Atlantic to the east, twenty yards away, the adjacent dunes, the angle of the moon. The cabin had electricity but there were no lights on. She didn't smell any food cooking. However, she caught a strong whiff of chemicals, an acrid combination of ammonia and paint thinner, mixed with the odor of burnt wood. It seemed there'd been a fire recently.

She stood still and listened for two minutes, long minutes that felt like hours.

Nothing. Hank could be in bed. If injured badly, he might be convalescing. Then again, he could be lying in wait for them, either inside or nearby. She waited for two more minutes, willing her body to remain motionless.

Nothing. Silence was a good sign, yet she kept waiting and watching. No movements or sounds. It was time to act.

An owl hooted from somewhere to her right, emitting a deep, startling cry. Owls didn't hoot for no reason. Something had moved, or was continuing to move. The owl hooted again. It wasn't far off. She motioned for Hosken to freeze and stood stock still, preternaturally conscious of everything: every sound, every second.

Breathing slowly, she turned her body toward the owl, focused her eyes and waited for the bird to hoot again.

Nothing. Still she waited. On most ops, impatience was the enemy, not fear. The bird remained silent. Was it reacting to her and Hosken, or to other officers in the dunes? Or to Hank?

Suddenly, the owl took wing. She listened hard. No follow-up sounds, no indication of someone, or something, shifting after the bird took flight, having waited for a safe window to move.

After a few long minutes, she beckoned to Hosken. It was time to go in. Quietly, she pulled off her backpack, eased out the megaphone, and took twenty paces forward, still beyond a short .22's accuracy range. Nonetheless, due to the possibility of Hank having a long .22, she stood behind a rare thick pine, her handgun ready. She wanted to be close enough to see Hank's face if he showed himself. It would help if she could track his eyes.

Activating the megaphone, she called out: "Hank, are you there? It's Lieutenant Bourque."

No reply. No sounds, no movement.

"I'm here to help you," she calmly stated.

Still no reply. She half-expected the owl to answer her.

"I heard you could be in trouble," she called. "If you are, I can help you."

All quiet.

"I can help you," she repeated.

"How?" Hank's faint voice came from behind the window to the left.

"However you like," she amiably replied, scrutinizing the window for a rifle barrel. She didn't see one.

"*However?*" Hank mimicked. He sounded tired. "Get real. You can't help me."

"Why not?" She signaled for Hosken to zero in on the door. If Hank exited the cabin from the front, he wouldn't likely come through the broken windows.

"I've done what I've done," Hank answered.

"It doesn't matter what you did. I can help you."

"I don't think so."

"Are you hurt, Hank? Do you need medical help?"

"What do you care?"

"Do you need bandages? Painkillers?"

Hank didn't reply.

"I have a first-aid kit with me," she said. "It's yours. You can come out and get it."

Still no reply.

"It's yours."

"Bring it to me."

Time to switch from magnanimous to realistic. "That's not how it works."

"I thought you wanted to help."

She sensed she had him on the hook. "I do, Hank, but it's a two-way street. I help you, you help me. You need to come out, hands up, no guns."

"What guns?"

"You have a twenty-two."

"That old thing? It doesn't work."

She didn't believe him. "Come on out."

"I didn't really do anything."

"Okay. The law will look at whatever you did. Come out."

"I didn't finish the job."

Correct in one sense, she thought. He hadn't killed Zupan. "Cooperate. It'll be better for you."

"I didn't do anything. I was trying to cook some meth. It blew up on me."

If true, that explained the chemical smell. "We'll talk about that later," she said. "Come out. I'll get a doc to patch you up."

"When?"

"When you come out."

□   □   □

Bourque soon learned Hank wasn't lying. A day and a half ago, his first batch of meth had blown up on him. His hands had been cut by a shattered beaker and broken windows, not Zupan's bites. His face had been battered by an exploding hotplate, not Zupan's elbows.

The youngster figured he'd added too much nail polish. Bourque didn't disagree. Acetone was highly flammable. She arrested him for attempting to produce an unlawful substance.

She was worried about him. Meth fumes could cause liver, heart, or brain damage. In the moonlight, his face looked ghostly white, as if he'd lost a lot of blood. Although his eyes were still wolverine-like, he moved slowly, like a person in a trance. She called a doctor to treat him.

Re Hank tracking her in the woods, she had that wrong. He'd given a statement which included his timeline. The night she'd left the castle with the shepherd letter, he'd been in Plymouth buying meth ingredients. She decided her imagination had bested her on that occasion. Maybe she'd been couped up in Novak's library too long. She relegated the episode to the work of an overwrought mind.

It was almost midnight when Bourque reached her cruiser. Donnelly was waiting for her.

"Good job. No collateral damage," he intoned, then grinned. "That's what the paper-pushers will say. You know what I say? You outsmarted the bastard."

"Ah, you're making me blush."

"Must be my language."

She chuckled. "Did you have to disarm Nate Hayden?"

"Nah. We became buddies. No thanks to you."

"What?"

"That stuff about talking 'gridiron.' I almost puked laughing. What was next? The 'pigskin sport'?"

"Hey, I play hockey, not football."

"You're forgiven."

As Donnelly left, her duty phone crooned Elvis Costello. "Watching the detectives—"

"Bourque here," she answered.

"Hello, Lieutenant Bourque. Lieutenant Colonel Hyslop. I'd like to express my appreciation. Fine work."

She involuntarily stood straight up. "Thank you, Sir. Sorry," she fumbled, "I usually answer with Lieutenant Bourque, State Police."

"I see."

"It's been a long day."

"No apology required. You showed a great sense of duty, not to mention composure."

"Thank you, Sir."

"Very fine work."

After Hyslop disconnected, she chided herself for sounding so meek. *I usually answer.* She shook her head. What should she expect of herself? Her reaction was reflexive, baked in forever. That was life in a hierarchy. It'd be no different if the chief super happened to be a woman.

Bourque got in the cruiser. *You just got kudos from the big boss.*

Nice, she thought, but not a big deal. In truth, it meant far less than Donnelly's compliment. As he'd shown with Nate, policing was often about how wily you were—like Ulysses outfoxing Polyphemus, besting the one-eyed giant with guile, not force. If she had kids—*when* she had kids—and they asked her why it took twenty cops to bring in one person, she wouldn't be able to tell them. She couldn't explain it to herself.

She shook her head. She had to laugh at herself. She was a strange amalgam: a cop who was a nature-loving nutbar, one who hated leaving lights on or throwing out recyclable cans but who often drove 100 mph, burned rubber, and spent months hunting murderers, regardless of the cost.

She didn't start the cruiser, thinking she should phone Eller. She felt a hint of trepidation. How would he take her little success? Certain men didn't like it when female colleagues got kudos. She called him.

"Bourque here," she said when Eller answered. "Did you hear about Hank Payne's arrest?"

"Sure did. Good work. Maybe he'll straighten himself out now."

"I don't think so."

"Huh. Too bad. Get some sleep."

Chapter 28

DAY SEVEN: *May 20th*

The next morning, Bourque arrived at the detective unit at 0800, intending to put the previous day's minor success behind her. There'd been enough fanfare. She wanted to be treated like a regular cop. A pallid sun sat in a milky-white sky, making the day feel washed out before it had begun.

She entered her office to find it empty. Eller was still in Boston. Eating a lifeless muffin, she checked her email. Gronski had delivered an initial report on Tomaz and Marta Ravlic. The couple were IT professionals in their late-twenties who'd been educated in Llujbana. Well-educated, Bourque saw. They held double majors in computer science and linguistics, and minors in English. Marta had served in the Slovenian military. Her maiden name was Kemet, the same as Melanya's. Bingo, Bourque thought. A possible Old Country connection. Maybe the Ravlics would provide a useful lead, a long-awaited one.

"Watching the detectives …"

She fished out her duty phone. "Lieutenant Bourque, State Police."

"Dagleish here."

"Yes?" Less than a day had passed since she'd emailed the videos. Either they were clean or obviously doctored.

"All intact," Daggers said. "No Doctor Strangelove."

"Thank you."

"Glad to be of service."

Right. Bourque moved on, finally retrieving Novak's desk effects from the evidence locker and heading to a large table in the staffroom. She turned her phone ringer off. No more research interruptus. Fresh decaf coffee on the brew, she spread the evidence out.

One by one, she relegated papers and documents to the *nothing there* pile. She wondered about the efficacy of dusting off someone's memorabilia. A human's possessions weren't exactly a reliable indicator of their actions.

Nonetheless, she continued her inspection. When you worked a case, you were supposed to be detached and professional. However, for her, there was usually a personal side, even though the brass frowned on personal policing. In Novak's case, she felt obliged to him. From what she knew, he was an ethical man who'd quietly been giving his money away.

She soon uncovered a letter from Karnicar, the Slovenian mountain skier, in which he criticized Novak for berating him for stunts. Sure, Karnicar wrote, the world needed aid, but it also needed entertainment. Novak hadn't agreed. The rich man going through changes, she thought, recalling Vega's Bowie analogy.

Three cups of coffee later, she had nothing. However, she was thankful for decaf. Not long ago, her whole body would have been fizzing. Marty was pointing her in the right direction: decaf, no donuts, salads. Not a day too soon. She'd watched many cops get diabetes or, worse yet, succumb to heart attacks. It was almost a rite of passage.

By noon, she still had nothing. After lunch at her desk, she kept digging, coming across a small leather notebook with handwritten entries. In the first half-dozen, Novak complained of Hayden's spending habits. Later, he wrote of their increasing rift. His wife didn't agree with him giving money away. She was selfish. Her covetousness spoke of shallowness. He wrote of the need to "divorce" oneself from greed and excess and empty pursuits.

Divorce, Bourque noted. He'd used the word four times. Maybe Vega was right about the impending end of Novak's second marriage. But who wanted to divorce whom? Did Novak intend to divorce Hayden or, was Vega correct and Hayden was about to divorce Novak? If that were the case, there was some fuel for the theory that Novak wanted Hayden dead.

Bourque shook her head. The usual can of worms. No certainty. Private possessions often delivered a lead or two. Everyone hid a few things from prying eyes. However, the leads in the notebook didn't seem to go anywhere. They hinted a marriage was under stress, but every marriage was under stress. Besides, Novak hadn't written anything remotely incriminating.

Bourque plowed ahead. Finally, she reached the last of the haul, a collection of Confucian sayings written on four-by-six notecards in Novak's hand. It was a strong hand, generating tall, wide letters. She could reduce all the sayings to one axiom: *Wisdom accrues from doing good deeds. Wealth accrues from doing bad deeds.* Under the

Confucian notes, she found a final card, not attributed to Confucius:

Family is *not* of utmost importance. Do *not* indulge them.
The poor are your true family.

The *nots* were heavily emphasized. Were the words Novak's own? Regardless, the message wouldn't make his heirs happy. She wondered if any members of his family had seen the final card.

She sat back, musing about families and the mysteries they harbored. From the outside, it was hard to establish what was happening inside a family. She knew power couples often lived separate lives, sharing conquests but also hiding peccadillos. The leather notebook spoke of a growing rift between Novak and Hayden. Who had he been when he was alone? Who had she been? Bourque had some idea about Novak: he had a big heart. But why was he doing good? Was he assuaging some kind of guilt? Had he once been an oligarch? Or was he simply a man who wanted to help others? Were they looking at a rare angel? Who the hell was he? As for Hayden, Bourque had much less to go on. Then there was Atlas. How did he get along with a stepmother who was scarcely five years older than him?

Assuming Vega and Snežana were correct, the Novak-Hayden match was less than perfect. Bourque imagined Novak's mindset. *His second wife was a socialite. His son was off in his own world. His ex was a dependent. Why indulge any of them?*

There could be consequences for that, Bourque reasoned, as in resentful heirs. The son was aware he was only getting twenty-five million. Did the ex know she was only getting two million? Bourque would have to ask her. She began reviewing Melanya's file in her mind. It seemed the ex liked money more than she let on. In the same vein, considering the sudden outburst in her last interview, she wasn't as stoic as she let on. Maybe she was pretending to be unassuming when, in fact, she was calculating.

Bourque considered the whole Novak family. What about Aunt Branka? Bourque recalled the videotapes of Branka's interviews. The maid claimed to love her nephew Rollo. She'd been a history professor in Slovenia. She'd never married. She'd been living in the U.S. for eighteen years, having come for academic freedom. However, she'd ended up as a maid, despite years of trying to enter American academia. Most people would find that frustrating, possibly infuriating.

Considering Luu's video proof of Atlas's presence, Bourque didn't think the maid had lied for Atlas. However, she could have been overstating her love of Novak. According to his will, he hadn't left her anything. Years of service and not a penny. That could rankle. There was another thing, Bourque mused, a small thing she'd seen in undercover work. Branka's mouth barely moved when she spoke. Shills were trained to speak without moving their mouths, to hide what they said. Was she a shill, a backroom operator? Someone hiding illegal business dealings? Although forensics told them she wasn't at the crime scene, perhaps she'd been a setup person. She was a family insider. She had a driver's license. While she didn't own a car, she could have rented or borrowed one and driven to the castle.

Bourque exhaled. Even if the maid visited the castle, it was only a first step. There'd have to be more. Why did she get involved? What was the payoff? Who was the payer?

As her mind cycled, Eller poked his head into the staffroom.

"Got a few minutes, Bourque?"

She didn't, but followed him down the corridor. She knew he'd noticed her cheek gash. Like Zupan, he hadn't commented. She appreciated that.

Inside her office, Eller smiled broadly. "HQ is very happy with yesterday's op. Full kudos to you."

"Thank you."

"No casualties, no complaints, no newshounds," he enthused. "A triple play."

She shrugged dismissively, wanting to move past the op.

Eller got the message. "Are the butler's wounds real?" he asked.

"I'd say so. I think he's clean."

"Huh." Eller looked disappointed. His frustration showed on his brow. "We're spinning our wheels. Who set the killers up?"

"I don't know."

Eller stared out the window.

She let him be and evaluated Branka. They had to re-interview her. Forget about stepping on Metro Homicide's toes. While she assessed the logistics—another trip to Boston—Eller turned back from the window. She scanned his brow. The dark cloud was gone. He seemed to have recovered his equanimity.

"On Day One," he said, "you suggested messaging was in play.

Who sent the message?"

"It could be Novak," she replied. "However, assuming he was attacked by surprise, he had no time to leave a message. I'd say the perps sent it. They didn't simply drown the victims, which could have been misruled as deaths by misadventure. No, they strung them up like carcasses. They got personal. Which says hate."

Some cops she knew insisted every killer was a psychopath. Worst trap ever. Most killers were focused on personal retribution or money. They were friends or family members, not indiscriminate madmen. "I don't mean they were psychopaths," she added. "I think they were revenge killers."

Eller waved her on.

"Let's rule out a few POIs. Neither Zupan nor Snežana showed any signs of harboring revenge. Neither did Vega. We have no motive, opportunity, or evidence against them. I'd say they're clean."

"I'll give you that," Eller replied. "Three more dead-ends."

She nodded. The case appeared to be a nexus of dead-ends.

"What about Cantor?" he asked. "Where does he fit in?"

"I don't know." Recently, it seemed to be her default reply.

"His alibi checks for the Novak murders," Eller noted. "He doesn't have any marks that tie him to the Zupan assault. However, he had a beef with Novak. He could be an accomplice."

"Possible," she said. "Whoever the perps were, they used the back pool gate because they had inside info or were insiders themselves."

Eller held up a stop sign hand. "Devil's advocate here. The back gate is the easiest way to breach the castle. That's why the perps used it."

"Intuition tells me otherwise." She didn't know where her intuitive deductions came from, but knew they developed for days, sometimes weeks. Then a series of synapses fired in her brain and suddenly she knew. It was like going from zero to ten without stopping at any numbers in between. Her father called it *gut instinct*, which, to him, didn't mean that it had no grounding in fact. It was just that the facts were random and recurrent, not straightforward and singular.

"Okay," Eller said, "I'm listening."

"I'm confident the perps came in the back gate because they knew Novak and Hayden would be swimming at the time. They knew about the pool stair rail. How did they know? They were family members. They were also smart. They used the back gate so they wouldn't drag their DNA through the house. They were forensically aware."

Eller nodded.

"Look at the money angle. One of Novak's heirs got twenty-five million. One got two million. However, other possible heirs, like Branka Novak, got nothing. Some people get resentful if their expectations are, let's say, unmet. Take a closer look at the family. We have no evidence against Hayden's relatives near Truro. Then there's Atlas. I'd rule him out. I saw Abbot's latest update on him. There's no incriminating evidence on Atlas's phone file. We have no DNA evidence. And he had no opportunity."

"No oppor—"

Bourque cut Eller off. "The videos we saw at Luu's office weren't tampered with. They were verified by E-Forensics a few hours ago. Another dead-end." She stopped to let that nail sink in. "On the other side of the ledger, there's Branka Novak. Novak didn't leave her anything. After years of service, that could breed resentment."

"We have nothing on her."

"Yet. We've never interviewed her. You or I, that is."

Eller didn't reply.

"She's an insider," Bourque pressed.

"All right." Eller sighed. "So, if the butler didn't do it, the maid did?"

"You never know."

"Okay. We'll re-interview her. But I want to keep going with Hayden's social media friends. With all the dead-ends, they look like the best avenue we have. If we rule Cantor out," Eller added. "But why would he run if he's not guilty?"

"He's guilty of something," Bourque said. "I don't think it's murder. Could be some financial malfeasance."

"Such as?" Eller asked.

She raised both hands apologetically. "I'd really like to have a bead on him, but I don't see anything. Maybe M and M will work some magic. As for remaining POIs, we have Branka Novak *and* Melanya Novak."

Eller shrugged. "Melanya's alibi was reconfirmed. We have no DNA on her and no prints. Motive is shaky at best. Ex-hubby bought her a condo and gave her two million. All things considered, her involvement seems unlikely."

For a moment, Bourque wondered if Eller had a soft spot for Melanya, but that wasn't Eller. He didn't have soft spots. "Point taken," she said. "Everything checks. No opportunity, no forensics, no motive. Usually equals no guilt. But I don't think Melanya's as quiet and harmless as she wants us to believe. She grew up in a Communist country. She knows how to hide in plain sight."

"What's she hiding?"

"I don't know." There it was again. "But a small detail is stuck in my craw. She doesn't own a cellphone. I don't imagine it's a financial thing. She can afford one. Doesn't that strike you as odd?"

"No. A little unusual, but not odd."

"I still wonder about that. I originally thought she was in the dating game but forget that. She seems emotionless. Let's drop that angle and take up her Communist youth. What do you do when Big Brother is watching? You learn how to keep secrets. You hide things. *Apparently,* Melanya doesn't own a cellphone. But I think she has one."

"A burner phone?"

"Yes. Like I said, a small detail."

"Maybe not."

"I think we should revisit her."

"How about you do that? Interview Branka, then her. I have to get things cracking on the Hayden POIs."

□ □ □

To Bourque's chagrin, as she was leaving the unit, Peabody ordered her into his office. She entered it wondering what he wanted. Her paperwork was up to date.

Peabody looked grim. "We're far behind the eight ball, Bourque. I need you to assist Landon and Eller with scheduling interviews for Hayden's social media friends. I know, you'll be at your desk, but I want that file cleared."

She nodded. At least he understood they had to sit on their butts to do it.

"Landon's having no luck getting results for eight friends in the former Yugoslavia. They're in Interpol's Southern European Region. Our contact there, a Colonel S. Cellini stationed in Milan, hasn't returned his calls. Here's the thing—and pardon the euphemism. A lot of Southern Europeans are *ladies' men*. It's the way it is over there."

A bit sexist, she thought, although she had to agree: a lot were ladies' men, Nico among them.

Peabody spoke pleasantly. "Good-looking dames are scarce. That might not be politically correct, Bourque, but it's true. And it's a compliment to you. If you make some videocalls, your looks might move matters along. I admit, it's chauvinistic as hell, but nothing else has worked."

"Okay." Bourque didn't care. In her view, she had certain tools, and she didn't mind using them for the team. She'd noticed Peabody still called women *dames,* even after completing his sensitivity training. She smiled to herself. That's why it was called sensitivity training, not mind alteration.

"Excellent." Peabody seemed relieved. "Thank you very much. You can head off now."

"*Can* I?"

"Okay. I invite you to head off now. How's that?"

She chuckled. She had to give Peabody his due. He was a decent man, albeit with some "old" habits. He did what he did for Central, not for himself.

For the remainder of the afternoon, Bourque worked exclusively on the Hayden friends file, trying again and again to reach Cellini—to no avail. It was six hours later in Milan. Cellini wasn't in the office. Bourque left the station not long after dark, thinking about eating a late dinner with Marty. Half way to Menauhant Road, she felt so tired she went home to her own bed.

Chapter 29

DAY EIGHT: *May 21st*

Bourque arose early, forewent a swim, and sped to Barnstable to resume her task. Just past 1300, after being transferred from one Interpol official to another, she finally reached Colonel S. Cellini. Sandrina Cellini was on holiday in Capri, drinking an aperitivo with a deep blue sea in the background. She was a stylish forty-something with a sensual voice. Bourque turned the videocall over to Landon, their Robert Redford look-alike. Reverse sexism to the rescue. Waving *ciao* to Eller, she strode to her car.

☐ ☐ ☐

As Bourque left Barnstable, the sky darkened. The air was thick with humidity. Her sailing nose recognized it: pre-storm air. A few minutes later, a convoy of rain clouds moved rapidly east, blown in from the Atlantic. She heard a menacing whistle in the wind and powered up her windows. Seconds later, rain fell with a vengeance. Drops the size and shape of wheat kernels battered her windscreen. The storm tracked swiftly across the Cape, punctured by bolts of lightning, followed by peals of thunder. Her wipers barely managed to clear the windscreen.

The deluge's fury caught her off-guard. In the heat of summer, storms often lasted for hours until cool night air sapped the solar power that spawned them. In May, the land was usually too cold to feed a storm front, and the bodies of water around it even colder.

She concentrated on driving. The surrounding land seemed to be in a daze, beaten down by the deluge. The smell of rain came through the car vents, mixed with the smell of spring on the Cape: pollen and newly tilled earth. The Novaks case fell by the wayside. West of Sandwich, the storm dissipated. The sky cleared, unveiling a watery sun.

A few miles later, the case broke through and rose to the top of her mind. Central had arranged for two Metro detectives to join her near Branka's residence. Bourque sensed Branka Novak could be the lynchpin—likely not a killer, but an accomplice. The maid lived by herself, in anonymity. She could do what she wanted, when she wanted.

Just after Bourne, Bourque got a call from Peabody and switched her cell to handsfree.

"Long story," he said. "You better pull off the road."

She did so and powered down her window. An apple freshness filled the air. She saw blossoming apple trees nearby. When she indicated all clear, Peabody spoke. "You're being joined by four Metro officers in full gear. Central's orders."

"Seven of us for an interview?"

"You're going to do a search. They're giving you backup. A warrant is being filed as we speak." Peabody paused. "As is one for Melanya Novak. M and M found more probable cause for both of them. Re Branka, about a year ago, Novak wrote her a five-hundred-thousand-dollar cheque and cancelled it the day before it was cashable. He did something similar with Hayden. The cheque was couriered to Branka Novak's home address two weeks prior to the date it was cancelled. She signed for it, so we know she received it. We can assume she saw it. The judge assumed it. He accepted the cancellation as potential motive."

Peabody's voice sped up. "M and M also discovered a Novak account that was shut three months ago. The last withdrawal was just over nine hundred dollars. All withdrawals were made using the same card, one registered to Melanya Novak. Now we have three Novak cancellations. That's what I call a pattern. Those kinds of patterns can make enemies, as I'm sure you know. We checked the withdrawal amounts. They match Melanya's monthly condo fee. I don't imagine she was happy with that. Poor woman is on a fixed income."

"So," Bourque said, "she killed Novak to get a two-million-dollar bequest? Presuming she knew it was two million dollars."

"She probably thought it was more. M and M reported Novak only started his penny-pinching four months before divorcing her. As your notes reveal, his miserly streak could have bred resentment. Add in the other details you noted about the maid and the ex, and the judge saw probable cause for both. I feel the warrants are solid but a little hasty."

Bourque agreed with Peabody's assessment. As much as she wanted to go at Branka and Melanya, they'd jumped the gun with

Atlas. Bourque didn't want to repeat that mistake. "How many of Hayden's social media friends have been cleared now?"

"Seventy-eight," he related.

"Hmm, roughly eighty-five percent. That got anything to do with the two new warrants?"

"No. Must be a coincidence. I'd like to have more ammo, Bourque, but we don't. Each warrant focuses on weapons, specifically wire and neckties, and shoes, as in Adidas Athletics and Reeboks. I'll email the documents as soon as they're registered. Don't get bothered. Warrants are always speculative."

Call over, she rejoined the road, telling herself the warrants were reasonable. She'd execute their orders as honestly and fairly as she could.

Driving toward Interstate 495, she focused on searching Branka's apartment. The maid resided in a triplex on Chestnut Street in Brookline, a block from Brookline Cemetery. The Metro team had scouted the two-centuries-old residence, a detached brick house surrounded by rose gardens, located in the middle of a sedate neighborhood. Branka lived alone in the basement apartment, a 560-square-foot studio. There were two entrances, one, the main door; the other, a back fire door.

The location seemed innocuous. The maid wasn't physically imposing. She hadn't shown any signs of aggression. She appeared to be a refined woman. Yet Bourque felt a sense of anxiety. *Appeared to be*, she reflected. How did most perps hide their guilt? They projected innocence. So, what was ominous about Branka Novak? The operative slant? Was that it?

□ □ □

Bourque reached the outskirts of Boston half an hour before sundown. With every mile she drove, the traffic got heavier, indicative of the five million people living in the greater Metro area. A mile from her planned exit, she was stuck behind a bus. She signaled, changed lanes, and zipped past the bus. The right lane was occupied by a semi-trailer. She pushed her Mazda to eighty mph. The semi sped up. Welcome to Boston.

Bourque finally left Interstate 93 two exits later. As the streetlights came on, she parked in a secluded lane near Brookline Cemetery. Leaving her car, she heard chirping birds. The air smelled of damp soil and budding plants.

A tall man stepped from the shadows, Metro Detective Mike Williams, a relaxed-looking guy in his forties. He'd interviewed Branka in the past.

"Evening," he said and pointed to his sidekick. "Detective Al Canon." Williams winked. "Watch out for 'im at karaoke. He cranks it out."

Canon bowed deeply. "My claim to fame." He looked like a fitness junkie: wiry and wired.

She shook hands with the detectives. "What's your read on Branka Novak?" she asked.

"Could be trouble," Williams replied. "I assume your Colonel thinks so. He ordered the cavalry."

She shrugged.

"Go with the flow," Williams counselled. "Sometimes the big hats know things we don't."

She pulled on her Kevlar vest. It seemed Williams was an accepter, not a doubter. Probably why he was relaxed. It looked like he enjoyed himself. His face was etched with laugh lines.

As she unholstered her Smith & Wesson, a quartet of fully-armed Metro officers emerged from a smaller alley, forming a phalanx of helmets, Kevlar vests, and long rifles. In their gear, the men—she saw they were all men—were over six feet tall and looked four feet wide. In for a dime, she thought, in for a dollar.

On Bourque's signal, the team readied their weapons and moved out. The lane was deserted; the neighborhood, hushed. She saw no one outside. They continued down the lane single-file, treading softly, aiming for stealth as much as vigilance. Despite their gear and girth, the four Metro officers moved like foxes. One of them branched off for an alley behind Branka's residence, destined for the fire door. She and the Metro detectives made a beeline for the main entrance. The three trailing officers separated, fanning out to cover the whole house. The evening swallowed them.

With her team in place, Bourque knocked on the main door.

A woman's voice responded. "*Zdravo.*"

"Ms. Branka Novak?"

"Yes?"

"It's the police. We'd like to speak with you."

When the door opened revealing armed cops, the maid's eyes widened. She stepped back, clutching her chest. Although the apartment was small, it was high-ceilinged. The walls were lined with bookshelves.

"We have a warrant to search the premises," Bourque said and held it up on her phone screen. Canon swept past the POI, and headed for the bathroom. Toilet tanks were favorite hiding spots. The kitchen would be next, starting with the fridge freezer.

As Williams patted Branka down, the Metro officer at the fire door signaled *all secure*.

Within seconds, Williams gave Bourque a thumbs up. She studied Branka. The maid wore a blue housecoat, the color of the Novak castle tiles. Out of her crisp uniform, she looked older. Her black hair was disheveled. Unlike a week ago, it had visible grey roots. Bourque knew most women didn't stop dyeing their hair on a whim. They'd experienced change in their lives. Had Branka undergone an upheaval, as in being involved in murder?

"Ms. Branka Novak," Bourque began, "we need to ask you a few questions."

"Of course. It is no problem."

"Have a seat." Bourque pointed to a compact sofa. She and Williams remained standing, maintaining distance. She'd evaluated the videotapes of the maid's previous interviews. There were numerous theories about how to tell when someone was lying: they didn't look you in the eye; they did; they fidgeted; they kept still. However, there were no standard tells. You tried to pick out a person's unique tells. In Branka's case, Bourque hadn't detected any.

Branka's eyes were calm now. Despite the show of force, she appeared unperturbed. She smoothed her robe, pulling it over her legs.

"When do you start work at Mr. Atlas Novak's condo?" Bourque asked.

"Seven a.m."

"How do you get there?"

"I take the C Line Streetcar. I get off at Copley."

Branka spoke in the same manner as at Atlas's condo. Her lips barely moved. Her voice came from the back of her mouth. Not surprisingly, some of her words were difficult to understand. As with the first time Bourque had seen her, Branka's gaze was confusing, meek and self-assured at the same time. "How long does the trip take?" Bourque asked.

"Thirty minutes in the morning. Forty or forty-five in the afternoon."

Correct. "Do you like Atlas?"

"Yes, for the most part. He's a hard worker. However, as I told this other detective—" She gestured diffidently at Williams. "—occasionally he made me feel disappointed. He's profligate."

Spoken like a professor, Bourque reflected. "Go on."

"Officially, I was hired to work as the condo maid, but I was there as much to keep the young man on track. Rollo Novak asked me to make sure Atlas dated Slovenian girls, like a good Slovenian boy. He didn't. Not once. Then again, he's not really a Slovenian. He's American," Branka said with acceptance. "It can't be helped. That is what happens."

True, Bourque knew. You couldn't export Quebec to New England, or replicate Slovenia in Boston.

"We're a small nation," Branka lamented. "Every son we lose, every daughter we lose, makes the survival of the Slovenian nation that much more tenuous."

Again, spoken like an academic. "Why didn't you marry?" In other words, have children.

Branka didn't skip a beat. "The man I loved died young, in the Bosnian War. His mother was from Sarajevo."

Bourque remained silent. Sarajevo, again.

"He went to help her escape. They both died."

"Were you in Sarajevo?"

"No."

Bourque saw no signs of lying. The maid's mouth was relaxed. "How old were you then?"

"Thirty-one."

"Did your family push you to marry someone else?"

"They certainly did. You know Southern European families, Lieutenant. But I didn't listen. It was selfish," Branka admitted. "I should have married. I failed my country." Her eyes were full of regret.

Another serious Slovenian woman, Bourque reflected. Time to change the channel. "Did Atlas love his father?" she asked.

"Yes. Very much." Branka held up a polite *wait a moment* finger. "I'm not saying they always agreed."

"Did you serve breakfast to Atlas on Monday, May fourteenth?"

"Yes, at nine o'clock."

"Was Ms. Amber Luu there?"

"Yes."

"Do you like Ms. Luu?"

"She's certainly a fine young woman, but she's not Slovenian. In that regard, I feel the same as Mr. Novak. I'd like Atlas to marry a Slovenian woman."

Nothing unusual there, Bourque deemed. Her father had hoped she'd find a French-Canadian husband. Her mother, on the other hand, had campaigned for a rich one.

"But I can't stop him." Branka said. "This is a new country. His new country. I must accept things."

Bourque wondered if Branka was paying lip service, or if she truly accepted things. "His father, your nephew, married an American woman. Considering he wanted his son to marry a Slovenian, that's strange. Did Atlas resent that?"

"It was a point of friction." Branka paused. "Please don't misinterpret me. It caused friction, not outright animosity."

"What did you think of Rollo Novak's marriage to Katrina Hayden?"

"I couldn't stop it, even if I wanted to. In any case, I liked that woman. She had such zest." Branka dropped her head. When she looked up, she had tears in her eyes.

Manufactured tears, Bourque wondered. "You said you were a professor in Slovenia. Where?"

The maid pulled a Kleenex from her robe and dabbed her eyes. "The University of Ljubljana."

"Show me your credentials."

"Of course." She walked to an antique desk, retrieved some documents from a side drawer, and handed them to Bourque. "Here you are. Three degrees and a copy of my doctoral thesis, *Zakaj Je Balkan Balkaniziran* or *Why The Balkans are Balkanized*."

Bourque scanned the documents. All valid to her. She snapped photos of them, then scrutinized Branka. She looked composed. "Back to May fourteenth, Ms. Novak. Did you serve coffee to Mr. Atlas Novak and Ms. Luu that day?"

"Yes, at the usual time. Ten-fifteen. Atlas always wants coffee at that time."

Bourque saw no evidence of subterfuge. Branka hadn't fidgeted once or exhibited any ticks that spoke of anxiety or deceit. Time to throw an uppercut. "Did you love your nephew, Rollo Novak?"

The maid started sobbing. "*Ja, ja.* Very much."

"Then why did you have him killed?"

The maid stared at Bourque with incomprehension, tears streaming down her face.

"You arranged to kill him and his American wife. *American*, not Slovenian."

Branka seemed to be in shock.

"How many times did you visit Mr. Novak's house in Falmouth?"

Branka looked confused. "Pardon?" She rubbed her tears away.

"How many times did you visit Mr. Novak's house in Falmouth?"

"What house?"

"Mr. Novak's house in Falmouth."

"Never."

"You aided and abetted the killers. You told your accomplices where and how to get in the house and where Mr. Novak and his American wife would be."

"Me?"

"You, Ms. Novak."

"I did not." For the first time, she sounded offended.

"You helped them."

"I never went there," she said. "I don't know that house."

"It's all clear now. You slaved for years for Rollo Novak and his family. They lived in towers and castles. But look where you live." Bourque gestured around the small apartment.

"Yes. I live here. It's very good."

"It is? What did Mr. Novak leave you?"

"He didn't leave me anything." Branka seemed fully in accord with that. "Why should he? I can work."

"He left nothing," Bourque pressed. "Not a penny. Do you know he cancelled a five-hundred-thousand-dollar cheque to you?"

"Yes. I told him to."

"You told him to?"

"Yes. I didn't want the money."

"Explain."

"He was going to give me that money to buy a condo, but I told him I didn't want one." She smiled impishly, showing her teeth. They were white and straight. "I'm happy here."

Bourque eyed her silently.

"I have a good life."

"You left everything behind, Ms. Novak. Your home, your history, your career."

"I left behind war."

Bourque ignored her. "You left your whole life behind. For what? To work as a maid? Doesn't that make you resentful?"

Branka shook her head. "I didn't come here for worldly success. I came for peace. Don't you understand? After that horrible war, I wanted a safe life. You might think it's a boring life, but it's not, not to me. I came from nothing."

"So you wanted more."

"No. I do not want more." Branka spoke with quiet authority. "Why? For what?"

"More," Bourque repeated. Even as she said it, she knew she was *barking*, as Zupan would say. Intuition told her the POI was clean—which was disappointing. She'd hoped for a break in the case.

"My nephew also came from nothing. He told me he was giving everything back. I praised him. To nothing we all return."

Bourque nodded. More Saint Rollo. The non-oligarch with a heart. And yet he was murdered. Who killed saints? Dissatisfied acolytes. Resentful insiders. She still had a few of them on her list. She signaled for Williams to assist Canon.

While the two Metro detectives completed the search, she made notes on her phone, ignoring Branka, feeling embarrassed. She'd stepped over a line. She'd tried to intimidate a POI. In retrospect, she'd brought a gun to a fistfight. Wrong. Seven guns.

Half an hour later, Williams approached Bourque, holding his thumb and forefinger by his side in a zero sign. *Nada.*

She chalked up another dead-end. All too common, the kind of lead that had dogged the investigation. She sighed inwardly and stood. "Thank you for your time, Ms. Novak."

Leaving the apartment, Bourque chastised herself for bullying a cooperative POI. Although she'd felt pressured by the warrant, that was no excuse. Eller was right. Branka was the Novak family conscience. Bourque stared straight ahead, into the backs of the cavalry. Her ex was also right. Sometimes she manufactured guilt.

Chapter 30

Bourque and the six guns walked the alley from Branka's apartment under an anemic halfmoon. The first stars of the night were barely visible. It had cooled down suddenly, as it often did in mid-May. Bourque zipped up her jacket and walked faster.

Reaching her car, she scanned her email. Gronski had sent a second report on the Ravlics. They were living in Dorchester with a man named Arben Kodra, a trucker who was known to distribute goods for an Albanian gang.

She glanced at her watch: 2142. Melanya could wait. In fact, a later visit would be better; it would be more unexpected. While Bourque had no warrant to search the Ravlics, she had probable cause to question them. Having struck out with Branka, the investigation needed help. If the Ravlics were simply POIs and not suspects, after a little chat, they'd go back to their lives. No harm done. If Peabody griped about protocol, she'd remind him his hasty warrant pushed Branka. She phoned Gronski.

"It's your old buddy Bourque," she said when he answered. "Sorry about the late call."

"It's not late."

"What's the score on Arben Kodra?"

"He's a lackey. A few boxes 'fall' into his truck now and then and he delivers them."

"I'm going to hit his place now. His 'houseguests' might be implicated in a double murder."

"He could be carrying. Do you have backup?"

"A six-shooter."

"Good."

Bourque zipped through Brookline trailed by the Metro detectives and the cavalry's unmarked van. Near Dorchester Basin, they parked a few blocks from Kodra's property. Though the area was gentrified in places, it wasn't upscale. It hosted a mishmash of immigrants. She and the detectives would make a front door call with two shotguns in their wake, and the other two covering the back lane.

The team set off, moving with practiced silence. A streetlight fronted the Kodra property but the bulb was dead. There were no lights on in his house, the top half of a double-decker. The neighboring houses were dark as well.

Early to bed, Bourque thought, early to rise. Will it make Kodra wise? Reaching the porch, she waited for her four sidekicks to flank the door and rang the bell. No one answered.

She rang again.

No answer.

"Police," she called out. "Police!" she repeated.

No reply.

She called out again.

Eventually a short burly man slid the door partway open. He had a trucker's body—big arms and belly, but small legs—the shape of someone who relied on upper body strength and sat for hours on end. "What you want?" he belligerently asked.

"Are you Arben Kodra?"

"Yes, I do nothing wrong."

"No one said you did." She showed him her badge. "Are Tomaz and Marta Ravlic here?"

"I see your type every day. You look like TV star, you think you bigshot."

"I'll leave the thinking to you, Mr. Kodra. Are they here?"

"Are they here?" he querulously said.

Bourque knew he was repeating the question to gain time—but for what she didn't know.

He shrugged, as if to say *they could be here*. "They do nothing."

"Take us to them."

"You come to my house after dark. You order me around. You are like Albanian Police," he spat, "like Communists."

Williams guffawed. "If we were Communist police, comrade, we'd take you outside and beat you."

"See, you are threatening me."

"Mr. Kodra," Bourque said, "I believe your truck is due for an inspection."

"Was inspected last month."

"There'll be another inspection if you don't take us to the Ravlics. If even one wheel is misaligned, you'll be off the road. Now, take us."

Kodra eyed her. *I do it. You are lucky.*

Bourque directed Williams to frisk Kodra. She didn't care if he bellyached about it. She had a squad to protect. If he lodged a complaint later, she'd face the music, then sic Gronski on him.

Big Belly was clean. She told him to switch on some lights. He shrugged his shrug, then complied and led the officers up a stairwell to the second-floor apartment. At the top, two shotguns fanned out to secure the floor. The place smelled of incense. Icon paintings hung above a small table facing east: an Orthodox Christian home altar. Kodra stopped and bowed before the icons, as if apologizing to them for the intrusion. The altar displayed a pair of tall silver-hued crosses, palm branches, and an array of Easter candles. Continuing down a hall, he ascended a set of narrow stairs and knocked on a flimsy attic door.

"Po? Yes?" a tentative male voice asked.

"You have *visitors*," Kodra spat.

Bourque dug her fingers into his triceps tendon, restraining his right arm. "Time for you to leave." As she radioed one of the shotguns to escort him downstairs, she heard a lock being disengaged. The flimsy door opened, revealing a tall, hulking young man.

"Tomaz Ravlic?" she asked the hulk in the doorway.

He nodded. He wore the international uniform of the young: a hoodie and jeans. Through the hoodie, she could see well-developed shoulders, pecs, and triceps. His brown hair was long in the front and buzzed short on the sides and back.

"I'm Lieutenant Bourque, a detective with the State Police. Is your wife Marta here?"

"Yes." He called her and stood aside.

Marta Ravlic was dwarfed by her husband. She was dressed in yoga pants and a long-sleeved zip-up top. Although small, she looked fit. Her face was lean; her skin, smooth and olive-toned.

Bourque gestured for her Metro associates to frisk Tomaz and Marta. The couple were clean. Williams pointed them to two small chairs by a dormer window. The attic was stifling. And it was only May. Wait until summer, Bourque thought. The dormer window was blacked out and shut tight. The room was lit by a pair of faded fluorescent lights. It had a tiny kitchenette and a curtain drawn across the middle, cordoning off what she assumed to be a sleeping area. Two laptops were open on a trestle table against the far wall.

"What are you doing in Boston?" Bourque asked.

"We're working," Marta replied.

"What kind of work?"

Tomaz eyed Marta. *Say nothing.*

Marta ignored her husband. "We're making web sites, but they're not ours. They're for Kodra's boss."

"What kind of sites?"

"Doesn't matter," Tomaz interjected.

"Gambling," Marta said. "We're making them because we have a debt to people in Slovenia."

"What kind of debt?" Bourque asked.

Tomaz shrugged. "A minor debt."

Although his shrug was similar to Kodra's, like his wife, Tomaz spoke good English. "I suggest you talk, Mr. Ravlic. We're investigating a double murder. You're on our radar."

Marta looked shocked. *Murder*? her eyes said.

Tomaz sat calmly. "We had nothing to do with murder."

"Then talk."

Marta's eyes pleaded with Tomaz. *Tell her.*

He didn't move.

Marta's eyes widened. "Tell her, Tomaz."

He didn't speak.

"This place isn't bugged," Marta reminded him. "I swept it."

Tomaz nodded hesitantly. "Some men lent us money. It helped us pay off a few loans and fly here. Now we're using the last of it to buy food."

"What else?"

"Nothing else."

"Were the men Albanians?" Bourque asked.

Marta nodded instantly.

Tomaz looked away, as if pondering the wisdom of talking to Bourque, then he too nodded. "Yes. We met them in Llujbana, for maybe fifteen minutes. After we've paid our debt here, we're free."

Bourque wasn't sure about that. If their story was true, they might never be free. When you owed a debt to a gang, it had a habit of enslaving you.

"We're not criminals," Tomaz insisted. "We're web monkeys. You know, sit a million monkeys at typewriters and one will eventually write a novel. We're creating web sites, not novels."

"You came to Boston to create web sites? You could have done that in Llujbana."

"Yes, but soon we'll get real jobs. This work is temporary. I'm telling you the truth. We left Slovenia because of the death of my parents. It released us to go. We've been thinking about it for years. We don't fit in Slovenia. We're modern people. We're post-Slavic."

Bourque turned to Marta. "How long were you in the Slovenian military?"

"Three years. I was a communications reservist, an IT specialist, that is."

Bourque addressed Tomaz. "Why didn't you join the military?"

"I hate Balkan nationalism. All that fighting. Croatians hate Serbs. Serbs hate Bosnians. On and on. Even when Yugoslavia was created, people didn't stop hating each other. We Slovenians were always stuck in the middle. Peacemakers, some called us. Fools is more like it. Marta and I are finished with Slavic stubbornness."

Bourque had nothing to say to that. As usual, a person's past couldn't be unpacked in a few minutes, let alone a country's. "What can you tell me about Rollo Novak?"

"He's well-known in Slovenia. He's an IT mogul. *Was*, that is. I heard he was murdered."

"How did he die?"

"I don't know. I don't listen much to American news. We're busy, always coding."

Bourque addressed Marta. "Why aren't you working for Novak Enterprises?"

"We want to. We need to prove ourselves first. We'll work for a small IT company, then apply to Novak Enterprises."

"Who do you know here?"

"No one, yet. Just Kodra. He's our keeper. We work all day, we go out to get food, we come back to work. He watches us."

"Why don't you mingle with local Slovenians?"

Tomaz broke in. "We're finished with Slovenia."

"So are some of them, I'm sure."

Tomaz nodded. "Good point. But we're here to get a new life."

"When did you arrive in the U.S.?"

"May tenth."

"Where were you and Marta on Monday, May fourteenth?"

"Here."

"Can you prove that?"

"Kodra can."

Bourque raised an eyebrow.

"They saw us at the local 7-Eleven on Dorchester," Marta said. "We went there that day to get food, about seven a.m. They know us. We'll be on their security tape," she added.

Bourque decided to trust the Ravlics for now. She'd get Gronski to dig deeper into their backgrounds, to corroborate their stories. She sensed the young couple might need help. She handed Marta her State Police card. "If you run into trouble, any kind of trouble, call me."

Passing by the home altar downstairs, Bourque noted Kodra sitting next to it with a bowed head. He didn't look up. During her undercover years, she'd learned most Albanian gangsters were irreligious, like Albania itself under the Communists, when it became the world's first atheist state. Unless Kodra was paying lip service to the icons, he was likely a lackey, as Gronski had said, not a gang member. As for the Ravlics, from what she could see, they weren't even lackeys.

Walking away from the house, Bourque felt deflated. The two Slovenian immigrants looked clean. Another Old Country dead-end, she reflected. And another closed door. Their number was rising. Simultaneously, the number of open doors was rapidly falling. She surmised most of the legwork they'd done so far was useless.

Chapter 31

Bourque pulled Williams aside. She'd used enough heavy-handedness for one day. "Let's ditch the backup," she quietly said. She didn't need the long guns. She could handle Melanya Novak with two detectives. Three to one. The ex wouldn't get away.

Williams shrugged.

"I'm calling my boss." She hung back from the team.

"Bourque here," she said when Peabody answered. "Branka Novak is clean. Pending some follow-up, local and international, I'd say the Ravlics are as well."

"Why?"

"I'll deliver the details later. I'm on my way to Melanya Novak's with a shotgun squad in my back pocket. I don't need them."

"Like yesterday, Central's masters want them on board."

"We didn't need the extra guns yesterday."

"And Central doesn't need your input." Peabody signed off.

When she caught up to Williams, he didn't ask for the result of her call. He saw it in her face. "They're a good bunch, Lieutenant. We'll go out for drinks later," he said with a soft wink. "We can get into any club we want."

She smiled. Why fight it? Dancing with the cavalry.

□ □ □

At Melanya's building, the team wordlessly deployed, slipping through the air like shadows. They entered the tower through a security door and waited for two service elevators.

A few long minutes later, one arrived. It was too small for the whole team. The cavalry motioned for Bourque and the Metro detectives to take it, then started up the stairs, twenty-two flights of them.

She joined the two detectives in the elevator. On the ride up, she considered Melanya's condo. Unit 2212 had two balconies, one on each floor. Other than the front door, they were the only major exits, although neighboring balconies or the ground could be reached with ropes. The unit's airducts were too small for most adult bodies. Half the cavalry would enter 2212, search the apartment for occupants other than Melanya, and secure the premises, including the ducts. The other half would separate to seal the balconies and windows. She'd contacted Gronski to get the international goods on Rollo Novak's ex. There were none. Melanya didn't appear to have any European connections.

When the elevator reached the twenty-second floor, the detectives assembled in the service stairwell. Within seconds, Bourque heard the cavalry coming. In due course, the quartet arrived, breathing regularly.

Fit fellas, she thought. They could dance all night. As she was about to signal move off, her phone vibrated. She motioned for the team to wait, stepped aside, and answered the call. "Lieutenant Bourque, State Police."

"Captain Peabody. Where are you?"

"Melanya's building. About to storm the bunker."

"Hang on. We have more on the ex. Looks like she's collaborating with a known felon, a Teo Miocic, originally from Croatia."

Bourque wasn't surprised. She hadn't written off an Old Country connection.

"He's twenty-nine," Peabody said. "She might have herself a young lover."

Bourque didn't respond. Given the Ice Maiden angle, Miocic could be a friend or relative, not a lover.

"Coincidentally," Peabody continued, "Miocic hasn't been seen since the day of the murders. He has a long sheet. Two counts of armed robbery, three of aggravated assault. By the way, he might be there. I requested seven more officers."

Seven more, she thought. The Battle of Berlin continued. Of course, Peabody knew the added septet would be on Metro's dime, not his.

"Two will join you upstairs. Five will stay below to lockdown the grounds. Proceed with caution. Miocic's description matches that of Zupan's assailant. Tall, dark hair, wide forehead. We've updated the APB for the assailant. Here's the kicker. Miocic's a pilot. He owns a Piper Navajo Panther, a six-seater, kept at Hanscom Field, twenty miles north of Boston. There's a small public-use airport near Novak's castle called Falmouth Airpark. It takes about half an hour to fly there from Hanscom. Atlas could have committed murder in East Falmouth and returned to his Boston condo by oh-seven-hundred, as per Luu's testimony and a security video."

"Are you saying Atlas is involved?"

"Could be. We know there were three perps. We have a potential trio. The pilot, the ex, and the son." Peabody raced on. "Let me update you. A Metro detective did some legwork. He learned Miocic's Piper was active on May fourteenth, Murder Day. According to the Hanscom Field flight logs, the Piper took off at oh-five-thirty. It returned to Hanscom Field at oh-seven-thirty-three the same day. The flight plan said the plane was on a sunrise tourist excursion, with no touchdowns. But the detective discovered it landed at Falmouth Airpark at oh-five-fifty-nine and departed at oh-seven-oh-five." Peabody paused to emphasize the finding. "Falmouth Airpark is small. Only one daytime staff, on duty oh-eight-thirty to seventeen-hundred. However, the plane was captured on security camera. Flights from the Boston area are common in May. The plane's activity wasn't considered unusual. When it landed and departed, there were two people aboard, Miocic and one passenger."

"Two?"

"I know, that looks like a fly in our ointment, but we only need three perps at the CS, not onboard the plane. The third perp could have driven to Falmouth."

"True."

"Miocic's passenger was a female named 'Jill Reading.' Hanscom Field airport security checked her in. Of course, it's not like Logan. They ask passengers for two pieces of ID. 'Jill Reading' showed a D/L and a Massachusetts General Hospital staff card, both likely fake. The detective interviewed the security guard. The man remembered her. She was wearing a floppy hat and a long coat, which didn't hide the fact she was a knockout. He noticed her curves and lips. The detective showed him a few photos. He thinks it was Melanya Novak. We seem to have Miocic and the ex onboard. In short, we seem to have opportunity."

"But only for two perps."

"Agreed. If Atlas isn't the third perp, maybe it's Branka. Are you sure she's clean?"

Bourque hesitated. "Yes."

"I detect indecision. You're not sure."

"You can never be sure mid-game."

"Okay. Focus on Melanya."

"Roger that."

□ □ □

Outside the condo door, Bourque positioned herself so she was the only person in view of the peephole. Although her gun was holstered, the team's weapons were all drawn. She'd debriefed them on the condo layout and Peabody's latest intel. Four men flanked her on each side, flattened against the hall wall. She knocked on the door.

The ex opened it tentatively. Six armed officers stormed past her before she could speak.

You again, her eyes said to Bourque. She wore a different body-hugging leisure suit, this time bright pink. As usual, her perfume was front and center. It sucked the oxygen from the doorway.

The officers raced down the condo's spiral staircase, their boots reverberating like hammer blows. It was either race in or creep like foxes. Figuring Melanya's voice or words could alert collaborators, Bourque had recommended speed.

"We have a warrant to search the premises," she said.

"Show it."

Bourque obliged her. "In the meantime, we're going to have a chat." She gave Melanya a false smile, then directed Williams to frisk the POI in the hall, stood back, and calmly drew her Smith & Wesson. Canon circled to Melanya's side, covering her with his handgun. Given the fiasco with Cantor, Bourque was playing it safe. It was nine officers against one POI and perhaps a few more, but Melanya might have a gun. Having been a Yugoslavian army cadet, she'd know how to use it.

As Williams worked, Melanya's chin rose. When he searched her inner thighs, her whole body stiffened. "How dare you!" Her eyes bulged. "Stop!"

Williams kept going, taking his time. He found no weapons.

Bourque motioned for him to search for personal effects.

Melanya squirmed and twisted, muttering under her breath.

Bourque watched with interest. After Melanya's previous interview, Bourque had suspected the ex was tightly wound. She'd revealed an irritable side that evening. Now the irritable side was more obvious.

Search over, Williams stepped back. Melanya had no personal effects.

Bourque was disappointed. After weapons, her top priority was to confiscate smartphones, precluding POIs from contacting anyone or deleting anything.

Seconds later, the lead officer caught Bourque's eye and signaled *all secure, no other occupants.*

She dispatched Williams and Canon to execute the warrant, then escorted Melanya down the condo stairs. In the living room, it was night and day at once. Although the furniture was dark and heavy, the lights were all on, cranked to the max. Melanya dropped into an armchair and indignantly crossed her legs.

Bourque detailed two officers to guard her and four to cover stairwells and elevators, then started scrolling her phone. She'd decided to give Melanya the silent treatment, suspecting it would increase her irritation.

Melanya stared out the window, apparently gazing at a plane approaching Logan Airport, aloofly ignoring her Metro guards.

Bourque held her fire.

Five minutes later, the ex's top leg began bouncing.

Bourque waited.

The leg sped up.

Bourque nodded inwardly. Mission accomplished. "How much money did your ex-husband leave you?" she began.

"None of your business."

"Does two million dollars sound familiar?"

Melanya said nothing.

"Your son is getting much more than you. How does that make you feel?"

"None of your business," she repeated.

"Frustrated? Angry? You're only getting two million dollars."

The ex shrugged.

"And your condo fee withdrawal was recently cut off."

Melanya's eyes narrowed. *You know that?* She quickly looked away.

"That would make me angry," Bourque said.

"Pardon?"

"That loss would make me angry."

Melanya tried to look untroubled, but failed.

"Are you angry?"

The ex didn't answer.

Strike one, Bourque deemed. No answer was an answer in itself.

She had a probable hit on the financial front. She resumed her scrolling, simultaneously watching Melanya.

The suspect barely moved.

Thirty minutes later, Williams and Canon approached and gestured for Bourque to join them. In the master bedroom, Williams beckoned her to a walk-in closet. Inside, he indicated an open jewelry box and pointed to a mound of chunky necklaces. "My wife makes necklaces. What do you think of those? Homemade?"

Bourque pulled on CS gloves and picked up a necklace, a series of large glass beads strung on silver-toned wire. The clasp work was passable but not professional. She shifted a few beads aside and twisted the wire. It didn't break. She estimated the circumference. It looked the same as the crime scene wire. She picked up another necklace and examined the wire. The identical flexibility and circumference. Could be strike two. She regarded Williams. "I'd say homemade, with what looks like our CS wire."

He nodded.

"Got something else," Canon said. "I found some wire-working tools in a kitchen drawer. Cutters and three pairs of pliers. Innocent, you might say, but possibly not. Could be hiding in plain sight, like the necklaces."

Bourque agreed.

Back in the condo living room, she sat across from Melanya. "You own a lot of nice craft jewelry," she said, adopting good cop mode. "Do you make jewelry?"

"No."

"What about in the past?" Bourque respectfully asked.

"I used to."

"What kind?"

Melanya hesitated before answering. "Necklaces. But I don't make things anymore."

"When did you stop?"

"A while ago." Melanya's eyelids flickered. Her pupils contracted.

Bourque had seen that tell before, not with Melanya, but with many other people. "When?" she prodded Melanya.

"Five years ago." Melanya's pupils contracted again.

Bourque smelled a lie. "Why did you stop?"

"I don't wear jewelry often."

Bourque nodded politely. That seemed true. She'd never seen Melanya wearing jewelry. "Do you have any of the necklaces you made?"

"Yes. I kept some."

Bourque sensed Melanya's game. The ex was covering her lies with a truth: she admitted to making jewelry in the past. For now, Bourque wouldn't mention Miocic. "Why do you still have wire-working equipment?"

"I don't."

"You do. At least four tools."

Melanya's pupils contracted again. Her cheeks flushed.

Abruptly, Bourque felt a tremor run up her back. She stared into Melanya's eyes. The ex was definitely lying. That's it, Bourque decided. Three strikes. Not conclusive guilt, but good enough. She walked over to Williams. "We're taking her in."

"Good thing we have the firepower."

She chuckled. "Oh yeah."

Chapter 32

DAY NINE: *May 22nd*

Bourque assessed the suspect. Her back was rigid; her chin, tilted upward. Her face looked angular and cold, like a Swarovski crystal. Bourque gestured for her to stand.

Melanya slowly complied.

"Mrs. Melanya Novak," Bourque stated, "you are being apprehended for questioning regarding the murders of Rollo Novak and Katrina Hayden. You have the right to remain silent until you engage an attorney."

The suspect looked indifferent.

Bourque scrutinized her. Maybe she believed there wasn't enough evidence against her. She might claim the wire-working tools were planted. As for the cancelled monthly withdrawal, it was nothing. She didn't need the money.

A bell went off in Bourque's head. The burner phone. The ex had to have one. It could hold valuable data. She signaled Williams and Canon to the balcony. Canon looked hollow-cheeked and spent, as if he'd run a marathon. Williams, on the other hand, appeared energized and eager for more. She directed the two to keep searching, specifically for a smartphone.

Re-entering the living room, Bourque gauged Melanya's body language. The ex stood patiently, the embodiment of conceited stoicism. *You arrested me. So what?*

Bourque turned away and called Eller.

"We're taking Melanya into Boston A-1," she said when he answered. "The ex knew about the two-million-dollar bequest and the condo fee cancellation. She also has jewelry wire tools in her condo. Tell Peabody."

"Roger. I'm coming to A-1."

□ □ □

At A-1, Melanya Novak was granted permission to call a lawyer and immediately confined to a cell. Bourque left the precinct and walked three blocks to the nearest Dunkin'.

The air was moist. It felt like rain was on the way, but she wasn't sure. Once, she'd been able to detect rain approaching Boston by how the air moved over her bare skin. Although she'd only left the city five years ago, it seemed like a lifetime.

Sipping a decaf, she replayed Melanya's file in her mind. The ex had a few things stacked against her. And they were just over a week into the case. Everything had fallen into place quickly. The possible Miocic link. The timeline. The three apparent strikes. It was unusual. Was it too good to be true? The public thought most homicides were solved in a straightforward manner, A to Z, two hundred miles an hour. They didn't know about the POIs who fed detectives doublespeak, the false leads, the wobbly evidence, the hours of waiting and searching. Hundreds of hours. Since becoming a detective, Bourque had formed two tenets about homicides. One, most murders weren't solved by forensic evidence. Two, most murder cases needed a break. If Melanya was their break, exactly how was she involved?

Bourque brought up Miocic's sheet on her phone: born in Dubrovnik; raised in Boston; six years in the US Air Force, reaching the rank of technical sergeant; dishonorable discharge for theft. After that, a regular offender, apprehended every year or so when he wasn't inside. Almost like clockwork. He didn't seem to have any self-restraint. She studied his mug shots. The guy had an old-school military look: a brush cut, direct eyes, no facial hair. He was handsome—chiseled and intense-looking. A good match for Melanya. Maybe she wasn't an Ice Maiden. The Miocic connection appeared to be more than coincidental. Then again, it could all be too good to be true.

Bourque took a swig of coffee. *The worst thing you can have is early success.* Suitably cautioned, she evaluated Melanya's possible motive. Was two million dollars enough to murder Novak for? Maybe. How about two million dollars and revenge? Novak had left her. What if she hated him and despised Hayden? Better, but not good enough. Emotions were difficult to substantiate.

As Bourque was mulling the case over, her phone trilled. "Watching the detectives ..."

"Eller here."

She walked to an unoccupied corner and lowered her voice. "Clear."

"Got an update from Landon. Ninety-four percent of Hayden's social media friends are dead-ends." His tone indicated he was itching to move on. "Let's assume Melanya's guilty and she'd need help to carry out the murders. Let's also assume she'd have to share her two-million-dollar windfall. According to the CS, she'd have to share with at least two people."

"True."

"Well, Abbot ran a trace on Gene Cantor's cell. He phoned Melanya's landline seven times the last week in March, which happens to be two weeks after he lost the civil case to Vega and Novak. Why did Cantor call her? Perhaps to collaborate. There's more. The calls resumed the day after the Novak murders. There've been five calls in the past five days. Were the two tying up loose ends? Getting their post-murder plans in synch? Cantor could be the third wheel."

"Any news on his APB?" Bourque asked.

Eller paused. "Yes," he almost hesitantly said. "As a matter of fact, Cantor just called and offered to turn himself in. I wasn't going to tell you until we had him in custody, but Revere PD is close to arresting him."

She exhaled. She felt an intense sense of relief.

"He was hiding out in a house near Revere Beach," Eller went on. "Didn't go far from home. Often the case. They're bringing him to A-1. Assuming Cantor is successfully apprehended, let's interview him first, then Melanya. Incidentally, some detectives would wait until dawn, let detainees get a little sleep. Screw that. I'm past good cop mode," he rumbled. "It's all bad cop from here."

Okay with her. Cranky could be useful on Melanya—and hopefully Cantor. She wouldn't count that chicken until it hatched. "Melanya already lawyered up."

"No surprise."

Call finished, Bourque decided against another coffee and steadfastly ignored ten shelves of muffins and pastries as she walked out of Dunkin'. Willpower. Plus she wanted to impress Marty. A supersize muffin top wouldn't do that.

Having re-cleared security at A-1, she headed to the underground garage, got in her car, and tilted the seat back. She checked her watch: 0120. Alarm set for 0250, she closed her eyes.

□ □ □

Bourque emerged from her underground den surprisingly refreshed. In the staff cafeteria, she poured a real coffee, a dark roast. No decaf today. At the duty desk, the officer informed her Gene Cantor was in Interview Room Three.

She almost pumped her fist.

Bourque entered the appropriate shadow room to find Eller chugging a coffee. His face was haggard; his beady eyes said *don't mess with me.* Think on the bright side, she reasoned. It was a good look for an interrogator.

"How was the trip?" she asked.

"Fine," he intoned and pointed at the monitor.

She followed his finger. Cantor sat calmly at the interview table. Despite the early hour, he was wearing a dark-blue-checked suit with a crisp open-necked white shirt.

"Looks like a playboy," Eller said. "Hasn't he heard? Clothes make the killer."

"Sounds like a Donnellyism," she replied.

"No way." Eller grinned. "I'm not up to his standard. As for Cantor, his DNA and prints were in the pipeline from his first interview. Both came back clean. No evidence of him at the murder scene or Zupan's assault scene."

"The usual."

"Before we take a run at him, I've got an update on the Miocic APB. Looks like Miocic landed near the Maine-New-Brunswick border yesterday around twenty-two-thirty, at Lubec Airport. There was a pending storm. Seems he 'borrowed' a Piper Cherokee at Cape Cod Airfield. The Cherokee was just reported stolen. No one at Lubec Airport suspected anything. The pilot was caught on videotape: a tall man wearing a wide hat and loose clothes. Central is ninety-percent sure it was Miocic. The bad news is that whoever landed the plane went to ground. A few other things. One, someone stole a car from a summer property near Falmouth Airpark. The owners arrived last night and phoned in a missing car. Two, Donnelly found it an hour ago, abandoned behind the airpark. The car theft might be a connection to Miocic and Melanya. The big ducks could be aligning, Bourque. Maybe two ducks in one day. Okay, back to Cantor. He told the arresting officers he ran because he was scared. Never heard that before," Eller mocked.

"Never ever. Scared of what?" she asked.

"Ending up in court again. He thinks Vega will prosecute him.

Let's find out why."

"I'll watch from here. My *presence* could complicate matters." As in she might feel the urge to mess with Cantor's beautiful chin.

□ □ □

Eller started Cantor off with his trademark shtick. "Detective Lieutenant Eller, State Police. Homicide," he added.

"Nice to meet you," Cantor replied.

"Nice of you to come in," Eller snidely countered.

"Lieutenant, I'd appreciate some respect. I admit, I ran, but now I'm here."

"Sorry to interview you so early," Eller said, but his eyes said he wasn't sorry at all.

"No problem," Cantor politely replied.

"Where's your lawyer?" Eller asked.

"I can speak for myself. In fact, I want to. I have no money left for lawyers."

"You have money for an expensive SUV."

"That's on a lease. I tried to cancel it, but I can't."

"Why did you run from your previous interview?"

"I admit, it was a stupid idea. I got nervous. I'm in a, let's say, sticky situation. I don't want my name linked to Vega's or Novak's again. Some people think I took advantage of them."

"What people?"

"Bio-techies. If they hear I'm being questioned regarding Novak's murder, it won't look good. Too late now, I know. The media is going to be all over this."

"How did you take advantage of Vega and Novak?"

"I didn't, but, well, I got research money from them that I spent on other things."

"What other things?" Eller asked.

"I leased warehouse space," Cantor tentatively said, "and some expensive machinery."

"Go on."

"I could owe Vega and Novak as much as three hundred thousand. If I do, it's going to ruin me completely. That's why I ran." He regarded Eller pleadingly. "It didn't have anything to do with the murders."

Eller didn't reply.

"I was afraid—irrationally afraid. Bitten by FEAR, as in Fuck Everything And Run." Cantor shook his head. "Even with Novak dead, I'll have to pay. Vega will pursue the matter himself. I'll have to declare bankruptcy. After thinking about it, I finally decided bankruptcy isn't such a bad thing. That's when I called the police."

"Do you have proof of the leases?"

"Yes. I'll send them to you."

Eller switched gears. "You took a long time coming in."

"I had to think."

Bourque knew Eller's strategy. He was putting Cantor on the defensive. Sixteen hours wasn't long at all.

"When did you meet Teo Miocic?" Eller asked.

"Who?"

"Teo Miocic," Eller repeated.

"Never heard of him."

"We know you know him. When did you meet?"

"Lieutenant, I don't know him."

"I heard you had dinner with Tomaz and Marta Ravlic yesterday."

"Again, I never heard of them."

"Is that right?"

"Yes."

Worth a try, Bourque supposed.

Eller moved on. "Tell me about your relationship with Melanya Novak."

"Oh, that." Cantor appeared to be marshalling his thoughts. "Not my finest hour," he eventually said. "Let me explain. By the way, it wasn't a relationship. We talked on the phone. I was angry after losing a court battle to her ex-husband. I called her to vent." He sounded self-conscious. "I thought she'd be receptive."

"You called Novak's ex-wife to vent? Why not him?"

"I wanted to call him, believe me. But my lawyer—I had one then—convinced me to stand down." Cantor held up a stop sign gesture. "For good."

On the monitor, Bourque noted his muscular fingers again.

"What made you think his ex-wife would be receptive?" Eller asked.

"Human nature."

"Are you a sociologist, Mr. Cantor?"

"No, I'm a biochemist. I know," he good-humoredly said, "I should have stuck to my field. Sometimes you take a chance and it works.

And sometimes it doesn't. It was a dumb move."

Another one, Bourque thought.

"Did you 'borrow' money from Melanya Novak?" Eller asked.

"No."

"Why not? You need money."

"I want to get back on my feet myself. I'll get there. You learn fast when you lose everything."

Shades of Vega's investment advice, Bourque reflected.

"Back to Melanya Novak," Eller said. "Was she receptive?"

"At first. She said her husband was a fool who knew one thing: How to lose money. I heartily agreed with her. Then."

"Did you meet?"

"No."

Bourque studied his mouth. Lips straight and still. No facial tics.

"You said you agreed with her then," Eller stated. "What about now?"

"I was wrong. Mr. Novak wasn't at fault."

"So, Mr. Vega was?"

"No. I was. I acted like a spoiled kid." He continued shamefacedly. "BioCell was my toy. I was bent on making millions, and it had to be done my way."

"You mentioned Melanya Novak was receptive at first. Did that change?"

"Yes. She talked quite a lot the first two times, then got increasingly quiet. In the end, whenever I called, she hung up almost immediately. I deserved it."

Eller eyed Cantor. "Did you have designs on Melanya Novak?"

Cantor psshted. "She's a society belle. I'm a lab rat. I wanted commiseration, not company."

"Why did you call her a week ago?"

"When I heard about Mr. Novak's death, I wanted to offer my condolences. Despite her disgust with his business acumen, they had a past."

"How did she respond?"

"She didn't want to talk."

"Yet you kept calling?"

Cantor grimaced. "I know, it was wrong. I stopped yesterday."

Eller studied him. "We could charge you for impeding a murder investigation and wasting police resources."

"I sincerely apologize."

Mind seemingly set, Eller loosened his tie. "Get out of here. Next time, don't run."

Exactly, Bourque thought. She shook her head wryly. Eller, that old softy. Cantor was lucky. Peabody wouldn't have let him off so easily. Cantor had been a resource burner. Come to think of it, she might not have let him off either. He should be prosecuted and fined.

She sat back. Let it go. Cantor was a fool but a false alarm. And another cul-de-sac.

Chapter 33

As Cantor left the precinct, Eller called the duty officer and ordered Melanya Novak to the interview room.

Within seconds, Eller entered the shadow room. His eyes were beadier than before; his face, drawn. He appeared to be running on empty.

"I'd say Cantor's clean," he informed Bourque, "but let's put a tail on him, just in case. I'll start Melanya off."

Eller grabbed a bottle of water and returned to the interview room.

On the console screen, Bourque watched the ex. She looked confident and resolute. The short jail time seemed to have boosted her stoicism. Was she truly indifferent, truly unafraid of incarceration? Maybe she was fearless.

She glanced up when Eller strode into the room. *Good*, her eyes said. *Better than that other one.*

Bourque grinned to herself.

"Hello, Miss Novak," Eller began.

"Missus."

"Your lawyer hasn't arrived yet."

"It's not four fifteen."

"Correct, Ms. Novak. In the meantime, we're going to have a little chat. A pre-lawyer *tête-à-tête*, you might say."

"You can't ask me any questions. I called my lawyer."

"That's absolutely right. Once you've invoked your rights, we can't question you. But I'm not going to ask you anything. I'm going to tell you what *we* know."

The suspect shrugged.

"You flew into Falmouth Airpark on Monday, May fourteenth. You and a Mr. Teo Miocic arrived at five fifty-nine a.m. You're on security camera. You didn't smile, Ms. Novak. Tsk, tsk. You and your accomplice 'borrowed' a car from a property nearby. How did you know the place would be unoccupied?"

The suspect didn't reply.

"Oh, I forgot," Eller sarcastically said. "No questions. You then drove close to Mr. Rollo Novak's house in East Falmouth and walked in via a path from the beach. You arrived at the back pool gate at six twenty-five a.m. You departed Falmouth Airpark at seven five a.m. Allowing for a trip back to the airport, where you dumped the car, you were at the house roughly twenty minutes. Plenty of time to kill Mr. Novak and his wife."

The suspect didn't react.

"You knew the victims would be at the pool. You arrived with neckties and throttling wire. Jewelry wire."

The ex stared straight ahead.

"You and Mr. Miocic had another accomplice. How did he, or she, get there?"

No reply.

"Not talking, Ms. Novak?"

"Missus, I told you."

Eller stood abruptly and left the room.

□   □   □

A few minutes later, the suspect's lawyer arrived. Knowing the room was wired, the lawyer pulled out her phone, selected a song track, and turned up the volume. She and Melanya spoke behind their hands. Bourque had expected a male lawyer, possibly of Slavic descent, yet found herself watching a young woman who looked Scots-Irish. Flaming red hair, freckles, pert nose.

Confab complete, the lawyer made a beckoning gesture to the ceiling cameras. Eller asked Bourque to take the lead.

She stood. "You coming?"

He shook his head. He looked exhausted.

She walked to the interview room, leaving Eller to man the shadow room. He appeared truly beat.

"Lieutenant Bourque?" the lawyer asked.

"Yes."

"Counsel Flanagan, Amber Luu and Associates."

Bourque shook hands. She should have known. The family connection.

"Address all of your questions to me," Flanagan instructed, "and only me."

"When did your client meet Gene Cantor?" Bourque asked.

Flanagan gestured for Melanya to reply.

She'd adopted an *I'm a victim* façade. Hurt eyes, aggrieved pout.

"I never met this man."

"When was the last time you talked to him?" Bourque asked.

Flanagan signaled for Melanya to speak.

"Yesterday."

Bourque eyed her. The ex's perfume was evident, but no longer intense. On the other hand, her caustic attitude hadn't diminished. Bourque turned to Flanagan. "Why does the accused have wire-working equipment in her condo?"

"She doesn't."

"According to our search, she does."

"That's your opinion."

Bourque moved on. "The accused has a driver's license and a Mass General ID card in the name of Jill Reading. Why?"

"No comment."

"The accused used them on May fourteenth."

"No comment."

Bourque didn't react. The usual. Stonewall Flanagan. Lie and delay. Time to flip the script. When lawyers were involved, there were three magic words: *we have evidence*. "We have conclusive evidence the accused flew into Falmouth on the morning of May fourteenth. The evidence tells us she was at the murder scene for at least twenty minutes."

Flanagan smiled thinly. "That doesn't prove anything."

□ □ □

Early that afternoon Bourque lunched with Eller at the Sheraton. He looked worse for wear. His skin was sallow; his eyes, beadier than at three a.m. that morning. His suit was rumpled and smelled of stale coffee. Or maybe that was him. Bourque felt at ease. They'd done what they could. If a court case existed, time would deliver it.

On the downside, Melanya Novak had been released from jail. In the movies, cornered suspects spilled their guts. Not in real life. In real life, it took time to crack a perp—days, sometimes weeks. While there wasn't enough evidence to detain Melanya, she was ordered to remain in Massachusetts.

Central was working on charges against her and Miocic, but Luu and Associates had put a damper on the case. According to them, Mrs. Melanya Novak was a supportive ex-wife and a grieving mother of a distraught son. Luu claimed the State Police was on a witch hunt. The State Attorney General seemed to concur. Bourque wasn't surprised. As Eller said, Attorney Generals hated egg on their faces, especially upper-crust egg. A wrongful charge in the Novaks case would be a public relations nightmare.

Eller stirred his coffee belligerently, eyeing it as if it were an enemy. His spoon banged against the cup faster and faster. Finally, he looked up.

Bourque saw a man fighting increasing internal pressure, more pronounced by the day.

"Who do they think did it?" he ranted. "The ghosts of Sarajevo?"

She shrugged.

"We need to find Miocic, or that cellphone. The ex has to have one."

Exactly, Bourque thought.

"Peabody is getting Central to put another chopper on Miocic's APB. He's somewhere near Lubec. He has to be! Why don't you head back to Melanya's? We'll get you a warrant to search for her phone."

□ □ □

As dusk approached, Bourque sat in an Adirondack chair on the lawn fronting Melanya's condo. Behind the building, the sun was sinking rapidly. It looked huge—less than a mile away, rather than ninety-three million, hanging in the sky like an alien apparition, enflamed and engorged. Although the harbor smelled half-fetid, the water sparkled. The inner harbor bustled with water taxis skitter-bugging to the Boston islands. Ferries chugged rhythmically back and forth.

The warrant had failed to materialize. However, Bourque hadn't left. She had no illusions as to what she was doing. It wasn't surveillance. It wasn't intimidation. She was simply sending a message. She'd turned her chair to face the ex's two balconies. She wanted Melanya to look out a window or stand on a balcony and see Bourque there, to know she wasn't going anywhere. For she felt sure the ex was guilty. Murder Two? Murder One? Accessory to Murder? It didn't matter. The ex was guilty. The first time Bourque had interviewed her alone, she'd said, "He fell. Not me." Four simple words, but now Bourque realized their true meaning.

For Melanya, the marriage had always been a business arrangement. Despite insisting she was still Novak's wife; she didn't love her husband. She never had. Then along came Katrina, the Dancing Queen. *Rah, rah, Dancing Queen, Boston's greatest love machine.*

Bourque smiled. *Rah, rah.* She stretched her legs, thinking of Melanya. The first wife's marriage was a masquerade, a protracted deception. Now her freedom was coming to a close. Listen to the bell, Mel. It tolls for you.

Hold it, Bourque ordered herself. Don't jump to conclusions. Unbidden, one of her father's sayings winged into her mind. *Patience is a detective's best friend.*

She pulled out her laptop and began updating her case notes, keeping an eye on the balconies. Once, she saw someone looking out through a window blind. She couldn't tell if it was the ex. She hoped Melanya would step outside. She'd give her a cheeky wave. *I'm here. You're not getting away with anything.*

An hour later, Bourque was still sitting there, hungry and chilled. The harbor breeze had morphed into a damp shore wind. Daylight had leached from the sky. Orion was setting in the west, signaling the end of twilight.

She thought about calling her old friend Gigi Lambert. Then she thought again. It wasn't the right time. She couldn't discuss much with Gigi. The case was still too wide open. Regardless, Melanya's emotional state seemed clear. The ex was trying to hide the truth. Bourque nodded inwardly. She and Gigi would unpack the case after the fact. They'd uncork a bottle of wine as well. Plus down a raft of Grand Marniers. Hello hangover, which didn't matter. Hello great gab.

Bourque felt like leaving but the lights were on in Melanya's condo. She fished an apple from her bag, ate it, then dug out a granola bar and munched it. Afterward, she pulled her jacket tighter and hugged herself to keep warm.

Patience, she reminded herself. She started reviewing the complete case notes. Central had spent an arm and a leg on soil analysis.

Just after 2230, Melanya's lights went off.

Bourque sat tight for twenty minutes. She thought about staying longer but stamped her feet and stood. The condo was under watch. The ex wasn't going anywhere.

On the way to her car, her phone pealed. "Watching the detectives …"

"Lieutenant Bourque," she answered, "State Police."

"Eller here. Miocic was found in Nova Scotia. Apparently, he stole a yacht this afternoon. Sailed across to Canada."

"The RCMP got him?"

"Yes. There's a new Rule One for perps. Don't steal a boat from a guy who lives on it. The guy got home from work, saw his boat gone, and immediately called the Maine State Police. Rule Two. Don't steal a sailboat in a storm. When Miocic started out, the wind was blowing offshore at twenty-seven knots. I don't need to tell a sailor like you, but in a wind like that you furl your sails or go where it takes you."

"Fast. Hard to argue with that kind of tail wind. Good work by our Canadian cousins."

"Absolutely. I'm going to see Miocic."

"I'm sure we can extradite him," she said.

"I don't want to wait."

"I'll come with you."

"No need. When I interview him, I'll bring you in via videocall." She hesitated. "Okay."

"Before I'm done with him, he'll spill the beans. We'll have a warrant for Melanya."

Bourque wasn't sure about that. Miocic wasn't a greenhorn. If Eller went at him the wrong way, he'd likely clam up. Besides, she was a little worried about Eller's health. He'd looked awful that afternoon, listless and pale. No appetite. She hoped it was simply overwork.

Chapter 34

DAY TEN: *May 23rd*

Eller started Miocic's interview at 0700 Boston time. It was an hour later in Miocic's location, a police station in Digby, Nova Scotia, a harbor town on the province's Fundy Shore.

Bourque scanned the interview room on her laptop screen, registering the metal table, flimsy chairs, overhead fluorescents, and grey cinderblock. The standard interview room. Eller sat across from Miocic. Her eyes settled on the pilot. Same hair and clean-shaven face, but he looked washed out, as if he'd endured a transatlantic crossing. He'd made landfall at Digby, the most likely spot on the Fundy Shore east of Lubec, Maine. Considering the conditions, he'd done well. He'd brought a thirty-six-foot Catalina into harbor with no damage to the hull or sails. Although he was certainly handsome, at the moment he wasn't the intense-looking guy she'd seen in his mug shots. His eyes were vacant. His body was limp, like a sail that had lost its wind. Unlike Melanya, he seemed devoid of stoicism.

Bourque switched her gaze to Eller. He looked extremely pale. Or maybe the interview room's lighting was worse than usual.

Per his request, Bourque had muted her mike and disabled her image. She and Eller didn't want Miocic to know of her presence. If needed, she'd come in as a surprise.

"Mr. Teo Miocic," Eller began with a friendly lilt, "I'm a Massachusetts State Police officer."

Bourque noted Eller hadn't mentioned his homicide affiliation. He handed Miocic a large coffee and a few packets of cream and sugar. "You seem to have borrowed a sailboat without asking. Why did you do that?"

Miocic shrugged.

"Do you want to come back home?"

Miocic nodded.

"You have to be willing to talk. Are you an experienced sailor?"

"No."

"Yet you attempted a crossing of the Bay of Fundy in a storm."

"I succeeded. I know about wind."

"Why did you borrow the sailboat?" Eller asked, his voice curious as opposed to combative.

"To get away from a woman."

"What woman?"

Miocic shrugged.

"You have to talk, Teo."

Bourque noted the friendly tone and the *Teo*. The old Eller, before he'd blown a gasket.

"I'll talk." Miocic looked away.

"Okay, take your time." Eller sat back.

Miocic swallowed a slug of coffee. "Well," he said, "she's a bit of a two-face. Fantastic some of the time, but she can be a wacko."

Two-face, Bourque thought. That fit Melanya.

"Name?" Eller mildly asked.

"Don't want to say."

"Okay. So, you were getting away from this two-face. Why?"

"I'm done with her. She's deranged."

"Stealing a boat is a serious offence," Eller said. "She must be trouble."

"Big trouble." Miocic shook his head. "If I knew what I know now. Some women are beautiful. Some are crazy beautiful."

Eller nodded sympathetically. "Do you owe her money?"

"No, she owes me."

"What for?"

"This and that."

Eller coughed, seemingly telling Miocic to come to his senses.

"I'll talk in Boston," Miocic said.

Eller shook his head. "You have to talk here to get to Boston."

Bull, Bourque knew, but Eller sounded persuasive.

"That's the system," he continued. "The RCMP—the Royal Canadian Mounted Police—won't release you until I charge you, and I don't know what to charge you with."

"Boat theft. I confess."

Eller nodded. "There's something else. You 'borrowed' a Piper Cherokee at Cape Cod Airfield."

Miocic sighed.

Eller leaned forward. "We know a lot about you, Teo. You flew a beautiful woman named Melanya Novak from Hanscom Field to Falmouth Airpark and back on May fourteenth. You stole a car in

Falmouth. You assaulted a man." Eller paused. "There's more. You were at the scene of a crime, a life-sentence crime. A double murder."

Miocic blinked. Conflicting emotions played on his face. Fear, acceptance, relief, then utter relief. He spoke quickly, as if to get the words out before he could stop himself. "I wasn't there. I just flew her into Falmouth, then drove her close."

"There were three perpetrators at the scene."

"Three? I don't know. I waited in the car. She went in alone."

"She went in alone? Are you sure, Teo?"

"Yes."

Eller smiled avuncularly. "Okay. We'll get you a lawyer. You'll have to give a formal statement. You don't want to contradict what you're saying now. It's on tape. Well, you wouldn't want to. Judges don't look kindly on that."

"I won't change it," Miocic insisted "I don't want to. She asked me to help her, I helped her. I acknowledge that. I took her to her ex-husband's place, a huge house."

"Where exactly?" Eller amiably asked.

"After flying into Falmouth, I drove a few miles south, then along a beach track to a footpath."

"How did you know the way?"

"We scoped out the place last month. She had ordnance survey maps. She's crazy but intelligent. Very intelligent. Don't let the blonde thing fool you."

Eller smiled. "Thanks."

Bourque didn't doubt Melanya's intelligence. The soft-spoken "Stepford Wife" was no bimbo. It took smarts to hide one's true self.

"I could see the house from the car," Miocic stated, "about three hundred yards away. She walked in."

"What did she do in there?"

"I don't know."

"I think you do."

"I do now," Miocic admitted. "But not then."

"Surely she talked to you, Teo."

He shook his head. "No talking. That was the agreement. I didn't want to know."

"Surely you guessed?"

"I didn't guess murder. I thought she was going to rob them. She said there'd be cash in a safe. She claimed she knew the combo. I believed her."

"What did she take to the scene?" Eller asked.

"A backpack."

"What was in it?"

"I don't know."

"You assaulted a man five days later at the same house. The man was Rollo Novak's house manager. Did you know that?"

"Yes."

"Why did you assault him?"

"Melanya drove me to it. She went nuts. Said he'd eventually connect the dots and finger her. I just wanted to scare him, not kill him."

"Did you plan the assault or did she?"

"I did," Miocic admitted. "I shadowed your officers the night before. I knew when to go in."

Bourque sat straight up. That was the night she'd left Novak's library. So, someone *had* been watching her. Her intuition had been correct.

"Why did you do Melanya's dirty work?" Eller asked.

"She paid me. A hundred grand, twenty to start, eighty to follow. I had my eye on a bigger plane, a nice upgrade."

"Besides the money, Teo."

"She wasn't someone to cross. I decided to play along, do whatever she wanted."

"Were you afraid of her?"

"No." Miocic looked away, then regarded Eller directly. "A little," he acknowledged. "I could handle her physically but I figured she might surprise me. You know, come at me with a gun. She can do anything she sets her mind to. She's bad news. Medusa masquerading as Little Miss Muffet."

"How did you get away from Falmouth afterward?" Eller asked.

"On foot, mostly farm tracks and dirt roads." Miocic shrugged. "It was pretty easy. I holed up during the day. It was a cloudy night, but the way was clear enough."

Bourque knew Miocic was underplaying his woodsman skills. He'd eluded sniffer dogs and manhunt teams. It had been cold the night Zupan was attacked and wet the day after.

"Did you walk to Cape Cod Airfield?" Eller asked.

"Yes, using a disguise. I tried to look thirty years older. Wore baggy clothes and a big hat. Used a cane. Simple stuff."

"How did you steal the Cherokee?"

"Waited until dusk. When no one was around, I cut the power to the security cameras and checked the planes until I found one with keys."

"What about fuel?"

"Half a tank was good enough. The Cherokee had three-quarters."

Simple again, Bourque reflected. Miocic was a "short-term borrower." He stole something, took a trip, and ditched the borrowed transportation.

"Suppose you didn't find a plane with keys," Eller said. "What would you do?"

"No prob. I'd find a car somewhere."

Eller nodded. "I'm curious. Why Canada?"

"You can disappear up there."

"For a while."

"Yep."

□   □   □

Bourque remained in her hotel room, waiting for Eller to call. In her view, he'd gone at Miocic in exactly the right way.

"Watching the detectives ..."

When she answered her phone, Eller spoke humbly. "I think that worked."

"Like a charm," she replied. "Love your avuncular side."

He chuckled. "Sometimes it's best to talk softly and sweetly."

"And not show your badge."

"Well. I gave Miocic plenty of rope and let him hang himself."

"You did. Just wondering, are things okay at home?"

"Not bad."

"But you got a little shock recently."

He paused. "How did you know?"

"I'm a detective."

"The Big C. My wife. She's being operated on soon, but the docs tell us not to worry."

Bourque waited.

"They're going to remove a tumor. If they can get it all, remission is rare."

"Excellent."

"One more thing. Peabody called the Attorney General's office. They're ordering an arrest warrant for Melanya Novak."

Chapter 35

Bourque walked leisurely from the Sheraton to Boston A-1. The afternoon spoke of summer. The sun was high and hot; the breeze, sultry, almost subtropical. She passed a street stall selling plants and flowers.

"Roses for hubby!" the vendor called out to her.

She stopped and smiled. "How about a blueberry bush?"

"Blue what?"

"Blueberry."

"You from the Cape?"

She nodded.

"For you, beautiful, I have blue butterfly delphiniums. They'll grow to a foot-and-a-half."

She bought six plants and strolled onward, thinking of Marty's garden. He had a few high sunflowers. She'd plant the delphiniums in front of them. Before she knew it, she was near A-1. Her mind switched to the case. Eller had obtained a formal statement from Miocic. While it didn't address Melanya's motive, the prosecuting attorney would assert she'd been motivated by the loss of her husband to Hayden, as well as the loss of her social standing and financial standing. In addition, Miocic's statement firmly placed her at the scene during the murder window. On the other hand, there was no DNA evidence.

After signing in at the front desk, Bourque handed the delphiniums to the duty officer.

He opened the bag. "You shouldn't have."

"I know." She winked. "Guard them with your life."

She headed to the appointed shadow room and entered it to find Eller sitting with his tie loose. His eyes were shining. He looked rejuvenated.

He beamed at her. "My wife's in post op. She's doing well. They cut out the whole tumor."

"Wonderful! Drinks all around." Bourque indicated the other side of the wall. "After this."

"I'm not worried. It's the Lieutenant Bourque show."

She shrugged uncomfortably.

"Go get her."

□   □   □

Bourque paced slowly to the interview room, collecting her thoughts. She had no surprise ammunition, no tricks up her sleeve, just the usual pile of binders. She always started suspects off with a mound of binders to suggest she had stacks of evidence against them. Of course, any decent lawyer knew that trick.

Inside, she sat across the table from Melanya and Counsel Flanagan. Melanya looked untroubled. No, cocky was the word.

Bourque told herself to forget the ex. As with most murder cases, eventually having a bead on who did it wasn't unusual. Proving it was another matter. She cut to the chase. "Does the accused admit to being at the crime scene?" she asked Flanagan.

The lawyer nodded.

"What does she plead?"

"Not guilty."

"Due to?" *Aggravated assault*? *Temporary insanity*? Bourque let Flanagan fill in the blank.

The lawyer ignored her.

"When did your client meet Teo Miocic?" Bourque asked.

Flanagan gestured for Melanya to answer.

"Four years ago," she haughtily replied.

"Where did you meet?" Bourque asked.

"Boston."

"How many people were at the Novaks murder scene?"

Flanagan motioned for her client to ignore the question.

Stonewalling again, Bourque saw. The shoeprint evidence pointed to three perps, but apparently Miocic wasn't at the scene. Bourque reassessed the evidence. Prints: inherently controversial. Not cast-iron proof. What if there were only two perps? Suddenly it came to her, like fusion. Two names colliding and creating an explosion: Melanya and Katrina. Both women were unhappy with Novak, more than unhappy. One had been divorced by him. If Vega was correct, the other wanted to divorce him. Bourque felt it in her whole body. The wives were co-conspirators. They weren't just passing acquaintances. They colluded to kill Novak. The second perp was also a victim: Katrina Hayden.

Bourque cold-shouldered Flanagan and spoke directly to

Melanya. "When did you meet Katrina Hayden?"

No reply.

"How did you know the victims would be at the pool?" Bourque sensed Melanya's mind working feverishly, trying to decide how much the police knew.

Flanagan leaned close to Melanya and began a whispered consultation. The ex seemed less sure of herself now. She regarded Bourque with what appeared to be apprehension.

"How did you know the victims would be at the pool?" Bourque asked again.

Melanya didn't answer. She was staring at a spot on the floor.

It was time to remind Melanya what they had. "We know you and Teo Miocic flew into Falmouth on May fourteenth. You stole a car, drove close to Mr. Rollo Novak's house in East Falmouth and walked in via a footpath. You—you alone, that is—arrived at the back pool gate at six twenty-five a.m." The team didn't know the exact time but Bourque wanted to imply they had the ex on camera. "You were at the house twenty-one minutes, giving you ample time to commit murder."

Melanya was still staring at the floor. Suddenly she sat straight up. Her eyes had hardened. She seemed to have made a momentous decision. "Katrina Hayden told me," she decisively said.

Flanagan immediately waved for Melanya to stop.

The ex shot Flanagan a withering look and kept going. "She disarmed the gate. She let me in."

"Why?" Bourque asked.

"She hated him too." Melanya looked energized. Her voice was no longer weak. "He was a tyrant! Kind and generous to everyone except his own family." She waved theatrically. "Did he care about me? Following him to America. Leaving everything behind. No!" she shouted.

Flanagan caught Melanya's eye. "Enough," she hurriedly said.

Melanya glared at her. "I'll tell what I want." She turned to Bourque with wild eyes. "Ask!"

"Did you kill Katrina Hayden?"

"Yes!"

Bourque sensed confession was part of Melanya's nature. Like many perps, she probably wanted the world to hear she was wronged and abused, maybe not physically, but emotionally, and wasn't that the worse kind of abuse. "How did you kill her?"

Bourque asked.

Flanagan raised a warning finger and pleaded with her eyes.

Melanya ignored the lawyer. "I sedated her," the ex smugly announced, "and then I strangled her."

Bourque wasn't surprised. Someone who could hide mental strength could hide murderous intent. It was an old story. Killers were rarely who they appeared to be. Melanya's meekness had been a façade. "Why did you sedate Katrina?" Bourque asked.

"She was strong."

"What did you use to sedate her?"

"Ketamine."

No lies so far. "Where did you get it?"

"A friend got it for me. I didn't really want to kill her."

So you say, Bourque thought. However, she saw a measure of regret in Melanya's eyes. Was it true regret?

"I liked her," Melanya divulged. "She was nice in her own way. Very friendly."

Bourque controlled her reaction. Did Melanya actually feel remorse, or was she trying to game the system? One thing was certain, regretful or not, she'd admitted to killing someone. She'd been desperate—desperate enough to commit murder. Bourque didn't find that shocking. In her view, it had just been a matter of time. "Who got the ketamine?" she asked.

"Teo Miocic."

"Do you love him?"

Melanya waved a hand dismissively.

"Was there money involved?"

"Yes, a hundred thousand. I paid twenty to start. I was going to pay the rest over time, to keep him quiet. All he cared about was money for a plane."

Not unusual, Bourque thought. Every accessory to murder was a mercenary. They just had different requirements. "There were three sets of shoeprints," she said. "Where did they come from?"

"I put two different pairs of size tens on my hands and made some marks. Teo said it would throw you off. It didn't work."

Oh, but it did, Bourque knew. Melanya's marks had misled the whitecoats. She must have pressed down hard with her hands, simulating the weight and load distribution of shoeprints. "How did you carry the shoes?" Bourque asked.

"In a backpack."

"What was the plan with Teo? Were you two going to leave the country?"

"No. We were going our separate ways."

"Were you going to keep in touch?"

Melanya shrugged.

"How did you meet Katrina?" Bourque asked.

"She was the instructor in a dance class I took."

"Was Mr. Novak in the class?"

Melanya nodded. "She was always flirting with him. Dancing with him, smiling at him. He couldn't ignore her. Then, one day, he told me it was over. I was angry. I wanted him dead. Her too, but it wasn't her fault. It was his! Later, much later, Katrina and I talked."

"How much later?"

"A year after she married him."

"How many times did you talk?" Bourque asked.

"Dozens."

"By cellphone?"

"Usually."

Ah ha, the ex had a cell. "Where's your cell?"

Melanya seemed to be debating whether to tell her. "It won't reveal anything new."

Bourque took that with a grain. "Where is it?"

"Walk-in closet," Melanya finally answered, "there's a loose floorboard under the bottom shoe tray."

"Did Katrina have a burner cellphone? A throwaway, that is?"

"I know burner phones," Melanya testily said. "Yes, she had one. I bought it for her. Americans are so stupid about privacy."

"When did you meet her?"

"Three years ago."

Bourque nodded to herself. The timeline fit with what Cal had told her. "Did you ever talk in person?"

"Yes. Three or four times."

"Where?"

"Boston Common. We wore long coats and head scarves. Sunglasses too. Katrina was always joking about our 'disguises.' She said we looked like a couple of babushkas. I stopped those meetings. We were too noticeable."

Bourque didn't respond. Melanya was right. Put those two beauties in head scarves and they wouldn't look like babushkas.

They'd look like blonde versions of Jackie Onassis. "Why did you turn to Katrina for help?"

"I saw what she wanted in a man. Anyone could see. Fun, adventure. I didn't think she'd be happy with Rollo. I was right. No one knew what he was really like. He didn't want them to know."

Another secretive billionaire, Bourque reflected, like Vega. Maybe it came with the territory. "It appears you two planned a lot together."

"We did. Even though Rollo left me for her, I liked her. We both hated Rollo. He was a miser. And a fool! You don't know. No one knew, only Katrina and I. He threw sticks," she scoffed, "to make multi-million-dollar decisions."

"Sticks?"

"The I Ching. Russian Roulette would be better. You survive five times out of six. If you throw sticks, your business has a fifty-fifty chance. In my last few years with him, he didn't even hide it. He threw them every morning, not caring if Atlas saw him running a business like that. A father's responsibility is to show his son the right way."

"He made a lot of money," Bourque commented.

"By luck alone," Melanya scorned, "not business sense. He had none."

Bourque kept her counsel. Novak had given away millions and millions of dollars, helping thousands of people. Did it matter how he did it?

"Chinese sticks?" Melanya sneered. "He didn't think like a Slovene man anymore. Maybe he dressed like one and ate like one, but he wasn't one. He wasn't! He was a madman. Don't you see?!"

Bourque remained silent. With her wild-eyed insistence, the ex could be mad herself.

"Katrina saw it too, I tell you! She told me he was getting worse. He had the sticks with him all the time. He was crazy," she jeered, "an idiot! We both decided we'd be better off without him."

"Why did you kill her?"

"I had to."

"Why?"

"Someday she'd talk. I couldn't pay her enough to keep quiet. She had much more money than me. She'd talk, or she'd kill me."

"Kill you?"

"Yes. I killed her so she wouldn't kill me. I knew her secrets."

"What secrets?"

"All of them. It was her idea. She planned it. She had sex with him to make him sleepy. She strangled him."

Bourque's mind spun, but her professional face held. "Confirm what you said. Katrina Hayden murdered Rollo Novak?"

"Yes!"

A curve ball, Bourque thought. Was Melanya playing her, or did Katrina actually kill Novak? Bourque couldn't be sure. Given what she'd learned about the dancer's marriage, it was possible. Vega had said Katrina was preparing for the end. Not just the end of the marriage, it appeared. She was strong enough to murder Novak. She likely resented her cancelled "allowance." Plus, twenty-five million was better than nothing. Then there was the ten minute or so difference in time of death, which gave Katrina time to kill Novak before Melanya killed her.

Bourque leaned forward. "Why did Katrina kill Rollo?"

"She hated him too. You don't know."

"Why did she need you?"

"I know computers. I taught her how to disarm the pool alarm."

"What else?"

"I bought the wire and the neckties. She helped me, I helped her."

Another bond of convenience, Bourque reflected. "Why did you use red neckties?"

"He loved that color. He called it Confucian Red. We hated it." Melanya pounded the table. "We hated his Confucian beliefs!"

"You both hated his beliefs?"

"His cheapness! His so-called equality!"

"But you, you didn't love him."

"So?"

"Why did you defect with him?"

"He had balls then. And later, after America? Nothing! He was not a man."

Chapter 36

Bourque trudged to the shadow room, thinking of the thin line between resentment and revenge. Everyone could kill, every human being. Melanya could be unhinged, a lost sheep. On the other hand, she'd killed at least one person without compunction. Bourque envisioned the wire around Hayden's neck and saw it tightening, saw her body and brain shutting down, function by function. She'd sunk into a torpor. She'd heard nothing but the pulse above her ear, fading, fading, then dying.

At times like this, Bourque was thankful she was a detective, not a judge. Like so many homicide cases, the Novaks case was a morality tale, one in which the perpetrators had no moral restraints, or, if they did, they ignored them.

Inside the room, she sat across from Eller.

"Good work!" he exclaimed. "You took her into deep water and drowned her. They'll put her away for life. There's at least one count of murder and one of accessory to murder. If it comes out that she killed Novak, that's two counts of murder. To put a positive spin on things, we had it right, but in the wrong way. The perps were definitely insiders, just not the ones we suspected. In any case, Central will be pleased."

Bourque didn't respond. She was thinking about the crime scene. Apparently, Hayden had used feminine wiles to distract Novak, which explained why she'd made love on the cold pool tiles. Then there was Melanya, suddenly frenetic Melanya. It seemed she was mentally unbalanced, or pretending to be. Bourque wouldn't be surprised if the ex's defense team lodged a temporary insanity plea. As for the color red, it had nothing to do with Communist red. She'd been off-base with that. The three sets of shoeprints had been off-base too. You couldn't trust prints.

Regardless, they'd reverse-engineered the *murder compound*. The whirling particles were now in their grasp: Melanya and Hayden colluding, Miocic collaborating, the jewelry wire and neckties.

Eller broke into her reverie. "How did you know Hayden was in the picture?"

She shrugged. "Somehow, it came to me."

"Understood." He sat back. "Beware female reprisal. Male reprisal pales in comparison. It's usually blunt and immediate."

Not female, she thought. Women hoarded their anger—incubating and multiplying it—until it burst forth.

She didn't feel like talking but Eller did. "So, Novak got killed for giving away too much, for being too generous. That's a rare thing. Be good to see more of it, although I doubt we will."

She nodded again. Eller was likely right. She understood his desire to unpack the case. No detective could close a murder book and walk away, regardless of what they told you. The case might play in her mind for months. She'd speculate on Katrina's and Melanya's motives, but she'd probably never get to the bottom of them. What could she conclude? Only that a man and a woman were murdered. Two lives had been abruptly ended, their futures forsaken. The planes, the stolen car, the wires, the ties—all were evidence yet entirely insignificant.

Maybe it was a cynical way for a homicide detective to think, but even when you solved a case, death won. It always did. Ashes to ashes, carbon to carbon. There was nothing she could do to bring the Novaks back. The golden sun, the grand beaches, the constellations spinning in the sky, all were inaccessible to them, all inextricably lost.

The End

ACKNOWLEDGEMENTS

My deepest thanks to Stark House Press, especially to Greg Shepard and Mark Shepard. Over the course of writing this book, my second, when the sophomore slump reared its head—as is its wont—many people helped me through it, among them Steven Heighton, Ken Haigh, Jane Bwye, David and Penny Hosken, Ilana Sophia, David Hoath, Jim Poling Sr., Judy Blum, Ed Schnurr, Fraser Mann, Fairlie Dalton, Mike Potter, John Potter, and, of course, Ninety-Nine.

Many thanks to all those readers who reached out to tell me my writing pleased or intrigued them. Writing is a conversation. Your words inform mine.

For your consideration, four hardboiled crime thrillers by

Timothy J. Lockhart

SMITH $15.95

"Smith — just Smith - is a tough as nails killer, a secret operative and tough fighter, and Timothy J. Lockhart makes this adventure a compelling must read."—Gary Lovisi, *Paperback Parade* & *Hardboiled* magazines

PIRATES $15.95

"...with bullets zinging and baddies converging from all sides, it's anyone's guess who will make it alive out of Lockhart's gruesome, exhilarating adventure."—Nicholas Litchfield, *Lancashire Post*

A CERTAIN MAN'S DAUGHTER $15.95

"...an enjoyable hardboiled read with snappy dialogue and a touch of humour." —Paul Burke, *Crime Fiction Lover*

UNLUCKY MONEY $15.95

"Lockhart's style is bare bones narrative. Just the facts in a linear investigation... future Wendy Lu books will be quite interesting..." —*Men Reading Books*

"Writer Timothy Lockhart delivers a straight forward, action thriller without frills."—*Pulp Fiction Reviews*

In trade paperback from:

STARK HOUSE

Stark House Press, 1315 H Street, Eureka, CA 95501
greg@starkhousepress.com / www.StarkHousePress.com
Available from your local bookstore, or order direct via our website.

Made in the USA
Las Vegas, NV
03 March 2023